DEAD COAST

A Novel of The Living Dead

L.I. Albemont

This is a work of fiction. Characters, locations, names and incidents are products of the author's imagination or are used fictitiously. Liberties have been taken with dates and geography. Any resemblance to anyone living or undead is purely coincidental.

The story thus far…

The origins of the outbreak were never in dispute although at first almost no one believed the dead were actually rising. When the island nation of Haiti was struck by wave after wave of violent earthquakes killing thousands, the Z-virus lurched spectacularly to life. Early reports of cannibalism from inside the country were disregarded until shocking live video splashed across the world's television and computer screens. Suddenly everyone was a believer.

Nevertheless, in many ways it still didn't seem real. Anything could happen out *there*, in the barbarous realm of the third world, beyond the pale of civilization. There were myriad reasons that it could never happen *here*. Health and security protocols, a literate, well-informed public, etc., were all on our side.

In truth, the virus was already here and spreading like the viral videos sent out from Haiti during the first days after the quake. News anchors and subject-matter experts (yes, there were subject-matter experts on the living dead) speculated and conjectured until theory gave way to the infected, pus-filled reality breaking down doors and smashing through windows with flailing, rotten hands.

Table of Contents

Prologue

The manners of the Androphagi are more savage than those of any other race. They neither observe justice nor are governed by any laws. They are nomads and their dress is Scythian but the language they speak is peculiar to themselves. Unlike any other nation in these parts, they are cannibals.

-Herodotus
5th Century B.C.

What shall I say of other nations- how when I was in Gaul as a youth I saw the Scots, a British race, eating human flesh, and how, when these men came upon the herds of swine and sheep, they ravaged the buttocks of shepherds and paps of the women and consume these for their horrid repasts.

-Saint Jerome
Anno Domini 400

And the god, tiring of the sacrifices of his children, gave a new command. Henceforth, the slaves slaughtered in the tombs of the mighty and left to serve the master in the after-life, should not die but, submitting themselves to the bite of Apophis, should arise in the darkness and live forever.

-Strabo
1st Century B.C.

"Aaron, you coming?"

Aaron looked up from his computer and grimaced. "Nope. Someone has to be here to keep the west coast from logistical meltdown. Besides, you know I'm trying to quit. I can't afford that nasty old habit anymore. "

Catherine laughed, "You and me both. I just can't give it up yet. Back in fifteen, sooner if it's still raining hard."

She walked away, taking a pack of cigarettes from her purse and pulling an umbrella from her coat pocket. She stopped at Jill's desk halfway down the aisle and said something Aaron couldn't hear. Laughter drifted his way, Jill's laughter, which sounded like heavenly silver bells to him. She had transferred to this office a week ago and so far he hadn't had the courage to do more than say "Hi" in passing.

The blue glow of computer screens shone from only three other desks. Because of the time difference between here and the west coast a skeleton staff was required to stay late in order to deal with logistic issues that arose out west. It averaged out to four evening shifts per month and Aaron didn't really mind it. Sometimes they all got together and ordered Chinese or pizza. He didn't know exactly all of whom were here tonight but was really hoping the consensus vote would be for pizza. The moo-goo gai pan last week had been gristly and flavorless.

The building, consisting of one floor honey-combed with cubicles and the whole enclosed with plate-glass walls, continued to empty out. It hadn't been that full to start with. An unprecedented fifty percent of staff called in sick or just hadn't shown up this morning.

The whole town (it was a small town) was still talking about what happened Monday night. Aaron knew more about it than some because his aunt was there when it happened. During a guest lecture series at the satellite campus of Ford-Emory, the assistant of the visiting lecturer from Haiti attacked a classroom of anthropology students, sending four to the hospital with bite wounds. The assistant was taken into police custody and was supposedly in the hospital, under guard.

Catherine finished her conversation with Jill and went outside, the briefly open door admitting the harsh shriek of an ambulance before it closed again. He caught a glimpse of flashing red lights near the parking lot before turning back to his computer.

His phone rang and he spent forty minutes trying to calm down an irate distributer in Portland who was still missing a shipment of shower doors that should have arrived yesterday. By the time he called around and found a shipment he could divert to Portland (taking them from a builder in Texas who wasn't quite ready for them anyway) it was after seven o'clock and he was hungry. No one messaged him or stopped by for his order.

Aaron stood up and looked across the cubicle sea all around him. He missed cigarette breaks more than he cared to admit and looked longingly at the side door that led to a small concrete patio, the one spot on which the company allowed smoking. He glanced away then turned back and looked again. Red lights still flashed outside and the siren- he listened- was still there, muted but wailing. Whatever was going on out there was taking a hell of a long time to sort out.

Time for a break and a little stroll around the office. The stroll just might take him by Jill's desk and he could ask her what happened to the supper plan. He looked at his reflection in the now night-black window. Half of his shirt collar had disappeared under his sweater. Sighing he fished it out. He always looked slightly rumpled no matter how much time he spent getting ready. This slight dishevelment aroused a desire in women to reach out and smooth his hair and straighten his collar just to have an excuse to get closer to him but he was unaware of this. He nervously made sure his collar tag wasn't sticking up again, took off his ID badge and hung it over his computer. Stupid thing looked like a necklace. Ok, good enough.

She wasn't there. Her computer was on and her jacket hung on the back of her chair but she was gone. A silver framed photograph of her with a group of friends on a white, sandy beach somewhere stood next to her phone. He studied it. Was one a boyfriend? It wasn't obvious if so.

Thinking she was in the break room, he headed that way but found her in the hallway, standing indecisively outside the ladies' room. The janitor had wedged the door partially open with a trashcan and from the sounds echoing off the hard tile surfaces someone was really losing their lunch in there. Jill saw him and raised her eyebrows a little comically. She wore a red, sweater dress and black, leather boots that stopped just below her knees. When she smiled, dimples appeared near the corners of her mouth. It's official, he thought, I am smitten.

"It's Trina. She felt sick at lunch but didn't want to go home. Some crazy guy attacked her last night outside her apartment. She got away and called the police but the guy *bit* her," Jill said.

"What? You're kidding!"

Jill shook her head. "No, she had to get antibiotics and whatnot. *I* would have taken the day off but she hasn't missed a day in something like four years and doesn't want to ruin her perfect record. You're Aaron, right? I'm Jill. I just transferred from Cleveland a week ago."

"Yeah, um, nice to meet you. Shouldn't one of us go in there and make sure she's ok?"

"I'm going. I have a really weak stomach so I'm trying to wait until she's finished, um…"

"Praying to the porcelain god?"

"Yes."

The vomiting ceased but a foul odor drifted into the hallway. Jill covered her mouth and nose preparing to go in but hadn't taken two steps before something slammed into the glass double-doors at the main entrance. They turned. A man pressed against the glass and pounded the doors until they shook, shouting something. Abandoning Trina for the moment they ran down the hallway.

Aaron recognized Hugh, the evening security guard. Screaming and banging on the glass he kept looking back over his shoulder. Aaron wondered why he didn't just run his ID through and come in. Then he noticed his face. One ear was gone and the flesh from his scalp and part of his cheek was torn away and hanging. Blood poured from his torn throat and covered the front of his shirt. Smears of blood soon streaked the glass.

Horrified, Aaron moved to open the door then stopped. Three figures, a woman, and two men emerged from the swirling mist and darkness. Even in the scanty illumination from the parking lot lights they were something out of a nightmare. The woman lurched forward on legs that were little more than bloody bones. Her mouth worked as if she were chewing on something and she clutched a pack of cigarettes in one bloody hand. It's Catherine, he thought with a shock of recognition.

One of the men was in better shape and he reached Hugh first, falling against him mouth wide and biting deeply into his shoulder. Hugh screamed, a shrill note of desperate agony that faded as he was knocked to the ground and pulled apart. Catherine hooked her fingers into his flesh and peeled the skin and tissue away in thick strips, pushing them eagerly into her mouth. Blood pooled then ran down the concrete steps, spilling over them in a trickling red cascade. The mist crept in and darkness swallowed the gruesome sight.

Jill was on her knees, staring at the scene outside with her hands pressed to her face. He pulled her up and away from the doors, back down the hallway just in time to watch Trina, oh-so professional Trina, crawl from the ladies' room on her hands and knees.

She appeared to have partially swallowed a dirty string mop with the strings hanging from her mouth. Then he realized that what dangled from her mouth was the shredded

11

and rotten tissue lining her throat. Her eyes bulged and she continued to retch, slowly choking to death before their eyes. Her legs jerked and kicked then slowly, slowly became still.

More people were pounding and scratching on the doors now. They were all wounded in some way, horribly, bloodily wounded. Aaron and Jill looked at each other then quietly moved farther away, deeper into the building, leaving Trina's body behind.

"We have to get out of here. There's a door to the side parking lot in the break room. My car is out there. Where did you park?" Aaron asked.

"Front parking lot. There's no way I'm going near those people."

"I'll drive you home."

They grabbed their coats and headed to the break room. The lights here were motion activated and came on as soon as they opened the door making it impossible to see out into the night. Aaron looked for a switch to turn them off but found nothing. Great. Just great. He really, really craved a cigarette right now, could almost taste the welcome burn of the smoke filling his lungs and feel the calming release of nicotine. They heard glass shatter somewhere in the building.

"We're going to have to run for it and just hope there's no one out there. Ready?"

"Wait. Do you hear that?" Jill took a few steps toward the hallway.

Someone was in the hall outside the break room door. Shoes squeaked on the floor, the sound gradually getting louder. Hands slapped on the door and they saw a face pressed to the glass. Trina, skin dead-white and skeins of tissue still spilling from her mouth, pushed on the door and had it halfway open before Aaron got there to slam it shut, catching some of the tissue hanging from her mouth in the process. She drew back, more and more rotten tissue pulled out through her mouth until it was at least a foot long. She finally pulled free, the tissue hitting the floor wetly before she began a new assault on the door. The expression in her eyes was dead and the eyes themselves glazing over with some sort of white film. Aaron stepped back, more frightened than he had ever been in his life.

Jill moved closer, saw Trina and screamed. Aaron pulled her toward the exit and out into the dark. They took deep gulps of the cold air. Somewhere around the corner the ambulance still keened.

"She's dead, she died; I saw her! I know I saw her die!" Jill shook and her breath formed vapor in the air.

"I thought so too but..." He felt a sense of unreality wash over him. "Dead people don't walk and bang on doors. Come on, the coast is-"

A nightmare mob, bloody flesh torn and hanging, materialized from the mist and rounded the corner of the building and more, some wearing only hospital gowns blowing in the chill wind, approached from among the cars in the lot, slow, clumsy but closing in.

"...not clear," Aaron finished. Jill made a soft, frightened sound and ran back to the door, pulling frenziedly on the handle, forgetting to run her ID card through the reader.

Aaron shouted, "Where's your card?!" She looked blank. "Your ID! Swipe it now!"

She screamed, "They gave me a temporary! That's all I have. It won't open the door!"

He fumbled for his then remembered it was hanging on his computer. He looked around for a weapon, anything. Decorative white gravel filled a shrub border next to the building and he scooped some up and threw it. Their attackers never even flinched.

They went for him first, tearing the skin from his face and throat, biting the hands he held up in defense. Striking out, punching, kicking, he was no match for his attackers who tore into his body while he was still alive. As he thrashed in pain, feeling the skin peeling from his flesh, Jill's screams were the last sounds he heard.

Chapter One

Five days later

"What was the name of this town again?"

Bea looked at the road atlas. "I think it's called Portsmouth or something like that. I didn't look for the sign."

Bea and David drove slowly past a sprawling, glass-walled office building. Masses of infected roamed the parking lot, among them a girl in a darkly-stained, red, sweater dress, who turned their way and bared blood-stained teeth before staggering toward them. The red dress stood out brightly against the gray, stark landscape though the effect was anything but cheerful.

Bea turned away, not wanting to see anymore. She felt tired even though they hadn't been on the road that long today and they had both slept last night in an actual house with beds. A *clean* house.

The houses were almost always infested. They learned that their second night on the road after three disastrous attempts to bunk in one particular neighborhood just outside of the Ohio state line. What do sick people want more than anything? Answer: to go home, rest and get better. They did rest but not for long and they certainly did not get better. Now they avoided the houses. Barns, if they could find them, were safer and often cleaner than a house where one or several people had "died."

But last night had been so very cold and they detoured so many times to avoid blocked roads and the roving creatures. They were exhausted and it was almost dark. The

Mcmansion at the end of the long, graveled drive looked so sturdy, so inviting, so *safe* that they hadn't been able to resist trying to get in. Anyone living this far out probably had a well-stocked pantry and possibly a well or spring for fresh water. Maybe they died out somewhere trying to get treatment in the first days of the pandemic and the house was empty. Maybe.

The car crunched heavily across the gravel forecourt as they coasted across and parked in the encircling woodland.

Watching the windows for movement, they circled around and approached the house from behind in case the homeowner was still alive and armed, prepared to fend off opportunistic wanderers (like themselves) and the undead hordes. Snow still covered the woodland in patches but most of it melted in the earlier sunshine. Pines gave off their fresh, sharp fragrance as they brushed against the needled branches. A tarp-covered swimming pool took up most of the lawn area back here and artfully crafted terraces with bedding plants filled the rest. Whoever these people were, they had spared no expense landscaping their home. Smooth, river rocks with words like 'Peace' or 'Family' carved into them lay randomly among the shrubs.

They stopped outside the French windows that gave onto the patio. They heard no sounds other than the splashing drops of the drizzle that sent needles of icy pain down their necks. Beatrice didn't detect the sickening scent that always accompanied the infected.

David laughed and Bea turned to see him triumphantly holding up a metal key.

"It was under the 'Home' rock."

Inside the house was cold and growing dark as the evening came on. Together they cleared every room and found no one, dead or living. No electricity but there were candles in a drawer and full cupboards in the kitchen held plenty of canned goods. They sat at the table and ate cold beef ravioli by candlelight. Bea carried their dishes to the sink. The tap gurgled briefly when she tried it but produced just a few dribbles of water. She wiped the dishes off with paper towels.

David said, "You keep doing that. Why? What difference does it make if we don't wash the dishes? I know it's a sanitation issue but we're not staying here. No one is."

"Civilized people wash their dishes. It's a small thing but it's important, maybe even more now than before. I wish I *could* stay here. If my brother were with me I probably would. This is exactly the kind of place I wanted to find." She placed the dishes in the drainer and turned around.

"So what do you think? Do we need to take turns standing watch or can we both get a full night's sleep? It's been hours since we saw anyone, living or not. This place is pretty isolated."

"Let's sleep. We'll hear if one of *them* tries to get in. They're not exactly stealthy, are they?" David stood and picked up his backpack.

All the bedrooms were upstairs. Bea chose the one at the end of the hallway at random. It was probably the master. Double doors led to a spa-like bath but it was too dark to see much and she was far too tired to spend time exploring. She locked the door and pushed a chair against it for good measure then checked her gun before placing it beside her pillow. The clip held fifteen rounds and she had another full clip in her backpack. The bed beckoned and she paused only to peel off her boots before crawling beneath the covers and falling asleep almost instantly.

When she awoke it seemed like only minutes had passed but morning sun streamed through the gap in the curtains. Struggling to wake up, she went into the bathroom and examined her face in the mirror. A drawer held cotton balls and astringent and she gratefully wiped the dirt from her face before twisting her hair into a knot at the nape of her neck. She went through the homeowner's extensive cosmetics collection and, finding an unopened tube of lipstick, put just a touch of sheer pink on her mouth.

Gravel crunched somewhere outside and she dropped the gloss. Easing the door open she saw nothing in the hallway.

A window in one of the empty bedrooms looked out over the front porch. She twitched the curtains aside and saw a lone figure wearing a torn, stained, white button-down shirt over a pair of equally stained khakis, shambling clumsily along the drive, weaving a path to the house. First it slammed into the closed garage door then pinball-like bounced over to the front door and began to slap its rotting hand against the wood. He held something out in front of him in his right hand but she couldn't tell what it was.

Drawing her weapon she held it pointing down in front of her. No one was visible from the top of the staircase and she eased down, cringing every time the steps creaked (and they creaked a lot). The front door shook but held as the dead man pounded it repeatedly. She backed up the stairs and returned to the window just in time to see the creature back up then make another staggering assault at the door. He stepped back too far, lost his balance and fell down, then floundered to get back up from the muddy ground.

David joined her at the window, looking like he just woke up but gun held ready. She shook her head, tucked her gun away and headed for the hallway where she paused. Framed photographs lined the walls, one showing three little girls in too-big, flowery, flounced dresses. They wore white gloves and picture hats and were sitting on the lawn near the pool, having a tea party. She wondered where the girls were now.

"Let's eat something and get out of here. The only threat he poses is that he's making enough noise to attract others. We'll take him down when we leave."

Breakfast was dry cereal and a few swallows of bottled water. Bea found a road atlas in the kitchen and took it, tucking it under her arm. They constantly had to find alternate routes around blockages and this might come in handy. Exiting the rear of the house they locked the door behind them and put the key back under the rock. They stood for a moment, surveying the peacefulness of the woodland scene spread out before them. The snow was almost completely gone and everything was quiet until the sound of dragging footfalls drifted their way.

The creature staggered around the side of the house just as they reached the driveway. Its face was so badly decomposed that one eye worked its way out of the sagging socket and now dangled next to its nose. As it swayed and lurched forward the bulbous, blackened orb dropped lower and dangled near the mouth. The dead man chomped on it, only to spit it out seconds later.

David looked inquiringly at Bea and she handed him her iron fence rail. He drove it home into the empty eye socket, churning it around to destroy the brain. The dead man slumped to the ground. David pulled the rod out with a moist-sounding *pop* and wiped it off in the snow.

The right hand still clutched something tightly and she prodded it with the tip of her boot, finally stomping the fingers open to reveal a key. Wondering, she took it and found it fitted the front door lock.

"Look at this!" she called back to David.

David stowed the rod in his pack and walked to the front of the house. He tried the key and shook his head before closing the door again and placing the key under the welcome mat.

"What do you think? Memory or coincidence?" Bea asked as they walked to the car.

"I'm voting for coincidence. He was trying to get in the house when he was attacked and just never let go. Heaven help us if these things are becoming intelligent."

"I wonder what happened to the rest of his family?"

"Probably nothing good."

"You know, he was really rotten. This whole thing might be over once it warms up enough for all of them to just decompose."

"Who knows? It's not a perfect solution but we'll take what we can get. One of the problems they're having in rural areas, according to Ian, is that the ground water in wells is becoming contaminated by all the decomposing infected. *That* situation will only get worse and it will affect the cities, too."

David started the car. The wheels spun briefly in the wet leaves and mud before gaining traction. They pulled out onto the graveled road. Bea watched the house behind them in the rearview grow smaller and smaller until it finally shrank from sight. Someone's rural dream house was just an abandoned pile of bricks that would eventually become ruins.

Now, driving through the brief main street of this town they saw no one other than the roaming dead. The girl in the red dress stumbled over the curb as she tried to get to the car and fell headfirst against a parking meter. Her skull cracked and black ooze dribbled onto the ground. She didn't get back up.

Ohio was dreary, wet, and cold. Staying away from major cities meant they drove through endless corn fields. The stubby brown stalks of winter stretched for miles. Large farmhouses, some intact, others partially burned, appeared sporadically. The dead shuffled mindlessly around some of the farmyards, always turning toward the car as they drove slowly past and following, at least for a short distance before they disappeared from sight.

"Other than west, where exactly are we trying to go?" Bea asked. "Where could the pilot have gone to find fuel?"

"There are small airfields, private and otherwise, all over the country. Unfortunately I don't have a map or list of them so we're winging it, Bea. I know there're at least two outside Cincinnati and that's where we're headed right now.

I landed there once. Engine problems," David said. "A lot of hospitals have helicopter landing pads but they're almost all infested and I really hope they don't try to go to any of those."

"They wouldn't have fuel there anyway, would they?" Bea stared out the window as they passed another smoking pile of rubble that used to be a house or barn. "We're going to need gas soon ourselves and I haven't seen a clear station."

"Keep an eye out for a pump near a house or more likely near a barn. Some farmers have tanks installed on their property for the farm equipment."

She looked but saw only desolate fields with an occasional clump of trees in the distance. The gas hand kept falling as did the rain. Twice they pulled up behind abandoned cars and tried to syphon gas but both were late model with anti-theft screens inside the tank. Neither car would start so they drove on.

Just past signs for Maryville they came upon a small compound consisting of a barn, sheds, and silos off to one side of a sprawling, white, clapboard-sided house. An old-fashioned-looking gas pump stood near a barn. The buildings stood in a pleasant semi-circle. There were no signs of the living or the dead as they turned down the driveway and coasted to a stop. David stepped out with his hands held high and faced the house, looking for movement in the windows. After a moment he lowered his hands. No one seemed to be watching them.

The pump had a lock on it. A thick, heavy, key lock. Crap, thought Bea. She went into the closest shed and fumbled around until she found an axe. It was rusty with a wobbly handle but it would do. The lock finally gave after repeated blows. David backed the car up and got out, preparing to fill the tank then he stopped.

"It's diesel. I should have checked. Great, this is just great." He hung the nozzle back up and kicked the pump in frustration.

A faint moan drifted their way and they immediately drew close to the car, back to back and scanning the area for anything moving. From behind the barn an overall-clad figure limped eagerly toward them, teeth gnashing in ghastly expectation. The bib of the overalls was stained with a dark ichor. It paused briefly and tilted its head back and made a keening, chittering sound before resuming its forward, staggering sprint.

David took the axe and met it before it reached the car, burying the axe in its forehead. "What was that? Was it calling to someone or was it exulting over a potential meal?" He put one foot on the thing's neck and tugged on the axe to free it but only succeeded in breaking off the handle.

Another moan sounded somewhere behind the barn. Then another.

Three men and two women, all dead, emerged from behind the barn. One of the men had a glistening red, gaping hole where his abdomen should be and a twisted leg dragging along behind him. The others were in better shape and dismayingly fast. Time to go.

The car started then died. David tried again but it only chugged. The third try resulted in a grinding sound with a few clicks then nothing. The infected were only yards away now.

"I don't get it! We still have an eighth of a tank." David tried again.

Rotten hands hit against the car windows. One of the men, taller and massively built, hit the roof so hard it dented and the car rocked.

Bea flinched and ducked her head. "If he hits a window next, we're-" The passenger side glass shattered and sprinkles and shards of glass rained down on her. A massive decaying hand groped as she scrambled out of the bucket seat over on top of David who was still trying to start the car.

The rest of the dead clustered around the destroyed window, reaching and clutching for them. The car rocked again.

"We're going to have to sprint for the house. Ready?"

David opened the door and they practically spilled out into the cold mud. Scrambling to their feet they ran for the porch to find the front door solidly locked against them. They dashed back down the steps and Bea fell, a sharp pain in her knee making her gasp before they were up again, sprinting around the house in hopes of finding a door, an open window. There was nothing except-

A truck, blue paint faded with a rusted tail-gate, stood parked under the gnarled branches of a looming oak tree. A plank swing hung by fraying ropes banged gently against the open driver-side door. The cab light was on and the bald tires had a gray look but the key was in the ignition.

A strong smell of wet dog rose from the torn, vinyl, bench seat. Bea slid behind the wheel and the engine turned over on the first try. She backed up, driving slowly across the rutted yard around the house back to the graveled forecourt.

Three infected still thronged the car, too stupid to understand their prey had escaped. Bea drove straight toward them until she smashed them against the passenger side of the car, splattering gobbets of black matter on the truck hood. They were pinned but still gibbering and all the noise attracted the attention of the others who began to stagger back.

"What're you doing? Let's go now!" David shouted.

Bea shook her head and got out. More dead were now less than twelve feet away. She opened the trunk of the car and began throwing bags and boxes into the truck bed. There were more new clothes, shoes, boots, et cetera in here than she or Brian ever owned in their lives. She wasn't going to leave all of it behind. Who knew when they would find more? She paused long enough to shoot the huge infected man in the face. Last of all she snagged their backpacks from the backseat then jumped into the truck. David glared at her as she put the truck in reverse and hit the gas.

The trapped dead hammered and scratched on the hood, still struggling to reach them. Worn tires spun briefly in the wet mud before making contact with the gravel and they backed away, unpinning the creatures. One of the women, split in half at the waist, fell to the ground with a sickening, soggy squelch. She immediately began to crawl toward the truck, dragging her torso along with clawing hands, guts fishtailing in the mud behind her.

They left the farm behind. The wind blew in cold through gaps at the top of the windows. They tried cranking them up but they wouldn't close. Bea turned the heat on and it blew out an even stronger wet dog odor. She groaned and covered her nose, slumping back against the seat and driving with one hand.

"Not traveling in your accustomed style, Beatrice Actually?" David asked.

"My accustomed style is not traveling at all. I never had the time. I only learned to drive because I took driver's ed in high school. Well, that plus *Simpson's Road Rage* and a little *Grand Theft Auto*. I've never had a car but I'm a pretty good driver."

She sailed serenely past the stop sign at a crossroads and David winced.

The landscape was changing. They left the cornfields behind and entered an area of tree-crowned hillocks with half-frozen streams winding their way across the countryside. The clouds had broken. A weak sun shone at intervals and the cold wind grew stronger.

"How far are we from an airport?"

"I don't know but that's not what we're looking for. An aerodrome is a better description of what we hope to find and we should be near the Holywell site in about an hour. There could be one closer, you never know, so keep an eye out for towers and wind-socks."

Occasionally fires and smoke appeared in the distance. Abandoned vehicles littered the landscape and they saw a few bodies, or body parts, scattered randomly. They glimpsed wandering dead who almost always turned their way and followed the truck until they disappeared from sight.

These grew more numerous as they reached the outskirts of Cincinnati and more abandoned vehicles littered the streets. The occasional stores they saw had shattered front windows and doors and looked looted.

"We're not going into the city, are we?"

He laughed. "Not a chance. You know what D.C. was like. If I am remembering this correctly the turn-off is somewhere near here."

After a few more minutes David told her to turn left onto a black macadam road that ran alongside a field. Savaged cattle lay scattered in irregular mounds, mostly stripped of flesh. The dead had been busy here but had moved on. She wondered why. Back in D.C. they concluded the creatures responded mostly to sound and she hadn't seen anything to contradict that. Dr. Osawy said something about them being able to hear heartbeats, rhythmic sounds attracting them the most. What did they do when there were no sounds?

Something buzzed then vibrated against her chest. She fumbled through the pockets and finally pulled out her phone.

It was a text sent yesterday from Brian.

"He's alive!" she laughed and held the little phone out exultantly in front of her.

"*On Wrigley Field to pick up another soldier. No fuel still going west not sure where. Battery low.*"

The phone chimed once and then died. "Oh well. At least that message got through. Wish I had a car charger." She put the phone away.

The blaze of joy on her face made David smile. "A baseball stadium is a good rendezvous point for an air rescue. A wide open field and great visibility all around. No point in trying for this air field now. We can turn around and get back on a main road. We'll make better time."

She stopped and put the truck in reverse, backing down the narrow lane with her hand on the back of the seat. She surprised him by taking his hand and pressing it to her cheek. Her hand was warm and her cheek soft and he almost, *almost* cupped her chin to turn her toward him but she stiffened and turned her head, looking through the rear window. Following her gaze he saw why.

The little lane had filled in behind them. The infected had already reached the truck bed and were moving around the sides. Advancing clumsily but with savage, rapacious intent, a man, shreds of skin hanging from his arms, grabbed the side view mirror and hung on as Bea tried to speed up. Dull thuds shook the truck and their heads hit the ceiling of the cab as they bowled over the fallen bodies. The man grasping the mirror hissed, hands scrabbling to hang on to the window. His fingers locked in the narrow gap at the top and the window began to slowly slide down.

Bea scrambled through her backpack. Where was her fence post?

"Just shoot him! Here!" David handed over his gun and she fired, the report painfully loud in the confined space. The dead man's face caved in and she saw daylight through the back of his head. He dropped off.

The window wouldn't roll back up. She pressed on it and pushed but it stayed down. More dead reached them and thrust searching hands into the truck. One caught her hair in a vise-like grip and wouldn't let go. Tears came to her eyes from the pain before she shot it in the head, closing her eyes and mouth tightly against spatter. Even then the grip didn't relax and she pried the dead fingers apart. The body fell under the truck and they bounced as they rolled over it. Bea's scalp burned.

The crowd became impenetrable and the truck almost bogged down. Seeing no other choice Bea put the truck in drive and they shot away from the moaning throng. Ahead was a fenced-in, paved area with razor wire and a locked gate. A sign read "Muncy Airfield". There were a few dead wandering inside the fence. They kept going.

The street dead-ended just past the airfield. Tall privet shrubs surrounded this end of the street blocking any view of what might be behind them. Far in the distance now but not slowing down the dead were staggering closer. Bea looked at David, shrugged and gunned the engine, speeding up to break through the shrubs. Terrified, David gripped the door handle. A maelstrom of branches whipped around them, hitting the windows and doors and then they came to an abrupt stop, nose down in a ditch. Bea's head hit the side window hard and she cried out then gunned the engine but the wheels spun uselessly.

David slammed his fist on the dash in frustration. They would have to go forward on foot. Bea was already climbing out, standing by the truck bed, swaying a little. Blood ran down her forehead and she wiped it away from her eyes with the palms of her hands then began taking boxes from the truck.

"Stop it! There's no time and we can't carry all of it." David took just his backpack and guns and handed her the Glock and backpack she left in the cab.

She kept removing the boxes with her free hand. "Brian needs these. He lost his shoe, don't you remember?" She set two boxes on the ground and went back for more.

"Bea, let's go!" David grabbed her arm and then noticed the blood on her forehead. He took her head in his hands and turned her face toward him. Her left pupil might be slightly larger than her right and if so that was a classic sign of concussion. A gash near her hairline bled freely.

He pulled her away from the truck and she didn't fight him, donning her backpack when he handed it to her. They climbed out of the ditch onto pavement.

"We have to find transportation. Come on." David began to stride down the street then looked back to see Bea still standing by the ditch. She wiped her forehead again and stared perplexedly at the blood on her hand. David took her arm and pulled her along.

They were in a residential area, a little on the shabby side. Several houses sported boarded-up windows and doors. Cars were parked randomly here and there but none had keys in them. The moans and shuffles were getting louder even though they couldn't see the dead through the privet yet.

Discarded items filled the streets, backpacks, fishing tackle, a pink, plastic Barbie dream house, all dropped by fleeing residents. A dead dog, white ribs facing upward and legs torn off, lay in a gutter. They passed a burned-out house containing an infected clawing at flame-scorched basement walls and trying to climb out. He or she had been so badly burned that it was impossible to make out any features; hair, nose and ears were all burned away.

Most of the houses appeared to be locked up tight with no evidence of living human habitation. David looked back down the street behind them. Four infected made it through the hedge and were coming their way. He could shoot them but the gunfire would inexorably draw the others their way. He gripped Bea's arm tighter and pulled her along. She stumbled and would have fallen if he hadn't been holding her up.

He glimpsed movement out of the corner of his eye. Someone raised an upstairs window in a red, clapboard, two-story house on the next block and was beckoning to them. He strained to see. The figure left the window.

Behind them more infected emerged from side streets and shambled along, heading their way.

Any port in a storm, David thought. The red house was just a little farther. Bea was starting to stagger. He put an arm around her waist and half dragged her across the street.

Here the houses were a little more spaced-out, some with detached garages left open when their owners fled. Smooth lawns sloped down to sidewalks littered with more detritus of the fleeing. Seemingly out of nowhere a man, wearing nothing but filthy, stained boxers, shreds of skin hanging from a ragged hole in his abdomen, slammed into David, taking him to the ground.

He felt the dead man's mouth chomp down hard on his arm, tearing away the nylon shell and the down underneath. Little puffs of feathers floated to the ground. Chewing for a few seconds before spitting them out, the man came in for another bite.

Spinning around, David kicked him hard in the face before scrambling backward and almost colliding with Bea who was standing, holding a Glock in shaking hands. She looked down at her hands almost as if they belonged to someone else and had nothing to do with her. When the gun fired twice she looked surprised.

The first shot hit pavement. The second hit the dead man in the side of his face, blowing off his jaw and the side of his skull. Black chunks splattered across the street. He went down.

"I think he wanted to hurt you." She struggled to get the words out and her speech was slurred.

David almost laughed. "I think you're right. Let's get inside."

More dead staggered into the street behind them. They ran for the red house, David hoping she didn't collapse before they got to the steps. Someone opened the door and they almost fell inside, finding themselves in near-total darkness. David froze when he heard a shotgun rack.

Chapter Two

David put his hands up and turned slowly, looking for the source of the sound. As his eyes adjusted to the darkness he saw they were in a small front room containing a sofa, a television and a gigantic fish aquarium. Heavy curtains covered the single window. A strong smell of cigarette smoke hung in the air.

A shadowed figure, shotgun held at the ready, strode angrily forward.

"What was that for? Don't you know that gunshot is going to draw a crowd of those monsters?"

A chunky, dark-haired man, wearing heavy-duty work boots and a camouflage vest, he seemed to be almost sparking with rage. Bea flinched and backed away then raised the Glock. He didn't slow down and knocked it from her hand then slammed her into the wall. She saw stars before the room seemed to recede down a narrowing hallway and all sounds ceased. She slumped to the ground.

Choked with rage, David raised the butt of his rifle and managed to land a good hit in the guy's substantial belly. His breath released with a startled *oomph* but he didn't go down. He launched himself at David and threw him to the floor, battering him with those steel-toed boots. David kicked him hard in the knees and he came down, almost on top of him.

The two men were silent during the whole struggle, both aware that the creatures would be drawn to sound. Just as David managed to sit on top of his opponent, ready to punch the man's head into the floor, a deep moan and then a keening snarl sounded outside. Both men froze.

The man sucker-punched David in the stomach then slid out from under him. Scrambling to his feet he twitched the curtain aside and looked out.

"Five or six of them now. In a few minutes it'll be a hundred." He glared at them then noticed that Bea was unconscious.

"What's wrong with her? I didn't hit her that hard."

"She has a concussion, you jackass. Who knows how much damage you caused when you hit her." David caught his breath then scooped her up and carried her to the sofa. Her eyelids fluttered but didn't open. He checked and found her pulse was racing.

"What was I supposed to do? She pulled a gun on me."

"Only after you racked that shotgun and came at us. Do you have any blankets?" He wanted to keep her warm.

"I know there are some upstairs. This isn't my house. I was getting ready to leave when I saw the two of you. We can't stay here."

"I'm going to have to stay here. At least until she gets back on her feet. Could you just look for some blankets? Please."

The man grunted and turned away. David heard a click and looked around. Their reluctant host had just turned on a closet light and was rummaging through the closet contents. Electricity?

"You have power here?"

"Yeah. Not sure why. This is a pretty old part of town. Maybe it's on a different sub-station from the rest of the area. I'm not using lights unless I have to and I'm trying to keep them from showing through the windows. Don't want to attract unwanted attention." He emerged from the closet with a knitted afghan.

David covered Bea. "I don't think they can see very well, if at all."

"Yeah, I kind of figured that but there are other threats. Lots of gangs and just plain old-fashioned bad guys in Cincinnati will thrive in situations like this. Like the ones down south that deliberately stayed in New Orleans during Katrina just to loot or worse."

"Should we be worried that the homeowner is going to come back and shoot us for trespassing? Do you know whose house this is?"

"My ex-wife's. I came over here looking for my two boys when all this broke. Everyone was gone when I got here and I've been trapped by the infected for two days. They had cleared out when you and your gun-happy girlfriend showed up. Thanks a lot."

The chorus of moaning outside rose to a disturbing pitch. David felt the hair on his neck prickle. How he hated that sound. It carried such driving, primal menace. No thought behind it, just the urgent hunger to kill and consume.

"Look, I'm sorry. That guy came on us so fast. I mean, we know how attracted they are to sounds but we had to get rid of it. My name is David and this is Beatrice. She's not my girlfriend, by the way. We're trying to get to the west coast. She's trying to find her brother and I have business out there."

"I'm Homer Hazard." He fished in his down vest and drew out a pack of cigarettes, lighting one and taking a deep drag.

"You're kidding."

"Nope."

"But you're-"

"Asian, I know. As far as the Christian name goes my mom liked reading the classics and the surname is supposed to be an anglicized version of Hsiao."

"So you're from Ohio?"

"My family is from Tennessee. Can we move on? Do you want to take your 'not girlfriend' upstairs to one of the bedrooms? She'll rest a lot better on a bed."

"No. It's fine. I want to keep an eye on her. Plus who knows when we'll have to bug out," David said.

"So you're headed to the west coast? That's a long way to travel with or without zombies blocking the way. You know the whole country is infested, right?"

"We assumed it was but we don't have any recent details."

"You need to educate yourself fast, buddy. The west coast was hit by an off-shore earthquake and the tsunami that rolled in smashed the harbors and beaches. They're a mess out there. You're on foot?"

"We are now. No keys in any of those vehicles in the streets. How were you going to get out?"

"The black truck out there is mine. I'd be long gone by now but I've got very limited ammo. Just a few shells left. Those things finally migrated to the next block. I can handle a few at a time but hundreds- I'm screwed. Lord knows when I'll get out of here now. I'm going up to get a better look at the street."

He left. David found the kitchen and ran water on a paper towel to wipe some of the blood from Bea's face. He hoped the water wasn't contaminated. If it wasn't now it soon would be. Municipal utilities probably hadn't been maintained since all of this started.

He peered out the window. The crowd had increased exponentially. The dead shuffled back and forth, bumping into one another or cars, sometimes falling but always getting back up eventually. As usual they showed no real awareness of one another. A woman fell down and he was close enough to see she had no skin left on the soles of her feet. She must have walked it off. Others were in worse shape.

Sitting on the floor he went through his backpack. Still plenty of ammo but not enough to shoot his way out of here. He double-checked all of his weapons, making sure they were loaded. He then inspected Bea's Glock and noticed a few light rust spots. He added two bullets to the magazine and snapped it back into place, thinking that he should look for some gun oil soon.

Bea murmured something and her hands moved restlessly. He took both hands and held them in his. She drew a shaky breath and seemed to slip into a deeper sleep. He sat beside her for a while.

There was a laptop on a kitchen counter and David booted it up, hoping it wasn't password protected. The blue light from the screen was comforting, a reminder of civilization and normalcy and being connected with the rest of the world. He checked his email (old habits die hard) but there was nothing helpful there. Searching he found the latest posting from WHO, dated three days ago.

World Health Organization
Z-virus now in Post-Pandemic Period

Director-General's statement at virtual press conference

*Update: **Canada***

Alberta Children's Hospital reports considerable anxiety among the international community since the reported bombing deaths of an entire ward of children of guest workers from Mali. Hospital spokesperson Monique Darr confirmed the auxiliary wing of the hospital was bombed by persons unknown at this time. Witnesses to the early morning attack described a group of men in military style uniforms all wearing knitted facemasks and arriving on the scene in black, late model SUVs with tinted windows.

The Canadian government has a press conference scheduled for later today and WHO applauds this move and all efforts to increase the flow of information concerning the virus.

This is not the first hospital bombing seen in Canada since the outbreak of the pandemic but is the first time children have been targeted specifically.

*Update: **China***

The Chinese Ministry of Health, before today, has denied the existence of any cases of the virus in the country. Following a surprise shake-up in the Ministry, newly appointed director Xaio Ling confirmed a large number of virus cases in Guangdon Province but insists the situation is under control and they do not expect the disease to spread any further. Doctors say they have found no evidence that the disease is airborne and state that all new cases have occurred within isolated areas. All cases have been traced back to one hospital that has since been placed under quarantine.

The ministry will now be providing daily updates on the illness. WHO is pleased with this effort at transparency that will help provide useful information to other nations dealing with the virus.

*Update: **Switzerland***

Traffic checkpoints have been set up outside Geneva in an effort to stem the flood of refugees from Italy, which remains in crisis having been particularly hard-hit. The disease has spread outside the circle of first responder groups and their families. Overwhelmed hospitals have turned away patients causing them and their families to seek help outside the country. Surveillance in Switzerland has been heightened for suspect cases. Authorities now consider refugee cases 85% contained.

***In conclusion**, as we move into the post-pandemic phase of the crisis we expect to see the disease spike in some areas with a gradual fade worldwide. Luck has been with us since the beginning in that cases were handled promptly and decisively and the virus itself did not mutate into an airborne transmittable form.*

David sat back and stared at the screen. He couldn't believe what he just read. Post-pandemic? The World Health Organization thought this was over? Did they really think they were fooling anyone with this garbage?

He heard footsteps on the stairs. Homer came in and started rummaging through the fridge, pulling out a beer. He popped the top, took a long, thirsty swig and then belched. David shut the browser and turned around.

"Where were you when it all started?" Homer asked.

"At work."

"Me too." Homer spoke between swigs. "I work downtown. Two of the major hospitals there- oh my gosh, you wouldn't believe the crowds waiting outside the ER that day they announced the outbreak. People downtown were supposed to be evacuating but really going nowhere since all the streets were blocked. It's amazing how just a few wrecks, stalls, and abandoned vehicles can shut down the entire traffic grid. On top of that a couple of water mains burst and everything was coated with ice. You could barely walk down them much less drive."

"How did they evacuate then?"

"Most of the city bus drivers parked the buses and left but the mayor tried to organize the evacuation anyway. They announced that buses would be picking up on the corner of Depot and Rhinehart and we'd be dropped off outside the city. So about three o'clock that afternoon people started queuing up all along the streets, hundreds of people. I'd been trying to call the boys' school all day then calling Janine to see if she had them. I was half out of my mind by then.

I was still up in my office trying to call Janine's folks to see if they were over there. I had a great view of the street. Like I said there were a ton of people down there waiting for the buses. The buses never came. Those walking cadavers showed up though. They must have come from the hospitals. A lot of them were wearing hospital gowns."

"How many dead?"

"At first probably a couple dozen. If people had known how to handle them, how to take them out, it would have been manageable. But of course no one did. Once they

37

started in on the crowd- well, everyone they took down was back up within minutes and now playing for the other team."

Suddenly a shrill scream pierced the continual moaning coming from outside. They ran to look out an upstairs window but couldn't see anyone living. Just the shuffling mass of dead.

"Whoever it was must have been insane to go out there." David still peered out at the crowd, looking for whoever just screamed.

"Where did you guys come from?" Homer asked.

"D.C. We made it out a few days ago."

"Really? Were the Feds still in operation? Everyone figured they were long gone and hiding out somewhere safe."

"Some branches were sheltering in place but the president and staff had already left. There is still a functioning government somewhere but those functions are greatly reduced."

Homer left while David continued to look for signs of life outside. That scream sounded like that of a child to him and the thought of a-

He heard a muffled shout from the floor below and ran for the stairs.

Downstairs Bea was sitting up, her Glock trained shakily on Homer who had his hands up and was whispering loudly.

"Wait! Don't shoot. I'm s-" Homer backed away.

David came forward. "Bea, it's ok."

She swung the gun in his direction then back toward Homer before slowly lowering it. "Aren't you the same guy who hit me?"

"Um, yes. I'm Homer Hazard and I think we got off on the wrong foot earlier. I'm glad you're feeling better."

David sat down beside her and took her face in both hands, looking at her closely. "*Are* you feeling better?"

She pulled his hands from her face. "I'm fine, just sore. Not sure why. How long was I asleep? Wait, *what* did you say your name was?"

Homer rolled his eyes and repeated his name.

David spoke up, "You've been asleep a couple of hours. It's almost dark. We'll have to stay here for at least the night. Homer's been trapped here for two days."

"How bad is it? We saw a lot of infected in the streets."

"Bad, really bad. Downtown is wall to wall zombies. Do you want a beer?"

Bea managed not to flinch at the alcohol on his breath. "No. Thanks, though."

He muttered to himself, "Cannibals and monsters. Never thought I'd find them in my own yard. Are you sure you don't want a beer?"

"I'm sure."

"Suit yourself." He ambled into the kitchen and got another beer from the fridge. "I'm going to warm up some soup. Are ya'll hungry?"

"Yes, very. You have electricity? Do you mind if I charge my phone?"

"Not at all. Charge a hundred phones if you like. I'll probably skip paying the electric bill this month."

She fumbled through her backpack then stood up, charger in hand, swaying and almost falling before she sat back down and leaned against the cushions.

"Take it slow; you hit your head really hard. There's no rush," David said.

Bea put her head down for a minute then tried standing again with better results. She found an outlet in the kitchen and plugged her phone in then turned to Homer who was perusing the sparse contents of the cupboards.

"Do you still have internet?"

"Did last time I checked."

"May I…?" She gestured toward the computer.

"Be my guest. Does vegetable beef sound good?"

"Sounds like a feast."

Bea pulled up her email but other than spam (even the end of the world as we know it didn't stop spam, apparently) the most recent mail she had were the docs from Sylvie. That seemed like a hundred years ago. So much had happened in the last week, so many horrible catastrophes. She hoped for an email from Brian, something that would let her know they were in a safe place. A part of her still hoped to hear from her mother or father. She still used the same email account she started out with as a teenager and even though she knew it was unlikely, she continued to check sporadically for some proof they were still alive. She checked now and found nothing, as usual.

She continued cruising, getting a lot of server error messages but a surprising number of websites were still up. Clicking on a link for the online paper *examiner.com* she read an article dated four days ago.

Headline India: Thousands throng Temples of Kali in Tarapith and Kamakhya

AP: Estimated thousands of ecstatic worshippers have converged on temples of the Hindu goddess Kali in the last week, celebrating the rise of the dead in honor of "Mother Kali." Devotees claim the Mother has called them to surrender to death in order to rise in a new, 'deathless' body.

Death cults are nothing new to India. The cult of Kali (members are known as the Thuggee) has existed in India for hundreds of years. Members of the cult were known to befriend and attach themselves to groups of travelers prior to killing and robbing them, supposedly as a sacrifice to the goddess. The traditional method of sacrifice was by strangulation.

Approximately 200 years ago the British Raj launched a military campaign to wipe out these practitioners of holy homicide/robbery throughout India. The cult was considered largely extinct by the 1860's but evidence has surfaced at various times and places that indicates it was never completely wiped out but merely went deeper underground.

On Tuesday, millions of onlookers watched as thousands of devotees scaled the walls of several compounds where victims of the Z-virus pandemic were quarantined, dropping their screaming children into the infected masses before leaping joyfully in to join them. The outbreak appears to have originated among the untouchables in the slum areas. Large areas of the city were barricaded then burned in an effort at sterilization. Anyone caught fleeing was shot on sight. Despite these efforts the disease has proved impossible to contain and satellite images show large groups of refugees migrating to the border with Nepal while others are attempting to board ships and flee by sea.

Bea clicked on the video embedded in the article and watched mobs converging on tall, mud-brick walls, throwing up rickety ladders and climbing up, most holding their shrieking babies in their arms and throwing them over the walls as enthralled crowds cheered them on. It was difficult to see a lot of detail for the dust kicked up by the crowds but in one shot a larger than life-sized painted image of a naked, many-armed woman wearing a necklace of human skulls was clearly visible on a wall. A long, red, pointed tongue lolled from her mouth and she held a curved sword in one of her hands while severed human heads dangled from others.

An update noted that the worshippers succeeded in overwhelming the guards at one of the compounds and released the infected into Tarapith and were believed to still be spreading throughout the entire state of West Bengal.

"Anything interesting?" Homer set two bowls on the table and sat down. She joined him.

"Gruesomely so but not helpful. At least the internet is still working so we know some technology still exists."

"A lot of it is automated of course. It will run until some component breaks down and no human is there to repair it."

"I just hope some people with those kind of skills and education survive all this. This has to end at some point and we can start rebuilding."

"Maybe we'll survive and maybe we won't. As a species I mean."

"We'll survive." She wouldn't consider any other option. Her brother was going to get the chance to grow up.

"I'm not so sure. I think it's a do over. Mother Nature got sick of us and she's exterminating us. Like the dinosaurs."

"That giant asteroid killed the dinosaurs."

"Nope. Just finished the rest of them off. Most of them were already dying from some kind of super-parasite growing inside them. Mother Nature plays nasty when she wants to."

Bea sighed. "She's definitely playing dirty now. Thanks for the meal. I can't tell you how good warm food tastes after days without it."

"That's the last of what I found in the cupboards. My ex isn't the kind to stock up for an emergency. I was really hoping to get out of here today."

He left. Bea placed the bowls in the sink then looked through a crack in the curtains at the back yard. A six foot privacy fence surrounded the small lawn and so far nothing had broken through. Plastic swings dangled forlornly from a small swing set and slide.

The front of the house was a different matter. Mutilated figures shuffled mindlessly along the sidewalks and streets. Two figures, heartbreakingly small, lurched amongst them, the smaller one with a firm grip on the backpack strap the taller boy still carried.

Tears blurred her vision and her breath caught in her throat. Dead children were more obscene than dead adults and she was never going to get used to it. It wasn't supposed to be like this. She cursed herself again for ever letting Brian go on ahead of her. How would she ever find him again in this howling, death-blasted fright-scape that used to be the United States? She pressed her face against the cool glass.

Someone came into the room but she didn't turn around, not wanting anyone to see her face at the moment. A hand, warm and comforting, came down on her shoulder.

"Turn around, Bea. I need to check your pupils," David said.

"What- why?"

"Because I think you were concussed when we hit that ditch in the truck and now you've had another blow to the head."

Annoyed she turned to face him and he checked her eyes then her pulse. "Any nausea or faintness? Are you crying?"

"No, no, and no. I was dizzy earlier but I'm better- it's just that- out there." She gestured toward the window.

He looked out then gave a faint groan. "Oh, no."

Footsteps came down the stairs and Homer walked over. "Hey. Have they cleared out at all?"

David dropped the curtain and moved away from the window hurriedly. "No, still out there. Maybe things will look better in the morning."

Homer twitched the curtain aside and his face went white. "Jonathan? Ethan? Oh, God please-"

Cold air, rank with the smell of death flowed into the room as the door banged against the wall. Homer raced into the mob of infected so fast they could do little more than turn in his direction as he flew by. He snatched up both boys, running back to the house holding them close, one under each arm. David slammed the door. Homer peered in

43

through the sidelights, an expression of shock and growing rage on his face.

He screamed, kicking the door furiously. "Open this door, open it RIGHT NOW or I SWEAR I will kill you both. I'll-"

The smaller boy, whitened eyes staring expressionlessly, opened his mouth wide and bit into his father's neck, skin and veins stretching then snapping free. Blood spurted onto his gray face as he chewed, then opened his mouth for more. Homer screamed and dropped both boys as he sank to his knees, clutching his neck in disbelief.

Now other infected reached the stoop, moaning excitedly. Bea pushed David aside and opened the door, grabbed the back of Homer's shirt and pulled him inside, kicking the door shut just as the dead fell upon it in a gibbering mass, trampling the two boys in the rush.

Homer collapsed against the wall, alternately cursing and crying. Blood poured from his neck in a steady pulsing rhythm. His lips looked blue.

"He's going into shock. Get that blanket." Bea applied pressure to the wound and the bleeding slowed. The child had missed the carotid.

They wrapped him in the afghan and moved him to the sofa. The assault on the house continued but the door held. For now.

The night grew darker and though it was difficult to be sure, David thought the dead were beginning to thin out. One of the small figures lay in the driveway, not moving anymore.

Homer's skin was cold and grew colder. He recovered enough to stagger to his feet and run for the bathroom where they heard him vomiting over and over again. When he stopped they helped him back to the sofa where he dozed. They kept vigil, checking his pulse and making sure he was warmly wrapped up but the outcome was inevitable. That bite was going to kill him.

"How long do you think?" David whispered.

"Hard to say but it was a deep bite in the neck not terribly far from the heart so the virus is being pumped rapidly through the bloodstream. If the bite had been in an extremity it would have taken longer, like with Mac. Dr. Osawy thought it also varied from person to person. A few hours maybe?"

Around three a.m. the wound was turning black and Homer's breathing became labored and liquid. He tried to speak but only made garbled sounds. Bea took his icy hand and he held on tightly. His eyes opened briefly and the grief and pain Bea saw there tore at her heart. He knew what was happening to him. The expression in his eyes faded to dull acceptance and he coughed; a horrible loose cough that sounded as if he were choking. A bubbling, liquid sound rattled his chest which slowly expanded and deflated one last time. Then he was still.

Chapter Three

They knew they had only minutes before the body reanimated but it was hard to make themselves do what they had to do.

David whispered, "Not a gunshot unless we have no choice. If those things hear it they'll trickle back and trap us here that much longer. Where's your fence rail?"

She couldn't find it. How could they have been this stupid? They knew how quickly the dead could revive. She dumped her back pack on the floor but no rail. Searching the kitchen yielded nothing but flimsy spoons and forks and a wooden rolling pin that looked as if it had never been used. Did they keep all the knives somewhere else? She continued looking for something more substantial but there was nothing.

David stood next to Homer's body, gun ready. Less than five minutes passed but the legs had already started to twitch. Another minute and the left hand clenched into a fist, went limp and clenched again. The eyes opened suddenly. There was no intelligence in them anymore and they were drying out and dull. A moan, faint but deep-pitched arose from the depths of its chest and escaped the open mouth, accompanied by a rush of fetid air. Homer struggled to his feet and stood swaying, as if he were testing his balance. David backed away into the kitchen.

Upstairs, Bea tossed items out of closets, strewing toys, coats, and shoes on the floor. Finally in the hall closet, on the very back of the top shelf, she found a carved wooden box about the length of a yard stick. Inside was a wicked-looking blade with a jagged edge and a complexly carved handle she thought might be ivory. It was fairly heavy and looked timeworn but there wasn't a spot of rust on it anywhere and the metal shone even in the dim closet light. A moaning sound drifted up the stairs and she lowered the sword to her side and ran.

Homer now stood in the kitchen doorway, yards away from David. Bea handed over the weapon. Homer only now seemed to become aware of them and staggered forward, still moaning as if in pain but with teeth gnashing hungrily. With a broad, downward movement David sliced into his neck but missed severing the spinal column. He swung again and the head rolled free, thumping to the floor. David gave Bea the sword and she split the skull in two.

Though they were both shaken they didn't talk about it. David started dragging the body out of the door way. Bea cleaned the sword on the blanket then started back up the stairs to put it away.

"Wait. Let's keep the sword," David said.

"It doesn't have a sheath and it's wicked sharp. I don't want to carry it," Bea responded.

"Put it in my pack then, would you?"

She unzipped his pack pulled out her fence rail. "Look what I found."

"Oh? Good. I forgot I put it in there. Does the sword fit?"

Bea tried it. "Not without slicing a hole in the bottom."

"Never mind then. We should probably try to move on once it's daylight." David finished wedging the body between the sofa and the wall, out of the way.

"I'm really tired, David. Also I must have lost some of the stuff out of my backpack. I only have a few packets of dried fruit left and no water. We'll have to find a store that hasn't been looted."

"We're bound to find something along the way. You sleep for a couple of hours and I'll stand watch."

"I don't know if I can. His children- what must it be like to have someone you love so much come back to you but then- they aren't who they were. They're something

47

monstrous and murderous, not even human. You'd still want to hold them and keep them safe but-"

"Don't overthink it. You won't make it if you do, Bea. Just go get some sleep."

She went upstairs and David placed the pieces of Homer's head in the coat closet. He didn't want to have to look at it.

Feeling as weary as he could ever remember he searched the kitchen cupboards but they were completely bare except for plastic wrap and aluminum foil, etc. He sat down and sighed. A few dead still scratched and clawed at the front of the house but most had moved on, drawn by who knows what. The computer screen glowed in the pre-dawn darkness and he fumbled through his pockets, pulled Bea's memory stick and plugged it in.

The race to conquer the Equatorial Poles and find the much-desired Northwest Passage linking the Atlantic and Pacific oceans during the 19th and early 20th centuries is well-documented. The horrifying failure of the Scott expedition and the triumphant story of the Peary venture are both well-known.

However, the burning ambition to conquer those frozen lands began long, long ago with figures such as Martin Frobisher, Godske Lindenov, and of course, the famous Erikson men, Eric and Leif.

A private journal from one such expedition of the 1700's survived the rigors and vagaries of time within the Lytton family of North Lancashire and was recently sold at auction. This researcher purchased it as part of a bulk lot, bought sight unseen as a favor, wishing to help a friend in greatly reduced circumstances. As is so often the case, the kindnesses we think we are extending selflessly to others, work to our own benefit, and this treasure of a journal is proof of that. Ensign E.G. Lytton's account of his quest for

48

*the Northwest Passage aboard HMS Hecca is an enthralling
and unusual read.*
    W.D. (Whitehall archivist, 1919)

*The morning of the 23rd found us near Cape Repulse.
Foggy, gray but sea calmer until we rounded a good-sized
berg and were drawn into a strong tide that sent us amongst
heavy streams of ice. We were certain to be dashed against
them when an eddying current spun us around and into
calmer waters near a large berg to which we anchored to
wait out the tide. Very little progress today but managed to
stay close to the bergs which, due to their deep draught,
afforded us some protection from the floes and smaller
drifting ice. That is to say, we crept like mice, avoiding our
frosty, hulking predators.*

*June 6th. Approaching Repulse Bay we were surprised
by a small flotilla of Esquimuax natives paddling furiously to
overtake us. In less than an hour we found ourselves in the
midst of at least twenty craft, which I shall later attempt to
describe. For now I will recount the appearance of their
occupants.*

*All had inky-black hair worn either in a knot on top
of the head or else free and lying about their shoulders
giving them a wild appearance. The men were mostly beard-
less. Both sexes were small and well-made with slender
hands and small eyes. Some sport spiraling blue tattoos
around their mouths.*

*Several were afflicted with a disease of the eye and
had no eyelashes. Those thus afflicted wore curious eye-
shades made of a light wood as did some not evidencing any
blindness. One wonders if the constant glare from the ice
does not contribute to their condition.*

*Complexions were of brown or copper hue, difficult to
be sure as they were covered with dirt, grease, and often
blood. Nosebleeds were seen frequently and to our disgust
they lick and drink the blood with relish as it pours.*

Made primarily of seal skins the dress of the sexes differed but little. The women's outer jackets had a large pouch attached to the shoulders and hung down the back. This was used as a hood during less temperate weather but also served to transport their infants whom they left quite naked while thus contained. Older children were wrapped as warmly as the adults and their wonderfully tanned seal skins appear impervious to water.

They were eager to trade and I fear were cheated as we were offered (and accepted) oil, skins, and ivory in exchange for paltry items such as buttons and iron nails. Saws they particularly prized. With each successful barter they licked the received item before putting it away. I never saw them omit this custom and the more they desired the item the more thoroughly they licked it.

As the evening came on they returned to their boats, some sleeping there but others withdrew to a small island about a mile distant and encamped there.

June 7th. Pressed on the next day, taking soundings as we went, always struggling to find a way through the ice. A small number of the natives continued to trail us in their boats but the majority turned back. We spied a group of sea unicorns* and though we dispatched a boat, could not get close enough to kill one.

About suppertime we came upon an island and took the opportunity to explore. Our Esquimuax escort attempted to dissuade us from disembarking, one old gentleman giving a long speech of which we understood not a word. His companions nodded fearfully throughout and when they found we were determined to go on they paddled sorrowfully away and were soon lost to sight.

We landed a small party, led by myself and on the lookout for any signs of the large, yellow-white bears often seen in the distance. We saw no animals other than the snow buntins abundant throughout the journey. Quantities of driftwood lay washed up by the tide, so high that the island must suffer near complete inundation at times. Stunted, twisting trees, little more than scrub, marked the mouth of an icy pool of fresh water, constantly replenished by a sparkling waterfall. There was no evidence of recent human habitation. A few old, ruined stone huts dotted the slope. One contained a human skull, broken in two.

Just past the broken, bleached bones of an ancient whale carcass we came upon a small, jagged rise of hills. A certain symmetry to their arrangement caused conjecture as to whether they had perhaps been made by humans but we never found convincing proof. An irregular opening, little more than four feet high, marked the largest hill.

Entering the yawning, black mouth we found a cave with a smooth pebbled floor that sloped down and presumably back into the hillside but the darkness revealed little else to our gaze. The ceiling was quite low though we were able to stand upright in the center. Water trickled down the walls and pooled shallowly in the middle of the pebble floor before running down and back out of sight. Retreating outside we made camp for the night.

Sometime after midnight, a gale set in and we were indeed sore beset. Stinging ice pelted us without mercy and our driftwood fire was extinguished. Stumbling in the darkness we made for the cave seeking shelter. Seaman Peabody rescued most of our firewood and we soon had a warm, though smoky, encampment in the little grotto.

Unable to sleep we improvised flambeaux and made to explore our surroundings more thoroughly. I greatly feared coming across one of the gigantic, white bears seen on the ice and we all had our weapons out and ready.

Descending the slight slope we found evidence of an ancient battle. Scattered alongside the trickling water but not in it were broad swords flaking with rust and an occasional dagger, jeweled hilts glinting dully in the torchlight. Human skeletons, none in one piece, were flung about the passage in great confusion.

51

The cold increased as we went deeper into the earth. Not very far along the passage we came upon a jumble of stones as though a portion of the ceiling had fallen. Ice, possibly condensed from ceiling drips throughout the years, covered the entire mass.

We could go no further. The rocks and ice completely blocked the remainder of the passageway (if more there was) and we had turned back when Peabody called a halt. His voice echoed eerily off the constricting walls as he shouted that something was in the ice.

He stood holding his torch over the rock fall. Indeed there was a body. Upon closer examination it appeared to be a man. The face, though blackened and distorted, did not resemble the natives of this land. European features and fair hair were clearly visible. The facial features, despite their Caucasian bent, gave an odd impression of brutishness and vacuity. Clothing, style or material, was impossible to make out. Clearly he died here long ago, probably in the rock fall, his body preserved by the ice.

Back at the cave entrance we were confronted again by the storm. It should have been close to dawn but of course little distinguishes day from night at this season. The ice and wind drove us back into the cave.

Trapped and restless as we were it took little for Peabody to persuade us to venture to melt the ice around the enclosed man for further inspection. An uneasiness, almost a fear, tugged at my mind each time I peered at the poor brute but I dismissed the notion. In short course we rekindled our fire the short distance to the back of the cave, leaving a guard posted back at the entrance. The light from the fire illuminated the low ceiling and Morgan pointed out marks there that looked like those of axes or picks, making me wonder if some human hand precipitated the long ago rock fall. Could they have been mining the cave? I saw nothing to indicate the presence of any precious mineral.

We dozed. The dark cave grew warm from the fire. The ice encasing the dead man cracked and popped as it melted but we paid it little mind until the clacking began.

It started with a rhythmic clicking, sounds just seconds apart. Startled, we assumed a defensive formation in preparation to battle we knew not what but the source of the sound was not hard to find.

Our ice man, blackened and decayed as he was, had come to life. His lower extremities remained ice-bound but his twisting head and clutching, writhing arms were thawed. The warmth also released an overpowering odor of putrefaction, so strong it was an assault on the senses. His teeth clashed together and he seemed possessed of a most desperate hunger.

Building up the fire and lighting the remains of our torches we inspected him closely whilst staying clear of his raking fingers which were only blackened bone but sharp. What remained of his eyes resembled withered, mold-covered polyps but as stated before his straight, hawk like nose and thin lips were overtly European engendering thoughts of Vikings sailing their dragon-bowed ships through the ice floes. If only we could devise some means of communicating with him! To actually converse with an adventurer of the remote past would be an opportunity unheard of in history!

His struggles and the warmth released one twisted leg and he pulled himself forward, to our disbelief slowly tearing off the leg still trapped and leaving it behind.

My only other language is German and in hope that a Norseman such as he might recognize some of the words I shouted at him to halt and stay where he was. To no avail. His struggles caused more and more of the rock pile to tumble and more blackened, wizened figures began to crawl from the rubble behind him.

We all had our cutlasses out but only I and Morgan carried flintlocks. Too close range for these anyway and our

53

task seemed straightforward. We all moved forward as one and impaled our attackers with less trouble than anticipated. These creatures made no attempt to defend themselves or slow their approach.

They did not die! They did not flinch or even seem aware of their impalement! Desiccated, rotten hands continued to flail and grapple for us. The man on my cutlass slid forward to the hilt, clawing and scratching at my face with those dagger-sharp finger bones. In disgust I placed my boot against his chest to push him back and only managed to sink my foot up past my ankle into a stinking mass of black ichor. My heel connected with the bones of his spine and I eventually pushed him back enough to extract my blade.

The cave was full of shouts and the creatures' harsh, eldritch moans. Peabody pushed at the creature attacking him and the man bit down on his arm, hanging on like a mad dog despite Peabody's screams and attempts to shake him off.

More and more of the loathsome things advanced, some dragging themselves forward along the cave floor like hideously overgrown creeping lizards. We were greatly outnumbered. Our only advantage over them was our speed and we retreated and regrouped at the mouth of the cave where Peabody began hacking frantically at the roof with a small axe he habitually carried at his belt. Discerning his intent we all attacked the low ceiling with our swords until we managed to set off a small rock fall. Continued efforts produced a large cave-in and our pursuers were once again trapped inside their icy tomb. With one exception.

Our fair-haired Norseman had beaten the rocks and still struggled after us. The sounds he made were only vaguely human, a sort of rasping, drawn-out moan of pain. Whatever else he was feeling he was clearly in agony. Pulling himself forward with mouth stretched wide he made as if to devour my crew.

We drove our swords through his body, pinning him to the ground, and watching his continued struggles. Were these creatures some collection of possessed ghouls? Finally we ended him with a crushing blow to the head using a stone.

We carried the body back to the Hecca for a closer examination, hoping to find some clue as to the creature's origins and cause of its incredible revival from frozen death.

I concluded, based on his visage and the style of weapons found in the cave that he was most probably a Norseman. Age was difficult to determine but surely no older than thirty or so. The body was emaciated and damaged, with extensive wounds to the abdomen and shoulders missing large areas of flesh. The neck was torn with a deep, ragged, leathery wound revealing the spinal column. Even if not killed by the rock fall, this man should have been dead from blood loss long ago. Did the ice somehow preserve his life?

Our savage little Esquimaux followers returned and seeing the body, drew back and refused to come any closer. Through much gesturing and pantomime they indicated the creature was dangerous and must be burned. Somehow they managed to gather enough driftwood to build a large fire and the dried, brittle corpse caught fire quickly and was soon a charred bundle of bones. Even then they insisted on scattering the ashes containing these. When they became aware that Seaman Peabody was wounded they avoided him with a fright that was almost comical.

With a stealthiness and savagery we did not suspect them capable of until now two of their number stole onto the Hecca where Seaman Peabody lay, suffering from an ague as well as the bite he received in the cave, and beheaded him as he slept. I made an example of both men, hanging them by the necks until dead and leaving the bodies aloft and dangling for a time from the mizzen-mast as a warning to their fellows.

"Wow," David said quietly to himself. He hadn't read this one back in the shelter. He downloaded the entire drive to the computer then pulled out his own memory stick and loaded the new file on it. He hadn't confided information about his own "Z file" to many people. Despite collecting the information over the last few years he had no way of verifying it and never had any plans for using it. He still didn't but who knew when it might come in handy. After a moment's thought he emailed the entire file to his user account. Then he placed the small laptop in his backpack and looked out the window.

Dawn had crept unnoticed into the sky revealing mostly clear streets. Homer's black truck gleamed as the sun hit it reminding David he had forgotten to search Homer's body for the keys. Reluctantly he pushed the sofa away from the wall and rolled the headless body onto its back. In a jeans pocket was a set of keys that hung from a plastic picture fob containing the images of two smiling boys, one with a cowlick and the other beaming with a gap-toothed grin. David crouched by the body, holding the keys in the palm of his hand, looking at the small pictures. Boys any father would be proud of. Boys who would never grow up.

The dead man's hand twitched, startling David into falling back against the wall, hitting his head and momentarily stunning him. The hand groped at the floor, only for a few seconds, then went flaccid.

David shoved the body against the wall and pushed the sofa back in place. They couldn't get out of here soon enough. He checked his weapon and looked out the window again. A small group stood at the bottom of the driveway, shuffling and jostling one another randomly.

He found Bea sleeping in one of the twin beds upstairs. The morning light coming through a crack in the curtains just touched her hair, turning it to warm gold. Her cheek was smudged and he tried to wipe it away then saw her eyes open. She watched him with a look of intense concentration while he gently dabbed at her cheek before moving on to trace the outline of her lips. She closed her eyes again for a moment then sat up, swinging her legs over the side of the bed onto the floor. David's hand dropped to his side.

"What does it look like outside?" she asked.

"Better. Fewer dead and the sun is out. It's a lot warmer. And I have a surprise." He jingled the keys in his hand.

Bea looked relieved. "Do you know what vehicle they go with?"

"Yeah, pretty sure I do."

"Let's do this then."

The dead came for them as soon as the door opened. David was ready and knocked an emaciated woman to the ground. Bea split her skull wide with a sharp blow from her rail. There was little left of her brain other than viscous black fluid.

Homer's truck was unlocked and started on the first try. The gas hand was on "F" and the heater warmed up the cab in minutes. Attempts to find something on the radio produced nothing but static.

Winding through the unfamiliar streets, it took them a while to find a way to I-71. Every time they found signs directing them to the interstate they would have to detour around pile-ups or the dead and find themselves lost again. Looted stores, glass fronts broken, were ever present reminders they were now in a post-apocalyptic world and that resources like food and water were finite and viciously fought for. When they did find an on-ramp they encountered blockages they were fortunately able to weave through. Many, many cars still contained their dead occupants, entombed within glass and steel, struggling to get out.

Bea checked her phone but found no new messages. She sent Brian a short text telling him their approximate location and that they were going to continue to head west.

"That might be the equivalent of a message in a bottle but I have to keep trying," she said, putting her phone in her pocket.

"You are nothing if not persistent. Does the thought of throwing in the towel never cross your mind?"

"What would be the point of that? Would you give up if it were your brother?"

"No, probably not. So where does the stubbornness come from? Your mother or your father? I'm betting it was your mom."

She was silent for several moments, face turned away and looking out at the fields flashing by in the sunlight. It was only when the light glinted on her cheeks that he realized she was crying.

"Sorry, I didn't even think before I said that. Your parents- they left you, right? I just thought it was a long time ago maybe and-"

"It *was* a long time ago but it still hurts. Sometimes I'm afraid they're dead. A lot of people are but I can't picture my parents dead. Sometimes I have trouble picturing them at all. You asked if my parents are stubborn. I equate stubbornness with strength and if I use that equation the answer is no. They were never strong, probably still aren't. They left us, first my dad, then my mom. Our social worker usually referred to them as a substance abuse case. Alcohol mainly with some prescription drug abuse. Even before they left, Brian and I were mostly on our own. " She pressed her palms against her face then wiped her cheeks. The tears were gone.

"You probably hated them for that."

Her eyes widened and she looked at him in surprise. "Why would you say that? I love them, I couldn't hate them. They were just weak, not bad. They tried to be real parents

58

but they were never strong enough. For years after they left Brian and I looked for them everywhere we went. I wish I could find them now."

"If I ever had kids I know I would never desert them," David persisted.

"We all wear different chains, David. What about you? I suppose you had a *Boy Meets World/* Cory Matthews childhood."

"Sort of. Except my dad was in the military and we moved every few years. I think that was hard on my mom. To my brother, sister,and me it was just normal, you know, status quo. Almost everyone we knew was in the same boat. My brother and I went into the service because it seemed like a logical next step after high school. Except that my brother stayed in. He was deployed to Cali when all this started. My mom hadn't heard from him the last time we talked and she's worried."

"Is he younger or older?"

"He's the baby of the family. Mom's blue-eyed baby boy. She's protective- we all are really. He was born with a heart defect and there were several years when we thought he wouldn't make it but he grew out of it. He ran track and played basketball and did everything the doctors said he couldn't."

"Blue eyes with dark hair like yours? I bet he had lots of girlfriends, then."

"Oh yeah," David laughed. "More than I did. But mostly, he was always just a genuinely good person. He joined the military because he wanted to do good things in the world. I hope that's what he's doing now."

"He's probably okay, right? The military were better prepared for this than civilians."

"No one was really prepared for this, Bea. Similar scenarios but not the living dead."

They continued on in silence, David thinking about the persistent and stubborn love she still bore for her obviously deadbeat parents. He wasn't sure he would have reacted the same. Then he wondered what it would be like to have someone love him like that.

They drove for hours. His stomach felt hollow and he hadn't slept and was starting to feel the drain. The MRE's were still in his backpack but they were a last resort only. Billboards along the way advertised restaurants, whetting his appetite even more.

"I'm starving. Do you think it's too risky to pull off and see what we can find?" Bea asked, unconsciously echoing his thoughts.

"I'm hungry too but let's wait until we're ready to stop for the night."

"What about gas?"

"We should be fine for a while. I'm trying to avoid Louisville. It's a good-sized city."

But they were cut off by vehicle pile-ups and had to double back. They were lost and the daylight was passing. The shadows grew longer and the sun soon dipped behind a copse of trees to the west. A river, running sluggishly below muddy exposed banks, ran alongside the two-lane road that gradually became steep and twisting, guard rails poor protection against a miscalculation that might end in a plunge into the river gorge below.

Bea observed, "The river is so low. Odd with all the rain and snow we've seen."

"I don't know for sure about this one but most large rivers have at least one hydroelectric dam. It's possible there hasn't been an upstream water release since the outbreak. If that's the case then heaven help anyone in the way when the gates finally burst."

David pulled into a graveled area designated as an overlook. They were up so high now they might be able to look out over the terrain and get their bearings. Bea reached the low stone border wall on the edge of the bluff first.

"Oh, no."

The overlook afforded a panoramic view of the city, river, and surrounding countryside. On a normal day she could see how it would be breathtakingly lovely but not today. Fires burned and smoke drifted, partially obscuring the view but what *was* visible was disheartening. A dark mass of shuffling, staggering dead surged across the land, spilling into the river, jamming the bridges and roads. How many were down there? A hundred thousand? More?

"We have to turn around. I think that's Louisville."

Bea said quietly, almost as if she were afraid the teaming crowd below would hear her, "I thought, *hoped* really, that we would find towns that were still normal. Someplace safe with running water and electricity and food. It's not going to happen, is it?"

"Probably not. It's everywhere."

Bea took a deep breath and released it. "Ok. We turn around. Then what? We got lost before, we're still lost. Look at this-" she gestured "they're all around us and it's getting dark."

"Do you want to spend the night in the truck?"

"We may not have a choice."

Below them the seething mass of dead began to swarm the river. They soon saw why. A double-decked riverboat, the kind used for river tours, packed to overflowing with people and riding low in the water, drifted into view. They were having engine trouble, a loud chugging, grinding sound echoed against the rock bluff. The passengers saw the infected on the bank and as more and more dead plunged into the water, frightened screams added to the engine noise.

The current was still strong enough to take some of the floundering dead downstream with it but more were floating and struggling toward the ailing riverboat. Reaching it they were unable to scale the sides but the panicked passengers all pressed toward the far side of the boat anyway. The overloaded boat began to tilt dangerously to the left. A warning bell, clanging harshly, added to the confusion and noise. Someone, presumably the captain, took up a bullhorn and pleaded with the passengers to help right the vessel but they were past rational thought.

Slowly but inexorably the boat continued to tilt and take on water. With a splashing boom the vessel collapsed onto its side. Both decks hit the water hard and began to sink. Some passengers fought their way back to the surface only to meet with the dead. Some got away and were swept downstream. Others grappled with their attackers but they were overwhelmed. The water was a boiling mass of the dead and the soon-to-be-dead. A boy, small but obviously a skillful swimmer, made it to the small pebbled ledge against the cliffs. As he lay, gasping and winded, a group of water-bloated dead groped their way onto the shore and ripped him to bloody pieces.

That was when Bea turned away and went back to the truck. She leaned against a door, slid to the ground and hugged her knees. The boy reminded her of Brian and despite an empty stomach she leaned to one side and was quietly sick. She wiped her mouth and sat there, shuddering.

"Are you okay?" David came around the side of the truck.

"Yes, fine." She stood up and opened the truck door. "I can drive for a while if you like. It's my turn."

"Are you sure your head doesn't hurt? Okay then, let's go."

The winding road brought them back down and even closer to the river. They had to get out of the area before dark. Impulsively she turned left off the main road, away from the river, and continued taking left turns, going deeper and deeper into a heavily wooded glade. The road turned to gravel and grew narrower but she didn't slow down and David reached for the grab-handle and held on, white-knuckled. She kept going, finally crossing a shallow running stream after which the road began to take them up again. The switchback curves barely slowed her down and David expected them to plunge to their deaths at any moment.

The view, when they finally crested the slope, showed they were farther from the city and the river. The last of the daylight faded from the ruddy sky and as the truck sputtered to a halt they realized they were out of gas.

Birds called in the surrounding woodland, one trilling with a particularly piercing sound before flying away, a dark blur in the evening air. An early moon hung low in the sky, giving a little light. Just over the ridge was the barely discernible outline of a building. With no options other than remaining in the truck for the night they climbed out and shouldered their backpacks, proceeding up and over the top of the hill with weapons drawn. Bea switched on her flashlight and walked ahead. She was starving and hoped to find a place with water and food. A bed would be a nice bonus but she would take a night on the floor if she could just find a sturdy shelter with a strong, dead-bolt on the door.

Small rustlings sounded all around them as the animals in the woods found shelter for the night and settled in. There was nothing to indicate the possible presence of the dead except-

A smell like rotted meat floated randomly on the slight breeze. Bea stopped and turned around in a slow circle, trying to see if she could tell the direction the smell came from but it was elusive, coming and going randomly. They continued to slog forward across the mossy forest floor and entered a small, level clearing.

At first she thought she had stumbled over a rotted log, foot sinking into a soft pile and nearly tripping. She trained her flashlight on the ground. A deep groan drifted up and she dropped the flashlight.

She stood in the decomposing mush of one of the infected. Revolted, she tried to pull free but, off-balance, she fell backward and found her hands inside the stinking guts of another. This one tried to bite her and she rolled to her left, scrambling to her feet and ran, leaving her flashlight behind in a blind panic.

The ground itself seemed to be moving. Grunting moans filled the night air in a hellish chorus. She ran, sure they would pull her down and devour her with what was left of their mouths. Her foot sank into another moist pile of rotten flesh and pus, scraping her boot on a bone when she pulled out. Teeth clacked together somewhere behind her and she ran until an arm reached up and grasped her ankle in an iron grip. She fell, sprawling headlong on top of a writhing corpse.

Gasping for air and fighting to get free, she kicked the dead arm until it broke off from the body. She gained her feet and began to climb the next ridge. There didn't seem to be any dead here and she sank down, prying off the arm still clutching her ankle and flinging it into the darkness.

A branch cracked behind her and she froze, listening. Footsteps approached steadily and she whispered, "David?"

"Yeah. Stay where you are. I don't think anything followed us but I want to be sure."

They sat in silence for a few moments but heard nothing other than faint groans in the distance. David turned on his flashlight and they carefully made their way back down the ridge and looked around.

A campground, tents torn, sleeping bags and coolers scattered about, took up most of the copse. Decomposing infected bodies, most still moving, lay at random intervals. Bea retrieved her flashlight and they slowly made their way back to the truck.

Chapter Four

He woke the next morning to a squeaking sound. His head hurt where it lay against the window and he turned, opening his eyes to see a noseless face pressed against the glass, blackened tongue licking. He jerked away, elbow hitting the middle of the steering wheel and the horn blared. Squinting in the morning light he surveyed the area around the truck and felt his tension ease. Only the one.

Next to him Bea lay sprawled across the seat, face pressed into the crack between the seat and the door, still sound asleep. One booted foot pressed against his thigh and the other was tucked up underneath her. Her hands were folded together and pressed against her chest making her look as if she had fallen asleep while saying her prayers. If so, it was probably a good move.

They were stranded. The occupied but destroyed campground indicated there should be vehicles somewhere but he didn't see any sign of them. Of course the rain probably would have obliterated any tire tracks. Some of the campers must have survived long enough to get in their cars and escape.

The ground, soft and moist, steamed where the heat of the sun hit it directly. Spring was farther along here and some of the trees, especially the willows, were covered with swelling buds on the branches. Shading his eyes he saw slight movement on the ground over near the trampled and torn tents. Another squeak. The infected corpse was now biting the side view mirror, broken teeth gnawing uselessly but resolutely on the splintering glass and plastic.

He spied Bea's fence rail poking out the top of her pack. Rolling the window down he plunged the rail deep into the dead man's eye socket. There was a sucking, wet sound as he pulled it out. The wagging tongue went slack. The rotting man sagged to the ground.

He grabbed his backpack. Opening the door and stepping over the body he found his MRE's and opened one of the foil packets. Chicken fajitas. One hundred sixty calories was not going to get him through the morning so he opened one more packet and, righting an overturned picnic table, sat down for breakfast.

The truck door opened and Bea joined him. He tossed her two of the foil packets.

She shook her head. "Thanks, but one is fine. I owe you a breakfast now."

"I want the Grand Slam at Denny's."

"You've got it. I'd pay a hundred dollars for a mocha cappuccino right now. A hundred more if I could get blueberry pancakes with it."

"Too sweet. Give me black coffee, bacon, eggs, and buckwheat pancakes. That's a real breakfast."

"You have no idea what you're missing. My blueberry pancakes are world class. You can ask my brother when we..."

She trailed off and turning away, finished the fajitas, swallowing past a sudden lump in her throat. Fear she had held at bay for days slithered into her mind and coiled there, darkening the bright morning and making the food taste like ashes. She told herself she was just tired. Once they found a way out of here she would be okay.

"Did I dream it or did you just kill an infected through the window?"

"Yeah, I did. He's on the other side of the truck. You ready?"

They skirted the campground as they headed up the ridge. Neither of them wanted to see the rotting infected again but despite their efforts to stay away, they ran into one more. A woman, belly bloated in decomposition, lay just off the trail. A rasping moan drifted from her mouth and she managed to drag what was left of her body into their path, ravening mouth open wide but she was no threat. Mushrooms sprouted from her nose and eyes and beetles crawled in the moist folds of her neck.

David crushed her head with his boot. "They're decomposing faster in the warmth. It's looking more and more like all we have to do is stay alive long enough to let them all rot."

The day was warm, warm enough that they tied their jackets around their waists after they walked just a few minutes. The building they glimpsed the night before turned out to be a barn with two dead and ravaged horses inside. The infected had wreaked their havoc and moved on.

Even though there was no evidence any of *them* were still in the area, David and Bea walked with weapons ready, listening for footsteps and sniffing the air for traces of decay. They thought they saw occasional footprints but the ground was a carpet of springy moss and it was hard to be sure. The trail emerged from the woods into a graveled parking lot. They were in a park, Salt Lick State Park, according to a grayed, wooden sign. Another sign directed them to a trail for the Nature Center and The Cascades.

They descended back into more woods briefly and soon heard the roar of water. Lots of water from the sound of it. Passing by a log built building, the Nature Center, they found stone steps leading down. The water was really loud now and turning a bend in the path, they stopped.

Just below them a magnificent series of waterfalls cascaded down a rocky bluff, ending in a white pool of churning water far below. Bea almost exclaimed in delight at the sight then abruptly closed her mouth.

An assembly of the dead stood below them on the apron of huge flat rocks leading to the cascade's first cataract. They shuffled agitatedly, almost in unison, clearly excited by the sound of the water. A white-eyed child in red-stained, footed pajamas, half his jaw gone and the other half dangling, stepped too close to the edge and went over, body splattering among the rocks below. His unheeding comrades continued their slow dance of the dead.

Bea and David backed away silently and climbed the rock steps, the sound of the water gradually fading. Bea kept glancing over her shoulder to see if they were followed but saw nothing.

Breaking into the Nature Center involved one hard kick to a decrepit metal door back near the tightly locked dumpster. The trash was more secure than the building. Probably to keep bears from coming around.

They entered through what was presumably a break room. There was a sink, microwave and mini-fridge that stank of spoiled food. David found an unopened box of crackers. A short hallway led into an atrium with various displays relating to the flora and fauna of the region. Skylights only dimly lit the room and the air smelled musty.

Bea went straight for the ladies' room. Clear water gushed from the tap and she splashed her face and neck then drank thirstily. The soap dispenser was empty or she would have attempted a sink bath. Instead did what she could with wet paper towels.

She found David in the atrium scrolling through something on his phone while absentmindedly eating crackers. He offered her the box and she grabbed a handful.

"Any news?

"Nothing. Just updates on personnel and contact information. We must be losing a lot of people. They keep changing."

Bea nodded and wandered off, looking at the glass display cases. There were several stuffed foxes and two chipmunks, all a little dusty. The glass eyes looked cloudy, reminding her uncomfortably of the dead. She shivered.

A faded series of illustrations on the wall caught her eye. They detailed the local effects of a swarm of earthquakes that struck the area in the winter of 1811-1812.

According to the text the Cascades, formerly a single, sheer waterfall, were created over a period of three months and three or four separate earthquake events. There was an ink sketch of the original fall then several more illustrations of the Cascades.

In addition there were enlarged photographs of various sand blows created by the quakes. One was so large it was known as the Kentucky Sahara and was a popular spot for campers who liked riding the dunes with ATVs.

The display further detailed a bit of local lore:

"This area was in many ways still considered the western frontier, sparsely populated and with towns few and far between.

One town, Elm's Corners, was cut off for months by rock slides and a river that changed course during the aftershocks. When outsiders finally reached the town, they found the entire population dead or missing. Mutilated bodies lay in the streets and teeth marks were found on the bones. Tales of cannibalism circulated in the region for decades."

She jumped at the sound of David's voice behind her. "I have something about that in my files. Not that exactly but something from around the same time frame. Remind me to show it to you when we have time. Are you ready to go?"

Outside, a formation of three jets streaked across the sky, leaving triple contrail clouds, heading west. Two hours later they reached State Highway 61 and another hour's walk brought them to a partially burned-out Quality Inn. Two cars were in the parking lot, both locked. A steady, pounding rhythm shook the door of a room close to where the fire had been and they left it alone.

Guns ready, they entered the lobby. Furniture and paper lay scattered about but while they encountered no one living or dead, a steady scratching came from a closed door behind the registration desk and the air was foul with a tell-tale odor.

Bea said, "I don't want to go back there. Let's just leave."

"We need a car. Help me look for keys."

"In movies someone always knows how to hotwire a car. Schools are really sleeping on the job these days. I can't recall a car-stealing class even being offered at my high school or university."

"Funny. Will you just help me look?"

Searching the drawers and cabinets behind the reception desk was a dead end except for a handful of toothbrushes in plastic packages. Bea pocketed those while keeping an eye on the door.

David said, "I'm going in. Be ready for whatever is in there to rush the door." Bea nodded and held her gun in front of her. "Ready? One, two, three!"

He threw open the door and a furry figure darted out so fast it was almost a blur. A hound, emaciated and whimpering, skittered across the tile floor, into the lobby door and began to claw frantically on the glass, frightened eyes pleading. Bea opened the door and the dog was gone, dashing into the woods and out of sight.

"Oh no." David pulled his shirt up over his nose and mouth. Four figures, two adults and the others children, dangled from ropes thrown over exposed ceiling beams. Blackened tongues protruded between decomposing lips. The ropes cut into the decaying flesh of their necks. The parents (presumably) struggled and clawed at the air, legs trying to find something to stand on. The children, one little more than a toddler, were truly dead. Their legs were chewed to the bone, answering the question of what the dog had eaten while trapped.

Eyes watering and trying not to gag at the smell they searched the room, finding a set of keys in a purse. Bea opened the woman's wallet. A picture of a smiling family gazed serenely at the camera. She snapped it closed and put it back down gently.

David stared at the writhing dead couple with a grimly resigned expression. "We have to end them. It would be irresponsible not to. Eventually those ropes will give way and they'll be free. No one needs to walk in on that."

Bea reluctantly agreed. After she cleaned the tip of her fence rail on the comforter she went outside and tried the keys in the car with a child seat in the back assuming this would be the woman's car. The Nissan was in good shape and held a half tank of gas. She removed the child seat and loaded their back packs. The sky was now overcast and clouds were banking in the western sky. The air held a hint of rain.

David drove. Once again they encountered wrecks they couldn't get around and soon found themselves shunted onto back roads. They passed through a town that was little more than a wide space in the road. Mutilated bodies shambled along the sidewalks and streets in front of burned out buildings.

The threatened rain came down in torrents, a heavy fog set in and they slowed to practically a crawl. Headlights only illuminated the gloom as far as five feet.

Bea asked, "What were you saying about the earthquake here? The one from the 1800's?"

"Get the laptop from my backpack and plug this in." He handed her his flash drive. "It should be fully charged. Look for the file labeled *Lewis and Clark.*"

Most school children in the United States are familiar with the expedition of Meriwether Lewis and William Clark, two explorers dispatched by Thomas Jefferson, third President of the infant United States to reconnoiter the newly purchased Louisiana Territory. President Jefferson was harshly criticized by some for the $15,000,000 purchase as they felt it exceeded the prerogatives of a president.

Jefferson was no doubt eager to prove the value of the land to his countrymen.

Lewis and Clark, with a select company of adventurers that included the now well-known Sacagawea, the sixteen-year-old Shoshone purchased bride of a French trapper, set out to map and report back on the terrain, flora and fauna*, peoples, and resources of the newly-purchased land.

It would be a daunting task. The purchase added some 828,000 square miles to the total area of the country, doubling it in size. The journals herein encompass the time frame from March 3rd 1804 thru 1806.

The Ohio River was exceptionally low that summer and autumn and Lewis and his party were forced to travel for some distance on land instead of the preferred method of floating down the river to Indiana Territory where he was to join Clark. This very brief excerpt deals with the partial excavation of an indigenous burial mound in western Ohio and, as far as this researcher knows, has never been published. The tale may well fill part of the gap in the journal timeline that has frustrated historians for over two-hundred years. (Journals have been corrected for spelling.)

"The mounds are made of soil covered completely by vegetation, mainly local grasses. Measurements taken showed this particular mound was well over thirty feet tall with a flattened top. Circumference of 130 feet constitutes a perfect circle at the base. This particular site is at the bend of the river, a strategic location commanding an uninterrupted view of large portions of the river and fields. Prime agricultural land surrounds the area.

Our Indian guide, while exhibiting pride in displaying the mounds, said his people claim no ownership or credit as builders saying these earth pyramids were built during the time of the Long Winter by another race altogether, wehn-te-

goh, the ancient ones, who were turned into monsters as a punishment for consuming human flesh.

Two former attempts made to open the mound yielded some bits of pottery and a large, perhaps over-large human skull, according to our guide. Our time being somewhat limited we focused our efforts on an area of the mound already ventured and thus already at least one level down into the whole. Breaking through a hardened layer of earth we found scores of skeletons folded in together in such fashion and in spaces only possible if the flesh had been removed previous to internment. They rested upon a thick layer of shells and hardened clay soil. All of the skulls were crushed, as if from repeated blows. The air was thick, moist and smelled strongly of the black mold covering the remains.

Piercing the level underneath we found a chamber containing numerous skeletal remains, all of them with spears thrust through the bodies, effectively pinning them to the ground. Oddly, there were depressions in the ground under the skeletal hands as if they had dug into the earth. Numerous fire-hardened sharp stakes all pointing inward were thrust through the exterior walls of the mound, completely surrounding the bodies. Various articles lay arranged in a circle. Most remarkable were a stone pipe carved in the shape of a crocodile and the skeleton of a very large snake. We continued tunneling down but merely encountered more of the hardened stakes.

Our guide informed us that the entire race of the mound builders perished over a period of years due to a disease that induced a violent madness in its victims although he knows few details of the disease or the perished race. His people consider the mounds forbidden and never approach them unarmed as they have a tradition that something still lives within them.

Plan to rejoin party at the river tomorrow. Water route will save us time and considerable expense as horses *are exorbitant here. Received message from Captain Clark and additional boats await us in Indiana Territory."*

President Jefferson, an enthusiastic amateur naturalist, had high hopes that the party would encounter active volcanoes as well as prehistoric creatures like the mammoth and giant ground sloth which he believed might still occupy the unexplored western plains.

"So this would have been a few years before the earthquake. Why haven't I heard of this? I'm a history major and went to some pretty decent schools. I wrote a paper on Lewis and Clark but I never saw any of this," Bea said.

"Probably because this is something more like pseudo-history or crypto-history. When information doesn't fit into the accepted and well-known parameters, it gets pushed aside or sometimes destroyed altogether. Think of the 'Lost Gospels.' There were also those Mayan texts that the Spanish priests destroyed. It happens in every field of study, including science."

"There *is* a lot of conspiracy theory nonsense floating around out there. I guess some of it has to be culled. Their native guide mentioned a punishment for consumption of human flesh. Do you remember that tribe in New Guinea? The one where the women and children ceremonially ate the brains of their dead and developed that prion disease? "

"Um, sort of."

"You remember, it was kind of like mad cow disease. Their brain proteins had that abnormal fold in them and as a result they literally wasted away to skeletons and died. Those brains were eaten and the disease was passed on. It finally started dying away in the 1950's and researchers thought it was because ritual cannibalism had been mostly wiped out. But that wasn't the reason."

"Why then?"

"Genetic mutation. Some of the women developed a gene that wouldn't let the unhealthy prion attach to normal prions in the brain."

"We're dealing with a virus though."

"I know but the human immune system can develop a gene that disables the virus. Or develop sufficient antibody response. Either works."

"That would be great but in all the time this virus has been around our bodies haven't developed a way to defeat it. Enough of us will have to survive to give it time to mutate and no one survives for more than a few days. And this virus spreads fast and isn't confined to an island somewhere in the South Pacific. I follow your reasoning but the two diseases are very different."

Bea closed the computer. "You're right. I'm grasping at straws. But the mutation in New Guinea was incredibly rapid in evolutionary terms. It could happen again."

"Maybe. If you're interested there's another one on there. I think it's entitled *New Madrid.* It deals specifically with the 1811-1812 earthquakes."

Bea scrolled through and eventually found it though it was simply labeled *Earthquakes.*

The following eyewitness account of the 1811-1812 New Madrid Earthquakes is from John H. Baker of Kentucky. Involving four separate, major quakes with possibly two thousand aftershocks this horrific event caused church bells to ring as far away as Boston, Massachusetts and Charleston, South Carolina.

Many newspapers carried survivor accounts of the earthquake (see Eliza Braxton and Samuel Cocke) and while Mr. Baker's handwritten tale was found in the offices of the defunct Ohio newspaper, The Clarion, it is unknown if it was ever printed or published as gaps exist in the archived copies of the paper.

December 16ᵗʰ, 1811

"We woke up in the pitch-dark cold, thrown from our bed onto the floor. A loud rumbling noise filled the air and I felt the room swaying all around. The wood groaned as it twisted and buckled. Florence was whispering, "John Jr., John Jr." over and over again. I heard her trying to crawl across that heaving floor to get to the baby who wasn't making any sound at all.

We couldn't see anything but when the rumbling stopped I heard screams, people and animals crying out in the cold dark. Through the window we saw flashes of light that looked like they were coming out of the ground. Florence finally made it to the baby, who hadn't woken up through the shaking.

When daylight finally came we saw some of the damage. Our house got off light, the chimney got thrown down and the door was jammed shut but we eventually got out.

The ground near the spring house was split open about three feet. We couldn't see the bottom. Water rushed into the fissure. The water stank, smelled like sulfur and it was warm to touch. We had to find a new spring fast.

Our neighbors weren't so lucky. Jeb and Mary's house was down, destroyed. Mary was going through the rubble to see what might have survived unbroken but I don't think she found much. They are moving into the smokehouse for now. Jeb was off in the woods, hollering and cussing. Mary said he was looking for their animals.

I looked around again and realized our horses and cow were gone too. They must have all run off. I decided to try to get us some potable water and find the animals later.

December 20, 1811

We are all going to die if we don't find a way out of here. The ground heaved again yesterday. The iron kettle fell off the ledge in the smokehouse and killed Jeb and Mary's Eliza Jane. We buried her this morning under the cottonwood next to the church. Mary is grieved near out of her mind and won't leave the grave.

Preacher said the Devil is alive and walking, walking to and fro in the earth. I do believe he is spending some time under the earth, too. There are cracks so deep you can't see the bottom and people have disappeared without a trace near them.

Jeb heard that Chickasaw Bluffs are gone, fell right into the Mississippi and took those Indian mounds with them. I say good riddance. Those red heathens are afraid to go near them after dark. The one time I was up there I swear I heard something a-scratching inside the earth and I didn't fancy staying after dark either.

We can't leave yet. We still don't have enough animals to pull the wagons. Jeb and I are going back into the woods to look for the horses tomorrow but I think they would have wandered back by now if they were still alive.

January 14, 1812

The land shakes almost every day now in gently rolling undulations with hard jolts from time to time. Sometimes I think my mind isn't right. Jeb says this is how the end of the world starts. Maybe so. I don't know how to fight something like this. With a storm you can watch the sky get dark and see the wind blowing the trees and you know what's coming. This is different. Trees just fall over with roots pulled up and holes open up in the ground and swallow houses. Yesterday I saw a whole mess of hibernating snakes swarm up out of the ground and slither away into the creek.

Yesterday I ran into a fellow who said he saw the whole Mississippi River run backwards, washing trees and buildings along with it. Said Elm's Corner is cut off now because the bluffs keep falling and there's a river where there used to be a valley. Maybe his mind isn't right either.

Jeb and I tracked the cattle all the way to a lake* neither of us had ever seen before. The whole area used to be just a wooded stretch, set in a valley that had several Indian burial mounds. The tops of trees were still visible, swaying in that muddy, roiling water. Dead deer and opossum, swollen and stinking, rolled with the waves.

We found the cattle. Torn apart and mostly eaten. Can't tell what got to them. Jeb says the tracks around them are small, human, bare foot prints. People would have used knives or hatchets to get the meat. These look like they were savaged with bare hands. We still haven't found any trace of the horses.

January 20th, 1812

On the western side of the new lake we met up with a group of Frenchies. They said they came from a town called Tonti where they made their home for nearly twenty years but were heading back north before the ground ate any more of them. We camped with them for the night in a clearing and were fortunate to have their company for an occurrence so strange that- well, like I keep saying, I think my mind isn't right.

In short we were attacked as we slept. Not by the Chickasaw as I half expected but rather by creatures out of a nightmare. I happened to be taking the midnight watch with a Frenchie called Jean- Pierre when we heard a fuss among the horses. It began with frightened whinnies and snorts. The whinnies turned to wild screams of pain but we couldn't see what was happening in the dark.

Jean-Pierre took up a burning brand from the fire and we made our way a short distance out of the clearing where we found three ponies down and in their death throes while wizened, withered figures fed on their entrails. These things were five feet tall or less but the ponies, tied as they were, made easy prey.

I shouted and two of the creatures left off their feeding and groped their way toward us. As before stated they were undersized and in addition had blackened, wrinkled skin and were thin as skeletons with long shocks of lank, black hair. Some wore brief, animal-hide loin cloths but most wore nothing. Blood ran down their chins to cover their chests.

I ran and snatched up my own branch from the fire and waved it in their faces to hold them back but they came on, unfazed, with no fear of the flame.

Most of the camp was awake by now. A shot rang out and one of the creatures was felled by a direct hit to the chest. It soon staggered back to its feet and wandered back to the ponies and commenced to feed again on the poor beasts.

With more lighted brands to cast light we destroyed the attackers, finally by chopping them to pieces. Despite the strength shown when they ripped the horses to pieces, they are slow and clumsy, though very difficult to kill.

Almost all kept watch the rest of that long night and at dawn we followed the creatures' tracks back as far as the new lake. From the prints found in the mud they must have come up from the water though we found no canoes or rafts. We didn't find tracks anywhere else around the lake.

The bodies rotted fast and we had little time to examine them but did note that they didn't look like any of the local Indian tribes. They were shorter and broader with small but wide feet, short legs, and large hooked noses. They had eye sockets but no eyes. I've never seen anything like it before and hope I never do again.

January 28th, 1812

We arrived home two days ago and found the horses had come back while we were gone. Florence already had the wagons nearly loaded and was fretting to leave. The east wall of the house fell in one of the small quakes and crushed John Jr.'s cot. Florence had him in bed with her or we'd have lost him.

Trying to make it to Florence's brother's place up in Ohio in the old Northwest Territory. Maybe they'll take us in or maybe they won't but we know we have to get out of here.

*Reelfoot Lake was formed when the Mississippi ran backwards for a period of several hours. The eerie, swamp-like lake is located in western Tennessee.

Bea powered off the laptop and put it back in David's pack. "Skeletally thin, flesh-eaters and hard to kill? That sounds like our problem now. And *wehn-te-goh*? Canadian tribes had a tradition of an evil spirit or creature that used to be human but turned into a monster after consuming human flesh. Traditions like those are always dismissed as superstition. No one takes them seriously."

It was fully dark now and the rain was falling harder than ever. David switched the bright lights on but only illuminated more mist. It could be worse, he thought, this could be snow and ice.

"I know but there was no need, was there? Evil legends from ancient days were fun stories to scare ourselves with but had no relevance to-"

David flinched and Bea cried out as something thudded against the windshield and roof of the car. They had barely gone a few more feet when they were hit again and then yet again. David hit the brakes hard sending the car into a spin. He fought to get it under control, coming to a halt in the oncoming lane.

Chapter Five

Objects hung from the trees over-arching the road. David found his gun and flashlight. He got out in the lashing rain and hovering mist. Something touched the side of his face and he turned to see a foot, a woman's foot, still in a white Keds tennis shoe, dangling beside him. A few feet farther a man's bare feet twisted slowly.

He trained his flashlight up. Bodies hung all around him, some upside down, dangling from the trees. Some were really dead. Others, twisted in the wind, arms and legs flailing, uttering a chorus of dead groans. In some cases their throats were slit, others were disemboweled, their organs spilling down around them. There were children among them. One of them managed to grasp another, drawing in close as if for an embrace before biting into the dead flesh. The half-chewed lump of flesh fell through the open abdomen and hit David's shoulder in a sodden *splat*. He flicked it off in disgust.

The car door opened and Bea's flashlight wavered in the darkness. He almost called out then thought better of it. Whoever had done this might still be close by. Walking quickly back he took Bea's arm and they got in the car and locked the doors.

"Why would anyone do something like this? This is insane."

David replied, "This is about intimidation. Someone wanted to send a very definite message. As far as I'm concerned the message has been received. We're not-"

A loud peal of thunder crashed, drowning out whatever else he was going to say. The driver side window cracked, lines radiating out from a central hole and David slumped to one side. It took Bea a few seconds to recognize a bullet hole and that David was wounded. Another shot and

81

the glass disintegrated, showering little slivers of glass across both of them.   .

She tugged and finally rolled him awkwardly across the gear shift and into the passenger seat, climbing over him to reach the steering wheel. Another shot hit the side-view mirror splintering the glass and leaving it dangling, attached only by wires. Putting the car in gear she pulled out, spinning on the rain-slick asphalt before gaining traction and leaping forward.

Even with the wipers on high it was tough driving. She had no idea where she was going, only wanting to get away from their attackers. She kept glancing behind but nothing was following them as far as she could see. David wasn't moving and she couldn't see where he had been hit. Placing her hand on his chest she felt his heart beating and relief washed over her. He was alive.

Who killed all those people and then strung them up like that? What message had David been talking about?

Straining to see through the fogged-up windshield she looked for any sort of structure that might offer a chance to pull over and get David inside so she could at least assess his injury.

Suddenly he groaned and tried to sit up.

"Don't. Just lie still." He lay back. She put a hand on his shoulder and felt something warm and sticky.

Blood poured from the side of his head. A lot of blood. His breathing was shallow and rapid.

She drove on, through woods and more woods, bare tree branches swaying in the storm. Rain blew in through the broken window and stung the cuts on her face. When she finally came upon a split she turned right, with no clear plan other than to get off the main road. Almost immediately they began to go up. Just ahead she saw a split-rail fence and a faded, no trespassing sign.

"If they don't want us there then there must be something worth seeing at least." She turned sharply left.

The car bounced along the rutted and washed road. David's head hit the side window. In less than a minute the headlights shone on a barnlike structure surrounded by a railed paddock. Rain drummed on the car roof like an angry percussionist. Hunching her shoulders against the chill droplets, she opened the gate then drove through the muddy yard, straight into the barn.

The sudden cessation of noise was unnerving. She killed the engine and headlights and then sat for a moment, letting her eyes adjust to the darkness. The barn was a pretty basic structure with six stalls around a wide center pass through. The air smelled like a mixture of hay and dirt and perhaps a hint of manure but there weren't any animals in residence. Her hands stung with dozens of small cuts from the window glass.

Beside her, David was out again. She turned on one of the map lights and tilted his head gently toward her, looking for the source of the blood. There were no wounds in his head or neck, except- she ran her fingers along the side of his head and he groaned. His ear felt ragged as if part of it was missing.

The blood in his hair and on his neck was drying. She found one of their last bottles of water and cleaned the wound. Taking off her shirt she tied it around his head for a makeshift bandage, letting his head lean back against the seat to hold it in place. It was the best she could do for now. Glass still lay in slivers everywhere. Shrugging into her coat she opened the car door.

A ladder led up to a loft of scattered straw. Up here she found what she assumed were horse blankets. Climbing back down she covered David, reclining the seat back as far as it would go. She pushed her own seat back and settled in, hoping to get at least a little sleep.

She didn't. Just as she drifted off David began to snore noisily and heartily. Finally she got out and climbed the loft ladder, finding more blankets and, making a nest in the straw, she fell asleep.

~

A shaft of morning sunlight slanted in through a crack in the wall boards, illuminating dust motes rising and falling in the air. Somewhere in the woods a rooster crowed. She lay still, hearing the slow shuffle of feet in the dirt; that low moaning that raised the hair on her arms. The air was chokingly foul with the thick scent of rotten flesh. The dead had found them, they always found them. Where had they come from?

The floor boards up here gapped wide and all she had to do to look down was roll over and clear some straw away. Seven dead clustered the car but they weren't trying to reach in through the broken window. She could only assume David was still in there but there wasn't any movement visible inside.

The dead bodies below were some of the most grotesque she had seen to date. One, torn belly gaping wide, must have fed recently. Chewed, red lumps of flesh fell to the ground as he lurched forward. Maggots swarmed over the shredded, gray flesh of his rib cage and empty eye sockets. Another had arms that were nothing but sinew attached to bone.

She crept over to the loft access window, pushed the shudders apart a crack and looked outside. More dead were converging on the barn and she kicked herself mentally for not closing the paddock gate back last night. That was just sloppy and stupid.

Below, she heard something fall with a loud metallic *clang*. Peering through the floor, she saw David, not in the car as she supposed but backed into a corner and holding a rusty pitchfork in front of him. He looked dazed and still very pale and she saw him fumble for his weapon but he must have left it in the car. His neck and jacket were stained red.

More dead shambled in. David didn't stand a chance. She had her Glock with her but no extra magazines and she couldn't get them all. She looked around but only found a bottle of something dark that smelled like turpentine, sharp-looking shears, and some old issues of a magazine called *Garden and Gun.* She threw those down but the dead never looked up.

She shouted, "Hey, hey! I'm up here, here!" and stomped hard on the floor. A few stopped and turned her way but most ignored her. She grabbed the shears and, pushing up her coat sleeve, sliced her forearm, gasping at the pain. Leaning out as far as she dared she flung droplets of blood at their faces. Now they started moaning excitedly. A dead woman, torn blouse stained dark red, opened her mouth and gnashed her teeth in expectation.

More of them slowly turned her way. She pulled the ladder up into the loft, dragged it over to the outside access window and opened the shutters, lowering the ladder to the ground. Climbing down she shouted again, "Hey, this way!" and backed away toward the paddock gate.

The dead followed. Even out here their smell was overwhelming and she gagged. Banging hard on the metal gate with the shears she watched more and more leave the barn. It was working.

A familiar sound began to override the hoarse moans. An engine, faint but growing louder, labored to climb the hill. She listened, torn between hiding somewhere and staying and seeing if they could help her. As she stood in indecision, an ATV, quickly followed by another, crested the hill and rolled to a stop outside the paddock. Two men sat and looked at her, sizing her up.

They killed the engines and dismounted. Dirt was visible in the folds of their necks and she could smell them even above the stench of the dead. One had dark, greasy hair and the other, short and heavy-set, sported a swastika tattooed on his skull. The greasy one carried a very large hunting knife but Little Hitler (the name seemed to fit) held a rifle cradled loosely under one arm. The taller one smiled but it wasn't the kind of smile any woman ever enjoyed seeing.

"Hello there. What brings you to our little community?" He positively leered at her and put his knife away in a sheath hanging from his belt as if he didn't consider her much of a threat.

"Just passing through. I'm actually getting ready to leave right now." She tried to make sure her voice didn't waver but it betrayed her anyway and squeaked slightly. She swallowed hard.

The dead were almost out of the paddock gate. Greasy darted in front of her and slammed the gate shut. Little Hitler walked over until he was behind her and then he whistled appreciatively. She shuddered, repulsed and frightened. Her gun nestled against her hip in the waist of her jeans but she knew she had to get this right. It would have to be a kill shot. Missing would be bad but just wounding them might be worse; it would only make them angry. And she knew she wasn't a great shot.

The dead, thwarted at the gate, assembled along the rails, almost like spectators at a sporting event. The two men barely seemed to notice them.

Little Hitler spoke for the first time, "Did you try to drive through our welcoming committee in the trees down on the road last night? That was you, wasn't it? What'd you think? We spent a lot of time on the display. All of us."

Just keep them talking, she thought. "It was very effective. All of you? How many are in your group?"

"She doesn't like us; she wants to meet someone else. That's rude. We're not good-looking enough for you maybe?

I'm crushed." Greasy ambled closer and she automatically backed away, only to find Little Hitler closer behind her than she thought. He grabbed her arm where she had cut it and she cried out.

"Ah, crap." He pushed her sleeve up and saw the blood. "She's bit. I was hoping we had a breeder. Someone to help us re-start civilization. Just bash her head in; I don't want to waste a bullet. I got the baseball bat in the net on the four-wheeler."

Greasy went for the bat and Little Hitler threw her to the ground. Her gun fell out of her jeans and when she scrambled for it, he kicked it away. She turned to him.

"I'm not bitten but I'm still not your breeder, you Neanderthal!" She grabbed his foot and managed to bring him down with her. The rifle fell into the mud. She hooked her fingers and went for his eyes but could only scratch bloody furrows in his cheeks and he screamed, a sound she found oddly satisfying but not for long. He soon had her pinned and slapped her so hard she tasted blood and everything went dark for a moment. When her vision cleared she saw Greasy holding a baseball bat and walking her way. Little Hitler jerked her up by pulling on her jacket and she took the opportunity to slip her arms out of the sleeves and roll away, the ground cold and wet against her shoulders. He kicked her viciously.

"You're dead, you little-"

Whatever else he was going to say was abruptly cut off when a car crashed through the paddock gate and stopped, spinning mud and gravel over all of them. David, the makeshift shirt bandage slipped down around his neck, got out, grabbed Little Hitler and blew skull and brain matter out through the back of his head. The bright red blood was shockingly warm across her bare belly. Greasy stalked over with his knife but David dropped him with a shot between the eyes then kicked him until blood covered his boots.

Bea got to her feet, wiping mud and blood from her arms and breasts and retrieved her gun and the rifle as well. The dead reached them, some walking, others dragging mangled bodies across the mud, mouths open wide in ravenous anticipation. A little girl, soft pink nightgown stained and torn, dropped to her knees and began gnawing on the warm chunks from Little Hitler's shattered skull. A dead man grabbed Bea's calf and she shot him, his gray-white face collapsing into black, liquid goo.

"David," She took his arm and shook him but he ignored her and kept kicking Greasy. "David! Let's go."

David stopped, took her hand and almost threw her into the car. He spun out in the mud, spraying the oncoming dead with more dirt and gravel before leaving them behind.

He drove fast down the curving road. Too fast.

"David, slow down ! They can't catch us."

He ignored her but did finally slow down. A little. She continued to swipe at the mud but it was useless. She was filthy and cold and she had left her coat behind on the ground. She crossed her arms across her chest and thought longingly of all the clothes she pinched from the outlet mall. The horse blanket was still in the back and she wrapped it around her shoulders.

David stopped the car, took off his jacket and handed it to her, pointedly *not* looking at her until she had it on and buttoned up. She sighed and leaned back against the seat, relieved.

"Thanks. How do you feel?" She asked.

"Fine."

"You do remember being shot, right? Let me look at your head." She reached over but he brushed her hands away.

"I don't want you to look at my head. I want you to tell me what they did to you!"

Something was wrong with him. She had never seen him act this way before so she said patiently, "They wanted to be sure I hadn't been bitten so they took my coat to check. Apparently they had plans to re-populate the earth in their own image. They wanted a 'breeder'. Idiots."

"It's not funny. They could have done anything to you!"

"Well, they didn't."

"Then why aren't you wearing your shirt?" He clenched his teeth when he said it.

"Because you are," she said quietly.

"What the hell are you talking about?"

"The bandage around your head, David. That's my shirt. It was all I had to bandage your wound last night."

He reached up and pulled it off and threw it at her. She threw it back.

"I don't want that bloody shirt. You keep it and stop acting like such a jerk."

"Do you have any idea what it was like to look out and see you on the ground?"

"Probably no worse than *being* on the ground like that. Please stop talking like they did something to you. In fact, please stop talking to me at all."

For several miles they drove in silence. They eventually found signs directing them to 61 and began heading south again. The road was passable with few pile-ups but fuel was an issue now. Every station they passed was burned to the ground.

David's phone rang, surprising them both. He looked at the screen then answered, "Chambord here."

He listened for a moment.

"Yes, sir. I will make every effort. Fuel situation is in question at the moment. Still working on a solution. "

A pause.

"No, sir. That feature was disabled late last year for security purposes. Someone there should be able to turn it back on."

Another pause.

"No, sir. I will make every effort but I was never in the area. That will be a difficult situation to assess. I have been out of contact for several days."

And then.

"Thank you, sir. I will."

He rang off. "We have a rendezvous near Memphis. It's going to be difficult if we don't find gas."

"A rendezvous with whom?"

"West coast operations. They have a chopper arriving in seven hours. They'll take us to Cali."

"Who was it? Did they mention Brian?" She asked eagerly.

"No. That was Colonel Hamilton, acting head of operations on the west coast. He just now got notice that the helicopter I was supposed to be on didn't make it. Better late than never I guess."

His voice was raspy and he gripped the steering wheel so tightly his knuckles went white as he continued. "The government has fallen. Congress was in session when all this broke out so they all, almost all, evacuated to Mount Weather. Something, they don't know what, went wrong, the infection made it inside the shelter and once it got loose, there was no stopping it. The whole complex is a giant tomb of the walking dead."

Bea asked, "So it happened just now?"

"No. I'm sure it happened days ago but they hushed it up as much as possible. Don't want to appear vulnerable or other countries will take advantage of the situation. Now it seems there aren't a whole lot of functioning governments left anywhere. It's worldwide anarchy now, according to the colonel. They couldn't do a flyover of Mount Weather. They didn't know where I was and the colonel thought I might be in the area and wanted someone who could mount an on the ground rescue if needed. That reminds me, they're going to enable GPS tracking on my phone again. The colonel should be able to find us now."

"A colonel is in charge of west coast operations? I thought it would be someone with higher rank."

David laughed a short, bitter laugh. "The generals are almost all dead or nobody can find them. I'm sure Colonel Hamilton will get a field promotion soon. There probably isn't a lot of time for an investiture ceremony right now."

"I'm trying to remember the order of succession. The Vice-President follows the President and after the VP it's the Speaker of the House. Then the president of the Senate I guess but after that I can't remember."

"I think it goes through the Cabinet secretaries after that. The thing is, they *all* evacuated to Mount Weather at first, then they were going to divide up and go to other shelters. It never happened."

"I have to tell you I don't know what Mount Weather is. I assume it's like the Greenbrier?"

"Yeah, basically. It has everything needed for 'continuity of government'. A hospital, vast amounts of food, broadcast facilities, even an underground lake. All of it inside blast doors thick enough to deflect a nuclear event. It's carved from rock that dates back to the Pre-Cambrian period. None of that stood against a virus, did it?"

Bea felt surprisingly shaken by the news. Employed by the government she nevertheless shared the cynicism evinced by most for the feds. The jokes about government incompetence, intrusiveness, and inefficiency- she had heard them all and most were true. Still, it had been a constant in everyone's lives and during times of national emergency, they often came through. Especially the military. Almost everyone knew someone in the armed services, risking their lives and trying to do the right thing in extremely dangerous and difficult circumstances.

"By the way, those two guys back there were responsible for the tree decorations from last night. Or so they claimed. I got the impression they were trying to form

91

some sort of survivalist compound. They wouldn't tell me if there were others."

"There probably were more of them; that was too much work for just two people to string that many up. Incredibly dangerous too. I'll never understand what motivates people to do things like that. My grandad was in Vietnam and once saw an entire family, all dead, placed on chairs around their kitchen table and tied in place. Someone had even put dishes on the table in front of them. Insane."

Tree covered hillsides, punctuated by an occasional road sign, flashed by. The gas hand was below an eighth and dropping.

"I hear a thump, do you?"

Bea listened. "Yes, maybe it's this section of road?"

"I'm not sure. Almost sounds like a tire."

There was a sign advertising a travel station/truck stop at the next exit.

We're going to have to take a shot at this. Feel up to it?" David asked.

"Maybe we can find some food," she replied.

They coasted up the exit ramp and turned right. It was a pretty standard set-up, one area of pumps for cars and another for trucks. There was a "Doc in the Box", several fast-food places, and a mini-mart. Best of all, lights shone from inside the building and LED numbers glowed from the pump displays. Three large semi's remained parked next to the diesel pumps.

The car thumped as they cruised over to the gas pumps and got out. The left rear tire was flat. Dismayed, David checked the trunk for a spare, hoping the car had one. It did but it was flat, too.

"Do you have any change? I'll have to fill this before I can change it."

Bea didn't but they found a couple of dollars' worth in the console and under the floor mats.

"I'll go inside and try to turn on the gas."

"Thanks. We're pump five." David picked up the tire and she headed for the building.

Wind gusts, warm and smelling of damp earth and smoke, whipped her hair across her face and blew trash and dead leaves across the pavement. A crow, black and shiny, perched proprietarily over the glass entry doors, only flying away when she waved her arms and shouted at it. Gun held low, she went inside.

Behind the counter was a panel of switches. She flipped the one labeled "five", heard a *click* and then numbers started scrolling on the display.

The store had been robbed but not ransacked. All the beer was gone and the cash register drawers were open and empty. Wondering how much the thieves actually enjoyed that cash, she helped herself to a Coke and some cashews, savoring the sweet fizzy taste and the nutty crunch. The caffeine went to her head and she felt better and somehow clearer than she had in days.

Tee shirts with various logos hung from a rack near the Dunkin' Donuts counter. The only one in her size was emblazoned with a Superman "S" logo. It would do, in fact anything would do right now. Once again she regretted all her lost swag from the outlet mall, especially her coat. Before she changed in the ladies' room she scrubbed away as much mud and blood as she could. Splashing her face she inspected the new split in her swollen upper lip. This one would probably leave a scar.

Back in the mini-mart, she now began looting in earnest and took all the packaged food she could carry as well as bottled water. Chips, crackers, nuts and dried fruit, all looked heaven-sent to her, shiny plastic packaging crackling in her hands.

Outside, David aired up the spare tire and finished pumping the gas. Bea handed his coat back to him and he grunted and threw it in the car, raising an eyebrow at her Superman shirt. The day was still warming and it wasn't even noon yet. The car rocked precariously on the jack as he tackled the lug nuts but he waved away her offer to help.

The wind still whipped around the parking lot, rattling the aluminum roofs over the pumps. Another crow, very large with black wings spread wide, flapped overhead. It circled lazily then landed on one of the three semi-trucks. A Walmart truck. Carrying who knew what type of merchandise. She smiled.

Climbing up onto the bumper was easy but sliding the locking bars open was a different matter. Finding a rock she finally hammered them until they opened. Her hand was bleeding and she wiped it on her new shirt then threw the rock at another crow circling the truck. She pulled hard on the bar and then swung the door wide.

The odor rolled out like a rancid wave and immediately she pushed the door back but the wind caught it and slammed it open. Gouts of dark blood splattered the interior walls. Infected burst forth from the trailer like maggots from a dead dog. Stumbling forward they fell to the ground, dragging their entangled, blackened entrails behind them, collapsing in an ungainly heap on the pavement. They began to moan excitedly.

She backed away, shouting a warning to David over her shoulder.

"I'm sorry, David. Really, *really* sorry but-"

David turned and saw them, keeping one hand on the spare. "Don't. Just hold them off as long as you can." He turned back to the car.

The dead began struggling to their feet. Bea fired, one shot missing entirely, the other merely blowing out the knee of a shambling corpse. She was going to keep missing at this distance.

Hands shaking she walked closer, firing more carefully. A dead girl, faster than the others, reached her, shredded, rotted lips exposing broken, stained teeth. She wore a blue spandex tank dress covered with dark clots of flesh and still clutched a hemp purse in one hand. Bea shot her through the throat. She rocked with the blow but kept coming until Bea finally put a bullet through her left eye.

They were all on their feet now and coming in fast. She stopped another one with a headshot causing those behind her to fall but they were soon on their feet and she kept retreating, glancing over her shoulder at David. Most of them hadn't noticed him yet so she began to back toward the mini-mart, keeping them interested in her. The gun spat fire again, blowing reeking lumps of flesh and long black hair from a dead woman onto the child stumping eagerly along behind.

"Oh no." She squinted and fired again, not looking at the now headless bodies she had just felled. The dead behind stumbled over them and fell. She held the gun steady and kept backing away.

David had the spare in place and finished tightening the first nut. The little tire looked ridiculously undersized. Gunfire rang out somewhere close and he could only assume Bea was handling the situation. That familiar moaning and rotten meat smell drifted his way and he grabbed the wrench, accidentally knocking a nut under the car. He swore quietly, flattening himself on the ground, feeling under the car for the nut and not finding it. Something glinted on the pavement near the gas pumps. He walked around the car and snatched the nut up angrily only to glimpse dirty feet, shredded skin dragging, now waiting for him back on the other side of the car.

Adrenaline fueled he stalked back and buried the tire iron in a mouth of broken teeth, black fluid running down his arms. Pulling it free he pushed the slumped body aside and fumbled with the now gore-slick nuts. In the corner of his eye he saw more dead reeling his way. He twisted the last nut one more time then turned around and gored the ripe skull of a teen wearing nothing but the shreds of an Imagine

Dragons tee shirt. She went down like a collapsed wind sock. He heard a scream and looked around.

Bea had inadvertently backed into a corner beside the mini-mart where evergreens hid the dumpsters. She was out of ammo and the dead were closing in, their putrid smell overwhelming that of the rotting garbage. Climbing to the top of the fence behind her she looked down upon a deep ditch full of muddy water that ran the length of the fence. She hesitated.

A mold-covered woman reached her first and raked her shins with the sharp bone tips of her fingers, mouth stretched wide. Tiny mushrooms sprouted amongst her broken teeth and a stump of a tongue moved from side to side. The rest of the throng closed in fast.

She jumped and splashed down on top of a body, hidden just beneath the water, knees scraped painfully by a jutting ribcage. Crying out in pain she scrambled up the muddy bank, expecting to be pulled back down by rotting hands at any second.

Soaking wet and covered in mud, she stopped to catch her breath, eyeing the ditch warily. The water roiled and a detached arm floated to the surface followed by a torso, distended in decomposition. Bea flinched away but nothing else surfaced. Whoever was in there was really dead.

Wheels screeched around the corner and David came to a stop. She jumped inside, yanked the door closed and they were back on the road with the dead soon left far behind.

"Illegals," David said.

"What? Oh. They were being smuggled in, weren't they? I knew Walmart was evil but-"

"Funny. The truck was either stolen or a fake. Coyotes have a lot of tricks they use to get them across the border. I only saw women. They thought they were coming here for a better life but it was probably a prostitution ring."

Shivering, Bea turned the heat up. "I took some peroxide from the mini-mart. I'm going to try to clean your ear. This will sting a little."

"How bad is it? I haven't looked at it yet," he flipped the rearview mirror. "Crap! That's practically a hole."

It wasn't really but the tip of the ear was gone and the bullet had scorched a path through his hair. He didn't flinch when Bea drizzled peroxide on it.

"It bled a lot but scalp wounds do. I don't see any signs of infection." She brushed his hair away from his ear and blew on the peroxide to dry it.

The pleasure he felt at the touch of her hands was incredibly stirring but he deliberately tamped it down. He had done his best to forget their brief almost-tryst back in D.C. and she never referred to it again. But now she continued to touch him gently along his temple and neck. The nearness of her was intoxicating and when she sat back and buckled her seat belt he felt bereft.

"Don't worry. It's healing. Think of it as enhancing your rugged good looks." Her smile had a sweetness to it that took him by surprise.

"Kind of like that mud below your eye is a beauty mark."

She laughed and rubbed her face. "I know. I've never been this dirty in my life. I've been having shower fantasies for days."

At the sound of her laughter *he* began having shower fantasies too. To distract himself he turned the radio on and then hit scan. Static blared through the speakers.

The day grew warmer. This road was taking them south and they should be near Memphis in a few hours if their luck held. Road signs for various communities flashed by. On one for Newbern someone had painted out the population number and written, "All Dead, Keep Moving."

Bea said, "There was a body in that ditch I jumped into. It had decomposed to the point it was falling apart. I don't know if it had turned or if whoever it was just died."

"As it warms up we will probably see more and more of that," David replied.

"Where exactly are we going? It's not downtown Memphis is it?"

"No, I'm trying to avoid that. We need to get to the other side of the river. There are several bridges well above Memphis. I want to cross in Ripley; it's much smaller than Memphis."

"Why do we have to cross over? Couldn't they pick us up anywhere?"

"They're not flying any more missions across the Mississippi river. The eastern half of the country is considered lost and the Mississippi is the designated cut-off. It's sort of an arbitrary decision and I don't know who made it. They may be trying to save fuel."

"Cut-off as in quarantined? Will someone shoot us if we try to cross?"

"I don't think so. They don't have enough people to enforce a quarantine."

Again the enormity of the situation pressed in on her. All the immense means of commerce stopped. Vast ships at sea slowly turning into derelict, drifting hulks. Food rotting in warehouses or in the fields. Thousands of miles of paved roads overtaken by weeds and vines. Wharves and docks collapsing into harbors. Homes destroyed by leaking natural gas lines, their uncomprehending owners charred by the flames. Hydroelectric plants failing and concrete dams bursting due to lack of maintenance. Nuclear power facilities melting down. People dying from injuries or illnesses that were once easily treatable. Women dying in childbirth.

Bea filled their backpacks with as much of her stolen food and water as possible. She hoped they would drive across the bridge but who knew? It could be blocked, forcing them to travel on foot.

A pack of dogs emerged from a stand of trees and crossed the road in front of them. In the rearview mirror David saw a pack of dead stumble from the trees and cross after them. The dead were slow and clumsy; the dogs were in very little danger.

They took the exit for Ripley in the late afternoon. The two-lane road led them past farms and small local stores before they entered a stone-paved town square with a fountain and an ornately carved, wooden band-stand. A tattered American flag still waved in the breeze in front of a red-brick post office. Next to that was a rather grand building with massive, white columns and a door partially ajar. A brass plaque identified it as the local courthouse and police station. The only dead they saw were in the distance, shuffling around a Dairy Queen parking lot. David pulled into a space in front of the police station.

"We need ammo and more weapons if we can get them. Also, there might be shower facilities here. I can't guarantee they're working. Are you game?"

"Absolutely."

The smell hit them as soon as they entered the building. Slowly, guns at the ready, they scanned the atrium. Bea pulled her tee shirt up to cover her mouth and nose and they entered the door marked "County Sheriff." Chairs, phones, and computers were smashed and overturned and papers and files lay scattered. Bullet casings littered the area near the front door and bloody footprints crisscrossed the room before fading away out in the atrium. They saw no one, infected or otherwise, but the smell- where was it coming from?

A solid-looking wooden door with a small glass inset led to a hallway with four jail cells, two on each side. The door wasn't locked and hinges squeaked as they opened it and stepped onto the scuffed tile.

Chapter Six

Bed springs squeaked and a man, hair wild and wearing jailhouse orange, got slowly to his feet and stood beside his bunk. He stared at them as if he couldn't quite believe his eyes then ran to the bars, shaking them violently.

"Let me out! Please, you have to let me out of here. The keys is in that desk out in the front. I ain't seen nobody for a week."

He pressed against the bars, eyes pleading and arms reaching for them. The smell of rot and fecal matter was overwhelming. Bea backed away but David, noticing pooled, dried blood in the center of the hall tiles near a floor drain, moved in for a closer look.

"Move away from the bars! I want your hands up on that back wall. Now!" David punctuated the last word by gesturing with his gun. The man raised his hands and backed away.

"Don't kill me, mister!" He was crying now and snot ran down his upper lip. "I'm nearly dead already. You got to let me out! I'll starve if you don't let me out."

Bea left and searched the desks out front for keys. Finally finding a plastic key card dangling from a chair she went back to the cells, prepared to run it through the reader on the cell door but David gestured for her to wait. The man was still sniveling but it now seemed forced to her and she stopped, wondering what was going on.

"Where did everyone go?" David asked.

"I don't know! All I know is the cops got me for DUI on Friday but it wasn't my fault. I was home, minding my own business when my dad called to get a ride home from the bus station. Carl, he says, you got to come get your old dad. The only time he ever remembers me is when he needs something. Before I could get there I got pulled over and thrown in here. Half a six pack, that's all I'd drunk, I swear. The next morning I heard a bunch of screaming and gunshots out there and then nothing. We hollered for two days but ain't nobody ever answered. I've been drinking from the toilet but the water's all gone now. You can't leave me in here!"

David's eyes narrowed and he lifted the gun again. "We? Who was it who shouted with you for two days?"

The man's face went whiter than it already was. "There ain't no we, it's just me."

David gestured with the gun. "Pull that blanket up off that bunk and show me what's under the bed."

The man's face went utterly blank for a moment then he turned to Bea. "You, Supergirl, you gotta understand. I was gonna die if-"

David shouted, "Throw that blanket over here before I blow your head off!"

Trembling, the man reluctantly pulled the blanket off the bunk revealing a body, crammed under the bed and nude from the waist up. Chunks of flesh were missing from the arms, shoulders, and ribs. Bite-sized chunks. The smell of decay intensified.

"Don't try to tell me he conveniently died of natural causes. Did you kill him so you could eat him?"

"No! That's not how it started. We got in a fight about how much water he was drinking because the toilet stopped filling and I knew the water was- I never meant to hit him that hard but he was trying to kill me!"

"So you just got hungry and decided to carve up your compatriot there?"

"What was I supposed to do? Just starve when there was-" he stopped as if he couldn't bring himself to say it.

"Meat? Is that what's hard to say? But it wasn't that hard to take a bite, was it?"

David's hand shook and his finger tensed on the trigger. Bea put her hands over her ears and ran out into the offices, taking breaths of the cleaner air out here and waiting for the sound of the gunshot.

It never came. David followed her out, gun by his side. He grabbed a clipboard hanging on the wall and began flipping through the clipped pages. The prisoner began yelling again, the sound only slightly muffled by the closed door.

"What are you looking for?"

"This is the arrest sheet for the last two weeks. I see just two names. One for a Carl, charge is DUI and the other for Public Drunkenness, a guy named Roscoe. I just wanted to check the facts before I do anything."

"I know it's horrible but the circumstances were well…unprecedented. I mean, getting locked up for DUI just as civilization falls is a difficult situation to deal with," Bea said.

"Yeah, but is he telling the truth? Did he just kill the guy so he could eat him to survive?"

"He said it was an argument. As for eating him, there have been instances where the Catholic Church granted forgiveness for this kind of thing due to extreme circumstances. This was pretty extreme. And you know what they say about mercy."

"'It falleth as the gentle rain from heaven'? Shakespeare?"

"I mean the part about it being 'twice blest. 'It blesseth him that gives and him that takes.' We all could use some blessing right now."

David took the plastic key from her and went back to the cells. Metal clanged and the prisoner emerged, looking relieved and terrified at the same time. David held his gun on him.

"Get out of here."

"Thank you, thank you! If I can ever do you a favor, I will."

"Just go." David waved the gun.

Carl fled. The door down the hall banged and they saw him run past the windows.

"Did you tell him what's been happening in the world the last few days?"

David shook his head. "It didn't come up. Help me find the keys for the armory. I don't want to dwell on the fact that I just released a murderer and a cannibal back into the world."

Pickings were slim. The police here either didn't keep a lot of ammo on hand or else they took it with them when they left. They found two boxes of shells and pocketed them but the guns were gone.

"Let's hope they put them to good use. Let's go."

The dead down the street drew closer, attracted by all the noise. Bea and David left them behind and drove toward the setting sun, winding through lanes of lovely, old houses. They finally found a sign that directed them to River Road and they turned, hoping it would lead them to a bridge.

Starting out as rivulets the water soon ran across the road in a muddy stream. The road now sloped downhill and the lower they went the deeper the water rose. The floorboard was awash in several inches of water when they struck a submerged log and the car shuddered to a stop. They got out. The log wedged inside the wheel well.

They waded through water up to their knees and hung on to trees to stay upright. They reached an area where the road was washed completely away and stopped, not knowing the direction to take.

"Where's the river?" Bea looked through the trees for a road sign or anything that would tell them where they were.

David said, "I think we're in it. It's jumped the banks."

They struggled on a few yards more until they reached an overturned boat pressed solidly against the trees by the rushing water. Scrambling up the hull they hoisted themselves up to the lowest tree branches then began to climb.

The Muddy Mississippi. Old Man River. The Mighty Mississippi. All those nicknames came to mind when they looked down and out over the river valley. Dark water roared by in the mile-wide river, bringing with it trees, cars, even parts of houses. A huge barge swirled by in the strong current as if it weighed no more than a leaf.

"The bridge is gone. Swept away." David's voice was full of awe. A set of McDonald's golden arches bobbed up briefly in the muddy torrent then sank again. A dead cow, belly distended and legs jutting stiffly in rigor mortis bumped up against their tree before floating on.

"So what now? Where's the next closest bridge?" Bea asked.

"I'm not sure. I know Memphis has at least two or they used to. Maybe not anymore. We'll never make it through a city that size. It's not even an option."

The sound of the water grew louder as a dark, rolling current unfurled beneath them, carrying with it more debris. Steel pylons slammed against the trees and stayed there, crushing the wooden boat to matchsticks. The old oak tree shuddered but held as the water rose even higher. The road they had driven in on was no longer visible.

"It's getting dark and the water is still rising. I wish we had some way to tie ourselves to the tree. I'm afraid I'll fall asleep and fall out." Bea looked down at the surging water.

David pulled a hoodie from his pack and passed it to her. "We'll just have to keep each other awake. Put this on. It's going to get a lot colder once the sun goes down."

Bea put it on gratefully. The air was already chilly and they were both soaking wet. She positioned her pack behind a limb then leaned back and slipped her arms through the straps. The branch hurt her back but this should hold her in the tree unless the straps gave out.

David straddled a broad limb and leaned back. "Dams and locks upstream must have failed and caused the flooding. Once the water recedes we'll find a way across. If we survive the night things should be better tomorrow."

The sun set and the night grew dark. The only sound was the rush of the water and their desultory conversation.

~

The splash woke him. He opened his eyes to a gray morning with mist hovering above the water and the sight of Bea floundering below him in the dirty, much shallower water.

"Hey! Are you alright?"

She got to her feet and climbed the metal pylon. Out of breath after the shock of the cold water it was a few seconds before she could reply.

"I fell off the branch. I was sound asleep one minute then the next thing I know I'm under water. But I'm fine."

The good news was that they survived the night. An early morning mist drifted over the water. The bad news was that the water, while it had gone down, was still dangerously fast and rough. Trees, broken boats, and dead bodies bobbed in the turbulent water.

Or were they dead bodies? David took another look. The current eddied and sent a body straight toward them. Fleshless fingers clawed at the tree trunk and the infected gained its feet, only to fall again, the current pressing it up against the tree. Another body soon drifted their way. This one was swollen with water and the gaping hole where its abdomen used to be was full of insects and worms. Broken teeth gnashed in the lipless mouth but the creature had no legs and could only thrash about feebly with water-swollen arms.

106

The river swarmed with corpses, some animated, some truly dead. They were trapped and even if the water level kept dropping they would still be surrounded by the hungry infected. Bea dropped her head. She felt like crying but didn't want David to see.

David checked his ammunition before pulling out another MRE for breakfast.

"Hungry?" He offered her a packet but she was facing in the opposite direction and just shook her head no. He shrugged and peeled open the foil pouch. A light rain still fell but the sun was growing brighter and the fog should burn off soon. The bodies in the water writhed and bobbed as they-

A sputtering engine sounded somewhere in the distance. It died. Someone cursed enthusiastically then the engine started up again. It sputtered along and grew louder.

A battered aluminum boat with a small outboard motor slowly came into view. The chugging motor died again and the cursing, now accompanied by a metallic *clang*, resumed until the engine once more came to life.

"Hey! Up here!" David waved his arms.

"I see you! I'm getting there as fast as I can," shouted the boat operator.

Maneuvering through the debris and the occasional tussock of ground, their would-be rescuer pulled in closer. He wore a plastic rain jacket and hat.

"You! How did you guys get up there?" The voice sounded familiar.

It was the erstwhile jail inmate Carl. He grinned and stopped the boat. "Ya'll need help getting down?"

From their vantage point Bea and David saw two gray, water-logged hands grasp the side of the boat. They shouted out a warning and pointed. Carl picked up a small fire-axe, turned, and hacked both hands off at the wrist. The boat swayed violently and nearly capsized, Carl hanging on to the sides.

"Where're you headed?" Carl asked as soon as the boat steadied.

"Across the river. Can you get us there?" Bea asked.

"Let's find out, Supergirl. Climb down but be careful. I got a feeling there are more of those things down where we can't see them."

The river, while calmer, still carried dangerous debris. Knocks and scrapes on the hull were constant. A mutilated body surfaced, seeming dead until it reached for the boat. The little craft rocked dangerously before David chopped the hands away. Even after that they had to pry the fingers loose.

Something hit them hard underneath sending the boat into a spin. A cross-current carried them back toward the bank they just left. The motor snagged on weeds and vines and died.

Carl tugged but couldn't untangle them. "Someone's going to have to get out and unwrap that junk from the propeller."

David splashed down in the murky water. The thick, ropey vines were impossible to untwist so he used the axe.

"Be careful you don't hit the motor," Carl said.

Exasperated, David didn't reply, just kept chopping. Looking for attackers floating in, he saw nothing. Something bumped against his leg and he kicked out at it only to see a log surface and go spinning off into the current.

The vines finally broke free. "I'm going to push you out as far as I can before you start the motor. Ready?"

He pushed until the water reached his chest and he lost his footing. Bea pulled him in while Carl yanked on the starter. The engine coughed then began to *chug*. They turned the prow toward the opposite shore again.

Just as they reached the middle of the river a flotilla of infected drifted toward them. The bodies started slamming into the boat hard, slowing them down and making it difficult to steer. Bloated, gray hands clutched at the boat, making it rock dangerously. Bea leaned over the sides and punctured rotted skulls with her fence rail then kicked them back into the water.

They were surrounded and no matter how many they destroyed, more were there to take their place. Two women grabbed onto the motor and tried to climb aboard. Carl attacked them with the axe but before they dropped off, the motor stalled again. Infuriated, he stomped the reaching arms and both women slid backward into the river- taking the motor with them and capsizing the boat.

Bea and David spilled into the muddy, infested water, gasping at the cold. They tried to cling to the overturned boat but just before they grasped the side, the current turned the boat around abruptly, slamming it into David's head. He went down.

Screaming his name, Bea let herself sink and reached out with both hands to pull him up. It was impossible to see in the murky dark but she felt broad shoulders and grabbed him by the collar, pulling and tugging desperately. She broke the surface to find she had pulled an infected up with her. The cadaverous face had no eyes or ears and his throat was just a shredded black hole. Releasing him and kicking away she plunged down again, fighting a current that wanted to drag her down into the deep and sweep her away.

Her hands closed on hair and she opened her eyes but still couldn't see who or what she had. Struggling back to the surface she found she had David this time. He was unconscious and she struggled to keep them both from going back under.

She heard a shout. The boat was to their left, flipped back over with Carl clinging to the side and pulling it along as he paddled toward them.

Pushing David ahead of her she swam to the boat. Carl helped hoist David up and over the gunwale.

"Do we have any paddles?" she asked.

"No, Supergirl. Everything fell out."

"If we push together we might make it to shore. You stay here and guide. I'll take the back."

Carl nodded and she dived, swimming under the boat. Surfacing, she placed both hands on the hull and kicked as hard as she could. It was working. They were getting closer to the shore.

Steeling herself for a final push she took a deep breath and was immediately pulled under by a cold hand clutching her ankle in an iron grip. Down, deeper and deeper she went while kicking and prying at the dead hand holding her captive. Her lungs were on fire.

Finally her boot connected with the rotting shoulder and the arm broke free. She made a feeble attempt at swimming up but she had lost all sense of direction and wasn't sure where "up" was anymore. She was spent. Bright sparks of light floated briefly in front of her eyes then everything went black.

Somehow, she was on a muddy bank and on her knees, vomiting. The only sensations she felt were of cold and of rocks cutting into her knees and hands while she retched. She vaguely noted that someone or something was behind her and struggling to climb the bank. She vomited again and got to her feet.

The bloated monster behind her slipped backwards in the mud before climbing out of the water again. Droves of the infected were coming ashore up and down the banks, as far as she could see. A bright glint of metal shone far up the bank to her right. The aluminum boat. Were David and Carl still alive?

She jogged slowly up the bank, dodging the clumsy dead and looking for David. She came upon him just a few yards away. He lay with face pressed into the mud, not moving. His forehead still bled watery trickles of blood from a deep gash and she took that as a sign he was still alive. Two infected emerged from the water and began to climb the bank eagerly.

Training for emergency situations, especially terrorist situations (the term "man-caused disaster" never really caught on, even in politically correct D.C.) was routine for anyone working in the nation's capital. She knew how to carry someone in a fireman's lift but had never done it with anyone as tall as David.

A rusting metal silo loomed just up the bank. Debris lapped against its base indicating how high the water had risen. If they could get inside they might hold out for a little while. She moved below David on the bank and took his arms, tugging and shifting him until his body lay more or less across her shoulders.

The dead lurched after them as she stumbled up and over the weedy mud. Her feet sank into the ground and seemed to grow heavier with each step. Moans echoed around her, spurring her on but her strength was almost gone.

The dead were close. Their odor, dank and rotten, was suffocating. She couldn't see behind her or even to the side. An open door in the silo beckoned. So close.

She felt something tugging, trying to pull David from her shoulders and she fought back, kicking and aiming for the knees, hoping to break the decaying bones and at least knock the creature to the ground.

"Supergirl! Wait! It's me."

Carl lifted David and slung him easily over a shoulder. "Let's go."

They climbed the last few feet of the bank and cautiously entered the silo. Startled birds fled through a large hole in the silo's roof. Carl lowered David to the floor and Bea pulled the door closed on the following dead.

Bea assessed the building. They were in a cavernous, empty space, smelling of damp earth. A ladder ran up the side to a small platform near the damaged roof. Bird droppings formed a thick layer on the ground. The slime-covered, metal walls were rusted away in places and there were gaps near their base, large enough for something to crawl through. And from the sound of it something was approaching.

The blows started almost immediately, the metal vibrating under their force and echoing painfully inside. The dead knew they were in here. And they were hungry.

David started to vomit and she ran to roll him on his side. Dirty water mingled with the bird droppings and created a smelly soup. He retched one last time and sat up, shuddering.

"Where-?"

"Silo. On the west side of the river. Can your guy find us here?"

"Depends. Where's my pack?"

"We lost everything."

"My phone's gone then. That's what they were supposed to be tracking."

The noise from the attacking dead was deafening and worse, groping hands found the gaps in the walls. Broken nails dug ceaselessly at the ground, widening the gaps even more.

Bea went through her pockets and pulled out her phone. Water was behind the screen and she couldn't see anything on it. She shook it in frustration. Calming down, she touched the screen as if it were working and she was pulling up her contacts. Running her finger down the screen to where Brian's number usually appeared she tapped it. And waited. She heard nothing.

David tried to stand but staggered. His pants were shredded below the knee and his calf throbbed in pain. Lifting the shreds he saw a four-inch gash, wide and jagged. He tried again to stand and blood poured down his leg. He leaned one-legged against the silo wall, feeling faint.

"That needs stitches," Bea said. She thought she caught a glimpse of white bone deep in the wound.

David shook his head. "Eventually. Can you dial a number?"

"Maybe. That's what I've been trying to do but my screen isn't visible. Give me the number and I'll try it."

She tapped in the number he gave her and then put the phone on speaker. They heard the line ring then a sound as if someone had picked up, a garbled voice message, then silence. David took the phone and recited a rather long string of letters and numbers before handing it back.

"Well, we know something is working, somewhere. We should know if they're looking for us soon enough." His face was gray and strained just from the effort of staying upright and blackness flickered at the edge of his vision.

Just then they heard a loud moan and looked over to see an infected crawling under the wall, partially into the room. Carl stomped the head until the skull cracked and black fluid flowed into the ground. Two more broke through and grabbed Carl's ankle. He fell and a putrid mouth tore into the flesh of his calf. Dirty, skeletal hands pulled him under the jagged metal wall and out. Bea grabbed his arms and pulled him back but lost her grip and he was gone. Immediately more decaying hands appeared in the gaps and continued to dig, clawing at the soft, moist soil.

They were out of time. If a rescue were underway it was going to have to happen now. Not knowing what else to do they climbed the little ladder up to the platform, David's leg pouring blood the whole way. He missed his footing once and nearly fell but finally made it to the top and fell prone, exhausted. Just before he lost consciousness he heard thunderous hammering on the metal walls and felt vibration as if they were collapsing. Darkness, comforting and quiet, beckoned, and he surrendered without a struggle.

Chapter Seven

The following tale was gleaned from a collection of curious stories discovered in Greece by Thomas Bruce, the Earl of Elgin, British ambassador to the Ottoman Empire from 1799 to 1803. It is not, of course, as famous as the pieces of the priceless, marble Parthenon frieze he also "collected" during the same time frame and which still reside (somewhat controversially) in the British Museum. Nevertheless, it is a peek into the myths of a lost world that pre-dated and perhaps foreshadowed our own beloved Western Civilization.

The Greek historian Herodotus wrote of an antediluvian, scientifically-advanced people known for their healing abilities. Originally dismissed as another Atlantis type myth, recent textual and archaeological evidence has come to light in Russia that seems to confirm at least some version of the story. Recounted below is a compilation of various fragmented accounts of the tale.

"Now it came to pass that in the days before the Great Deluge a wise and learned people built a city of great renown, fairer than any city we know today, upon an island in the Mavri-Thalassa*. The people of this city, skilled healers, explored all of the known world for plants and minerals for their miraculous elixirs and poultices. They captured the venom of poisonous snakes for use in various curative decoctions. The ill journeyed hundreds of miles for treatment and the returned travelers spoke of withered limbs made whole, lepers made clean, and an elixir that alleviated all pain.

Snow-capped mountains ringed the city, leaving only a narrow passage through which ships were admitted by sentries at guard stations. Buildings with walls and roofs made of clear stone enclosed gardens where many strange and wonderful plants thrived, carefully tended by linen-clad acolytes.

But the learned people delved too deeply into arcane matters and in their pride and arrogance tried to make themselves immortal. They fell prey to an illness that destroyed their minds whilst leaving their once mortal bodies deathless. Travelers seeking treatment in the city at that time were never seen again or else returned with tales of besieged townspeople hunted by deranged cannibals from whom they themselves barely escaped.

Tales of the city soon faded into myth and legend. Herodotus tells us that, years later, explorers searching for the fabled city found an island in the midst of Mavir-Thalassa. Upon landing they found brutish creatures roaming a vast and once-beautiful city. Greatly outnumbered, the explorers fled and never returned.

Soon after, the gods grew weary of the wickedness of humanity and sent a Great Flood to cleanse the earth of man and his folly. The roaring, engulfing waters that covered the world swallowed the island and it never re-emerged.

The people of the region avoid swimming in the waters even now and parents frighten children with tales of monsters that emerge on moonless nights, searching for living prey.

*believed to be The Black Sea

~

*W*hite *Paper written by Department of Defense CDC liason, Hamm Schilling (Pro Tempore), on the decision to use tactical nukes within the continental United States. Post Urban-Shield.*

PRIORITY: URGENT
Overview:

Addressing the current plan involving the scheduled tactical bombing of population centers within the United States:

The effects of a nuclear blast are well documented. Hiroshima, Nagasaki, and the Tunguska event (strictly speaking not a nuclear bomb but a nuclear event nonetheless) have been thoroughly examined, dissected, discussed, and divulged. Most of us consider a nuclear bomb the most destructive and deadly weapon known, having been conditioned to do so from childhood. Yet how effective is it really?

At ground zero it is true the impact is devastating. With the explosion of a one megaton bomb anyone and anything within a radius of 2 kilometers will be obliterated. A bomb this size will generate hurricane-force winds. An enormous crater, over 60 meters deep and 300 meters wide will form. For anyone living, death will be instantaneous as their body is vaporized in the blast. The death toll at this range is approximately 100 percent. Destruction of the infected inside this area is a near certainty.

However, if we move beyond ground zero to an area 4 kilometers outside the blast zone the picture changes significantly. Here we will find the skeletons of some structures still standing. Poured concrete buildings often hold up against the hurricane force winds at this distance and underground shelters are quite effective. Approximately 50 percent of the population is dead here and 40 percent are seriously injured either from burns or being hurled into objects by the winds. A significant number will suffer "flash blindness" from the brightness of the explosion and everyone not inside a shelter will suffer deep flesh burns that reach to the bone. Most of these victims will linger just long enough to die in agony. Deleterious effects on the infected will be minimal.

Fallout:

The effects of fallout, long term and short, cannot be disregarded. Depending on wind speed and duration, radiation will continue to spread for some time. Within a 50 kilometer radius death will probably occur the same day of the blast and the area will be contaminated for years. A more gradual but still painful death awaits all those within a radius of 350 kilometers.

But what effect will it have on the infected?

Conclusion:

It is my expert opinion that the impact on the infected will be minimal outside of ground zero. The infected are not destroyed by burn wounds, blindness, or blunt force trauma unless it is applied to the cranial area. It is highly doubtful that they will succumb to radiation sickness. The long-term effects of nuclear bombing are known to be devastating to human beings as well as the environment.

I further contend that the bacteria destroying properties of radiation **may well retard the degradation and decomposition** we are already seeing in the virus victims and thus **I counsel patience rather than rash action**. By deploying nuclear weapons we may well be prolonging the 'life-span' of the infected while further damaging and weakening the living as well as poisoning our environment for decades and longer.

Therefore I urgently request that all preparations for tactical nuclear strikes be immediately abandoned and we pursue a course of patience and when possible, simple avoidance of the infected. Warm weather will soon blanket much of the country and will accelerate the decay of the dead.

Respectfully submitted for your consideration,
Commander Hamm Schilling (Pro Tempore) CDC liason

~

Office of the President of the United States

Dear Commander Schilling,
Your request has been received and after due consideration, is hereby denied. We believe the current crisis demands the utmost urgency and believe the "wait and see"

course you recommend is inadequate and would fail to secure the safety of the American people.

Desperate times often call for desperate measures and it is with full knowledge of the seriousness of our situation that we resolve to address this crisis to the full extent of our ability.

~

FOR IMMEDIATE RELEASE

U.S. Department of Defense Publication No. E-N549

Having determined that containment measures have failed to stop the spread of the Z-virus, beyond question the most destructive natural disaster the modern world has ever faced, and that large urban population centers must be considered high risk sources of infection the D.O.D. in cooperation with Homeland Security is issuing the following warning:

Strategic nuclear strikes to be the initial step in Operation Clean-Up and intended to replace failed Operation Urban Shield will begin immediately and are scheduled in the following order:

- *Dallas/Ft. Worth area- immediately*
- *Washington, District of Columbia-within advised time-frame*
- *Atlanta-to be determined*
- *New York Metropolitan area-to be determined*

These strikes will be in accord with our stated strategic policy of containment/elimination. Unintended casualties are inevitable but are within the limits of acceptable risks. Citizens unable to evacuate the intended strike zones should shelter in place as they are able and should keep in mind the following information:

Devices will be detonated as close to designated ground zero areas as possible, thus minimizing fallout but directly hitting intended targets.

Most damage will occur within 1.7 miles of ground zero. Above ground structures inside this radius will be destroyed. If you are within this area and cannot evacuate you should seek deep, underground shelter.

Severe damage will still occur outside of this area up to a 7.4 mile radius of ground zero. Anyone unable to evacuate these areas should also seek deep underground shelter.

Chapter Eight

In the 1930's, the "Golden Age" of Hollywood, California was one of the few places in the country where an enterprising entrepreneur could make a fortune. Everyone who could afford it went to movies or "pictures" as they were called then, to escape the hopelessness of life during the Great Depression. Errol Flynn, Charlie Chaplin, Mae West, and of course the delightful Shirley Temple, all cavorted on the silver screen and helped audiences forget their troubles, if only for a little while.

Vic Capra, an Italian-born film director, made his fortune with a series of noir thrillers. With that fortune he built his dream house high in the hills, secluded and secure. Elaborate wrought-iron fences surrounded the stucco house and small guest cottages that sprawled luxuriously across the rocky hillside. He and a successive string of wives gave lavish and scandalous parties that were legendary even in this land of excess.

Thick stucco walls kept the indoor temperature pleasant now and before the days of air conditioning. A cool stream from a spring on the property ran straight into and through a stream bed flowing through the large atrium before it exited into a rock pool outside. Rare plants from around the world were incorporated into the splendid gardens. Various magazines ran feature stories on the estate and its illustrious owners. That was before society fell. Before the property assumed its new function.

Refugee camps are seldom a pretty sight and the new western command center of the United States of America, which now doubled as a camp, was no exception. Makeshift tents and lines of laundry flapping in the shore breeze obscured the ocean view. Small campfires dotted the twelve acres of gardens. Full-sized marble statues of Mars, Neptune,

Jove, and the lovely Venus, were set into a thick hedge of myrtle that surrounded the rock pool. The Roman emperors Augustus and Hadrian were represented as well but all the statues looked less than dignified draped as they were with drying shirts, pants, and various types of undergarments. Small children, watched by parents, splashed in the rock pool. Primitive latrines, stinking in the hot afternoon, dotted the edges of the property.

Mounted at intervals on hastily constructed turrets, machine guns overlooked the receding hills as well as the vast throngs of teeming dead below. They shuffled and jostled but paid no real attention to each other. Many lay on the ground, some barely moving, some not moving at all. The offshore wind blew their decaying odor inland and up to the estate.

Two boys, one plump with dark hair almost the blue-black of a crow's plumage, the other thin with thick, blond hair in desperate need of a trim, ran along the wall's perimeter. Their feet kicked up dust as they pounded along the trail worn into the lawn by countless patrols. Just behind a barrier of orange cones encircling a cleared, level area of ground, they stopped. Both boys wore expressions of wariness and tiredness that looked out of place on faces so young. Rifles hung from straps across their narrow shoulders.

The sound of beating rotor blades, distant at first then growing louder as the shiny chopper came into view, drowned out all the other noises of the camp and most of the refugees looked up. The pilot deftly maneuvered the craft onto the area designated as a landing pad.

As the motor powered down another sound rose to take its place. The dead at the bottom of the hillside, excited by the noise the helicopter made, started up a moaning, cacophonous chorus, chilling to everyone in the camp. All the refugees had nightmares that included that sound.

Nightmares that often made them wake screaming in the night.

Two men ran up the hillside and eased a stretcher out of the chopper, carefully carrying the unmoving occupant down and through large doors into the main building. Two more figures emerged, one, a woman in a Superman tee shirt. The blond boy shouted, ran to her, and burst into tears. She scooped him up, crying and laughing at the same time. Putting him down she wrapped her arm around his shoulders and together they walked into the main house.

~

"So did you get my text when we picked up that guy in Wrigley Field? You should have seen it, Bea! The whole city was full of dead people. They were all jammed up around the stadium. You would have thrown up, the smell was so bad."

They were sitting on the floor outside a curtained-off passageway that had been dubbed the infirmary. Apparently the camp didn't have any doctors but did have several R.N.s and David had immediately been taken to them. That was late yesterday and so far she had heard nothing other than that he was in "stable" condition.

After everyone exited the helicopter they went through a checkpoint where a nurse examined them and they were thoroughly sniffed by two dogs. Bea's cut in her forearm was cleaned and bandaged and she spent the night in what amounted to quarantine, watched over by armed guards. She was examined again this morning and given a bill of health by the nurses.

The camp seemed to be preparing for an assault. Boards were being nailed to windows and some doors. Everything that could serve as a weapon, screwdrivers, utensils, iron skillets, and chainsaws was arranged for ease of access. Everyone, except for very young children, carried some form of self-defense.

Electricity came and went randomly. No one in the camp really knew why but Brian thought it was due to some sort of automatic brown-out system set up to deal with power blips.

Brian's new friend, Moshe, was with them, listening to Brian's story as if he hadn't heard it a hundred times already. Everyone here had a story of how they survived and what they had seen and often what they had lost but Moshe wasn't eager to share his, whatever it was. Telling their survival story was almost *de rigueur* for new arrivals and everyone regarded it as a form of therapy and a bonding experience but Moshe remained silent. She noticed that he watched everyone warily and once flinched visibly when a patient in the infirmary moaned aloud.

"We've been drilling with weapons every day but not with bullets. I mean, we know how to put them in but we can't waste them on target practice. Ian said it might be more useful to train with swords and I think that would be cool except we don't have enough of those either. They haven't let us go on any foraging raids yet but that's what we want to do, right, Moshe?"

Moshe nodded enthusiastically and added, "Ian says we should start going soon so we'll know our way around in case the 'regulars' don't come back. They don't always all make it back."

A slender woman wearing blue jeans, a red tee shirt, and tall, scuffed leather boots entered the hallway, holding a sleeping baby over one shoulder. Seeing them sitting on the floor, she hurried over.

"Bea! You made it! I knew they had located you guys but I didn't know exactly when you would get here." Virginia leaned over and ruffled Brian's and then Moshe's hair. The baby swayed down with her and didn't wake up but tightened his grip on his mother's hair. Wincing, she tried to disengage his fingers but the plump little fist was thoroughly entwined with the strands. She sighed and shifted her son higher on her shoulder.

"Have they told you how David is yet?"

"No. I'm still waiting for someone to come out and talk to us. He had a really bad cut on one leg and several blows to the head so- I just don't know."

Virginia was reassuring. "Barry, Pam, and Mei-Mei are really good. We're lucky to have them. Even with limited supplies they've practically performed miracles. Don't worry. By the way, Ian can't wait to talk to David about-well, a few things. Did you see much on the trip here?" Her tone was pointedly casual.

Bea stood and the two women walked down the hall, a little way from the boys. "We flew above clouds until Texas. After that, yes, I saw a lot."

"Tell me." Virginia's voice was low and urgent.

Bea swallowed and her voice shook a little as she said, "There were a lot of fires burning so even without cloud cover visibility wasn't that great but everywhere, as far as you could see, there were infected. I wouldn't have even thought there were that many people in the entire country. We stayed pretty high up. The pilot said some of the areas are still radioactive and will be for a long time. I didn't actually see the blast crater; the pilot said that was too hot even to fly over at this point. But I still saw more than I wanted to."

She continued, "They were fast; I had no idea they could move like that. Some were burned to the bone, no features left but they were more coordinated and faster than any I've seen before. There were herds of them, thousands, maybe millions."

"I guess you know about the bombing missions that didn't happen," said Virginia.

"No. I'm assuming they got D.C. I know it was scheduled."

"It was but they're pretty sure it didn't happen. Apparently it was a bitterly contested plan. I hate to say it but our president and his cronies- not the brightest bulbs in the lamp. They understood politics perfectly though, and couldn't break out of that mind-set. They had to be seen as strong and decisive leaders who aren't afraid to make the tough calls, even if those calls were pointless and/or stupid."

"What about Atlanta?"

"That one didn't happen. We're really relieved. The CDC is gone of course but a few of them managed to get out and are supposed to be coming here. We need medical personnel desperately. They definitely bombed Dallas/Ft. Worth but New York may not have gone off either. The fear now is that the radiation is going to preserve the infected and that could be a huge problem for us."

Bea reflected on the scenes she had witnessed from the sky. "I can understand why. How did you wind up out here? I thought you were going back down south."

"We thought so, too. Two of the airfields where we planned to refuel were overrun and heavily infested. The pilot wouldn't land. Fuel was pretty low when we got a call advising us we needed to head to Chicago for a pick-up. We were the only ones in the area and if we didn't pick him up, he wasn't going to get out. We finally did refuel at a little field west of Quincy and after that we were too far west to backtrack safely. So here we are."

"Thanks for looking out for Brian."

"He was no trouble at all. He's trained really hard with weapons and he's comfortable with a rifle now."

Virginia left and Bea walked back to the boys who were flicking a smooth pebble back and forth, trying to score points by sliding it past an imaginary goal. The game was childish but she noticed they carefully placed their rifles within easy reach and kept a more or less constant watch on the windows and anyone who walked by.

Footsteps approached behind the privacy curtains and pulled them aside. A heavily-muscled man who introduced himself as Barry told them one person could come in to talk to the patient.

"Five minutes, that's it."

Bea lifted the curtain and went inside. Four beds were occupied, three by barely conscious patients writhing in pain. She was shocked. There were tied to their beds with knotted sheets. The nurse, sensing her surprise, explained.

"They're not actually infected with the virus. They have bubos." She must have looked confused because he added, "Growths, boils. It's from the bacteria that result from the infection. If the boils burst or if we can lance them in time, the patients have a pretty good shot at getting better. If not, we have to deal with that, too."

"Like the bubonic plague?"

"Yeah, a lot like that."

She nodded and he left.

David occupied a bed nestled under a gothic, mullioned window. A petite woman with dark, shoulder-length hair and wearing scrubs sat casually on the edge of the bed, talking to him in a low voice.

Bea hesitated. The two seemed to know each other very well. David laughed then grimaced and put his hand to his forehead. The woman frowned slightly and put her hand over his. She looked up and saw Bea. She had exquisite, almond-shaped eyes that twinkled when she smiled.

"You must be Beatrice. I'm Mei. David and I are just catching up. We went to school together years ago."

"Hi. Nice to meet you."

She looked down at David. The bandage on his ear was very white in contrast to his hair. "How are you?"

"They tell me I'll mend. Your brother, is he here?"

"Yes, he made it."

"What about Carl?"

126

She shook her head then said, "Brian will want to come see you later when you're feeling up to it."

"Tell him I said to take care of his sister." He closed his eyes and Mei released his hand, put a finger to her lips and ushered Bea out.

"We stitched up that leg after we cleaned it out but it was a nice, straight cut and it should heal just fine. A good night's sleep and he'll be a new man tomorrow," Mei said. "Have they told you where you'll be bunking yet?"

"Not yet. We've been waiting to check on David. Is there someone in charge of newcomers?"

"I'm off duty in five minutes. If you can wait I'll walk you over to see the *concierge*."

"You have a *concierge*?"

Mei laughed and disappeared behind the curtain. In a few minutes she re-emerged and Bea, Brian, and Moshe all followed her out through a metal, scroll-work door and up a series of shallow, stone steps. They were now at almost the highest point on the property and Mei stopped and turned west toward the ocean, lifting a pair of mini-binoculars to her eyes.

The sun burned a hot, glowing orange over the Pacific. In the distance, masses of small figures moved slowly along the beach and streets. Seen through the drifting smoke they could have been locals out enjoying a day at the beach. Debris from smashed boats, docks, and houses floated in and out with the waves. Some of the dead drifted along with the flotsam.

"Before the tsunami there were huge beach houses down there. We had very little warning and most people didn't get out in time. A lot of the infected get pulled off shore at low tide then come back in with high tide. Not always in the same shape they washed out. Take a look." She handed the binoculars to Bea.

Bea trained them on the shore. Up and down the coast as far as she could see were smashed houses and jetties.

Huge ships lay on their sides, colossal, hulking wrecks. Dark, dorsal fins cut sleekly through the rippling waves, rising and falling almost in unison. Sharks were feeding amongst the corpses.

"Never thought I'd be cheering for the sharks," Mei said.

They continued up the hill. Behind them the hillside rose only a little higher before it ended in a sheer, rock cliff behind which the hill dropped off precipitously. Daring vandals climbed it in the past to spray-paint obscure graffiti symbols on its weathered face. Ghosts of old messages were still visible when the light hit it from a certain angle.

A natural break in the stone held scrubby bushes that didn't completely block a view of a construction site below. Gigantic concrete bases held panels of corrugated metal walls arranged to form a barrier behind a scree-covered slope that ascended to a section of cliffs. The site swarmed with workers using heavy-duty equipment to move more of the panels into place. They were obviously building a wall.

Armed sentries patrolled the area. A few infected roamed below the slope, unable to climb it more than a few feet before sliding back down. A shot rang out and brains and bone splattered across the rock and a figure slumped to the ground. Voices shouted angrily and sentries converged on the shooter, taking his gun away.

"No shots unless it's absolutely necessary, you idiot!" The shooter, head down, climbed a rope ladder back up the slope and disappeared behind a boulder. Another infected, possibly attracted by the gunfire, stumbled in closer where it was dispatched with a crushing blow from the butt of a rifle. The sentry muttered angrily while he cleaned the rifle.

The entire house and grounds were situated much like a medieval fortress, easily defended, but also easily cut-off.

"I love this view, don't you? I used to drive by this house and imagine what it would be like to live here. I couldn't have imagined these circumstances though. Let's go see what the *concierge* can help us with." Bea and the boys all jumped at the gun shot and the ensuing mess, but noticed that Mei didn't react at all, as if she were determined not to let it rattle her.

Down more stone steps and across a red, decorative, Japanese bridge they reached a small building almost hidden under a fragrant frangipani tree. The door was ajar so they tapped on it and went inside.

The tiled, single room was cool and dim especially after the heat and glare outside. Wooden crates containing sundry items filled the little space with just a narrow pass-through between them. Mei led them to the back of the room and down shallow steps into another section, this one lit only by flickering oil lanterns. There were more crates as far as they could see.

"A cave?" Bea asked.

"No. Capra's grandson had all this excavated in the late 1950's, early 1960's or so. Originally it was a bomb shelter I think, and they've modified it over the years. On the other side of the hill is where he put in-ground fuel tanks. That's how they're fueling the helicopters. Here is where we keep all the food and other supplies."

They heard footsteps and saw a light bobbing along in the distance, growing closer. A loud, phlegmy cough echoed in the cool dimness and the light illuminated small brown eyes peering at them suspiciously from a bearded, craggy face. He placed the lantern on a crate and cleared his throat.

"Another one? How much room do you think we have here, Mei?"

"As much as it takes, Fitz. This is Beatrice, Brian's sister, and she came all the way from D.C. just to bother you. Bea, this is Fitz. He is a retired quartermaster and he has no equal when it comes to proper and fair acquisition and distribution."

He grunted, picked up the lantern and held it in front of Bea. "Six or eight?"

"What?" Bea asked.

"Are you a size six or eight? I'm usually pretty good at guessing, but I'm tired right now so if you'll just tell me what size clothes you wear I'll take you to that section. You'll also get a blanket, and one roll of toilet paper. Don't waste it."

"I won't. Size six. I've lost some weight."

"Most people have over the last few weeks. Follow me." He said this mournfully as if he were inviting them to view the dead body of a loved one.

Mei left. Bea and the boys followed Fitz through a narrow aisle to a stack of plastic storage bins where he handed her a neatly-folded blanket. She rummaged through a box of clothing, some used, others with the store tags still on them, and pulled out two pairs of jeans, a couple of shirts, tennis shoes, flip flops, and a brand-new swimsuit top she could probably use as a bra. Digging deeper she found the matching bottom, tags still dangling. Good enough.

"I can't thank you enough, Fitz. I lost everything when my boat capsized."

"Don't thank me. I just organize it. People are risking their lives every day to bring this back. Each raiding party has to go a little farther out each time to find swag. Some of this stuff was bought with blood." He shook his head and his jowls wobbled ponderously.

Bea said quietly, "I know."

"Good. People don't understand this camp has an expiration date, and it's getting closer all the time. Some still think we're going to be rescued and then everything will get back to normal. Those people are fools. This many people in one place with virtually no sanitation facilities-it's a ticking time bomb."

Bea said nothing and turned to go but he stopped her.

"Just a few more questions. Religious affiliation?"

"Uh, Christian I guess."

"Denomination?"

"I don't know. Why?"

"Some people want certain prayers said for them before they die. We have a Catholic priest and one Holy Roller preacher type. Which do you want praying for you if you need it?"

"The priest, I suppose."

"Fine. Now, about housing. You can either stay in the tent with your brother and Moshe, or you can find a spot on the floor in one of the women's dormitories. We have almost 70 people here now and space is scarce. Some people say the ground is more comfortable than the tile floors, but I suppose it's a matter of preference."

"I'll think about it." She wanted out of here. The darkness and the towering mounds of supplies together made her feel claustrophobic.

"Okay, don't wait too long or the dormitory space may be gone. And don't forget, all told, typhoid fever and cholera have killed more people than the Z-virus."

Outside, the heat hit them again, but the brightness was welcome. She followed Brian and Moshe to the tent they occupied on the sloping ground and crawled into the muggy interior.

"It's better at night because it's cooler. We usually slide down to the lower section after we fall asleep. It's not that bad unless it rains. The lower part fills with water then and we both keep waking up wet. But it doesn't rain that much," Moshe informed her. "Ian and Virginia's tent is right next to this one."

Bea left her blanket and clothes inside and backed out. "It's got to be close to supper time, right? Where do we go for food?"

Brian led the way to an open breezeway between the main house and the north wing. A capacious pot hung from a beam over a good-sized fire. Sawhorses with planks on top made a long, narrow table. There were no chairs, everyone stood to eat or else sat on the ground.

They joined the line and eventually received a bowl of beef stew and a baked potato. The bowls and plates were of delicate china. Bea looked at the bottom of her plate. Noritake. They certainly dined in style here.

This was her first chance to see the camp assembled as a group. There were more men than women. One of the women wore jeweled rings on every finger and was weighted down with necklaces. She wore heels with denim shorts and clutched her purse tightly when anyone came near. Everyone looked dirty and hungry.

She and the boys took their food up to the highest part of the fence on the steep hillside and sat down. The stew and the potatoes were fairly flavorless, but they ate every bite anyway.

Bea needed to think. Seeing David in that bed, bandaged and vulnerable with Mei touching him aroused a fierce possessiveness that stunned her. How well did they know each other? And why should she care?

That kiss in the shelter was a lifetime ago and she deliberately avoided thinking about it. Now she recalled it in breathtaking detail. She remembered the sweet warmth of it and how amazing she felt-if only for a few moments.

The beat of helicopter blades interrupted her thoughts and she looked up. The chopper hovered for a moment over the rock pool, sending everyone there running. With jerky movements it approached the landing area then the tail rose and the nose tipped forward, wind from the blades scattering the orange cones. The blade then hit earth, throwing up chunks of dirt and sod, bringing the engine to an abrupt halt. The cockpit window shattered and one skid crumpled as the bird tilted to one side.

A helmeted figure staggered from the cockpit, looking over his shoulder and holding his right arm. Blood covered his jacket and he took a few steps then fell and lay still on the dusty ground.

Two women, both wearing grubby-looking white lab coats, stumbled out after him. One was clearly infected; her eyes were dead and dull, but bright-red blood ran down her chin, soaking the front of her shirt. Her left leg dragged behind her, shin bone jutting out through the skin. She fell clumsily to the ground and began to crawl toward the pilot, teeth gnashing.

The other woman was hurt but still in possession of her senses. Clutching her side she ran to the pilot and tried to get him to stand up and run, but he didn't respond. She stood between him and the infected woman, trying to shield him. Blood ran between the fingers of the hand she held to her side.

Four armed figures ran up to the landing pad and assumed a shooter's stance. A gunshot rang out. The crawling, infected woman lay still, the back of her head gone. The four stood around the pilot and the other woman. They seemed to be waiting.

A man with two leashed German shepherds dashed up the hillside. The dogs began barking as soon as they drew close to the pilot and the woman standing guard over him. She lowered her head then fell to her knees and began to plead for her life.

"It's just a little-bitty nip, that's all. If you'll just wait, there's something that might-" she said in a lilting, southern accent. She wrapped her arms protectively around her abdomen and more blood poured down her side. "Please, I need to find my children. There's no one to take care of them but me. I just want to go home. They said we could all go home after-" Tears ran down her face and she drew a shaky breath and began to plead again.

The dogs pulled back, sat on their haunches and were silent. The group of four closed in and two shots were fired in rapid succession.

Almost everyone turned away. Bea sat back down on the ground, stunned and shaken. Brian looked carefully toward the ocean, away from the three bodies being thrown up and over the fence, left to roll down the cliffs to the streets and to whatever fate scavengers inflicted on them.

"What? We don't bury them?" Bea asked.

A gruff, British voice spoke behind her. "You want to go out there and dig the graves, love?"

She turned and saw a giant of a man staring stoically down the cliff. "We all die and the dead are blissfully unaware of what happens after." He turned. "No sense in more dying, I say."

Bea nodded, a little embarrassed, "You're right. I still wish..."

"As do I. The apocalypse takes some getting used to. Let's unload whatever it is they thought was so important they flew it all that way."

She was bemused by his accent. He had fiery, red hair, vividly blue eyes, and broad shoulders. Muscles in his arms bulged as he pulled himself up into the chopper and began to hand down cargo. Brian seemed to know him already and introduced him as Cam.

There wasn't much to unload. Styrofoam containers, tightly sealed, took up most of the cargo space. They were cool to the touch and marked with biohazard symbols. An Atlanta, Georgia address was stamped on the bottom of each container.

"Brian, go get Barry or Pam. They'll let us know where they want these stored. We'd best keep them away from the food supplies," he said.

Brian returned with Barry, the muscular nurse Bea met earlier in the infirmary. His eyes widened at the sight of the Styrofoam containers. "Looks like the CDC has sent us a special surprise. Follow me."

He led the way into one of the small cottages and down a short hallway. It was cool here, surrounded by thick, adobe walls. Barry took one of the oil lamps sitting on a small table then they went down a narrow flight of steps to a stout, locked wooden door. He flipped through a set of keys and unlocked the door, lit the oil lamp and beckoned them inside.

The dark room was cold with a stone floor. The walls were damp and they heard water trickling somewhere.

"This is the old springhouse where they would have stored perishables back in the day. It's the coolest spot we have so we're keeping some meds in here. Not that we have a whole lot. Let's see what Atlanta sent us."

He carefully peeled off the tape holding one of the little boxes closed. Bubble-wrap encased vials nestled snugly inside. The rest of the boxes contained identical contents. All the vials were labeled either *P. ovale* or *P. malariae*. The accompanying paperwork was torn and bloodstained. Barry leafed through it but pages were missing and out of sequence.

"Like we don't have enough problems? Why would they send us malaria samples?" Barry sounded angry.

Brian said, "I know why. This is what-"

Suddenly the ground heaved, throwing them to their knees, Barry barely catching the vial knocked from his hand. The oil lamp shattered on the old floor, flame snuffed out. An enormous blast that not even the thick walls could shut out rattled the contents of the room and ancient dust drifted down from the old walls and ceiling, choking them.

Chapter Nine

Muffled shouts came from outside as they groped their way out through the sudden darkness, leaving the sinister little vials behind. A continuous screaming grew louder and intensified.

They emerged into utter chaos. Acrid smoke drifted through the little compound, giving a surreal look to the evening twilight. A young father, charred left arm hanging uselessly, held his daughter, blood pouring from a head wound. As soon as he saw Barry he ran to him, holding out his child, pleading for help. Barry took the limp child and ran for the infirmary.

Similar scenes were all over the grounds. Scorched bodies lay about, some still, others screaming in unceasing agony, featureless, hair and skin burned away. The infirmary staff began a sort of mobile triage, sending some inside, leaving others where they lay. Scattered shots *popped* as the severely burned were put out of their misery. Moshe flinched with each shot.

The disabled helicopter had been hit and as a result, rolled down the hillside, smashing tents and refugees before it came to a stop against the fence.

A woman raged impotently, restrained by two others, as volunteers heaved her daughter's scorched, dead body over the wall. As the body bounced and rolled down the rocky hillside, the mother broke free and climbed the fence. She groped her way down to the shoreline where she was met by the hungry dead. She didn't scream long.

A small crowd gathered near the back of the property, looking down the cliff. A dirty column of smoke billowed up and hung in the air briefly before the evening breeze blew it into ugly, dark wisps and sent it east. A large section of the partially constructed wall was simply gone, twisted hunks of metal and blasted concrete strewn about the slope. Rocks and dirt were scorched and a bitter, burning smell filled the air.

Someone spoke. "They practically knocked it all the way to Mexico. That's where it was intended to go originally."

"All that work, just blasted all to hell. Makes me sick. Maybe we'll finally enforce radio silence now." The speaker turned away from the cliff edge and Bea recognized Ian Dare. He noticed her and walked over.

"Glad you're here. Virginia said she talked to you. I checked on David just a little while ago but he was still asleep."

"He's been through a lot. The nurse said he would be better once he's rested."

"Except that there's no rest for the wicked." The voice came from behind them.

Startled, Bea turned. David, pale but with a determined look on his face, limped towards them.

"I knew you'd be alright since, so they say, only the good die young," Ian said.

The two men clasped hands briefly then walked a few feet away. Bea overheard their conversation without even trying.

"I've been expecting it. They've been sitting silent for a while now. We tried to get out to the ship that's drifting. We thought we could take it and use it to evacuate, after we cleared all the dead out but the other ship fired on us. Didn't even come close to hitting us so I'm not sure it was on purpose but who knows? I'm not convinced they know our location but they might be monitoring our communications. I've been telling everyone that but no one would listen. I was just as relieved as anyone when the one foundered but at least one of them is still fully functional as they just proved."

"We have to find a way to take them out. Plastic explosives come to mind but how would we get them out there?"

"That is still under discussion. Those waters are full of corpses and now sharks. We have inflatables, enough to get us out there but we would probably be dragged down by the infected. Even if that didn't happen I doubt we would make it without being seen by someone on the active ship."

"Were you able to observe anything at all on the flight here?" Ian asked.

"A little. I was pretty out of it. What did the pilot say?"

"They're coming. Fast."

"How long do you think?"

"A week. Maybe less. They don't have to stop to sleep. Of course they might head off in another direction if something distracts them. The herds we saw in Nevada might be here even faster. We've sent a request to both Midwest and Northeast Command for air or naval support but we haven't heard back. One carrier ship could hold all of us with no problems." Ian stared worriedly down at the twisted metal chunks scattered across the dirt and rocks. He shook his head.

"Go back to the infirmary, David. There's nothing you can do here and I need you at full-strength. We're sending out another foraging party tomorrow. This could be an important one. I want to talk to the Colonel first, though."

David's face had changed to a sickly shade of gray and he nodded and turned around, making his way back to the infirmary.

Brian broke away and caught up with David just outside the building. He said something and David laughed then stumbled, swaying dangerously on his feet. Brian took his arm to steady him and together they walked slowly the rest of the way.

The smell of cordite and rot drifted through the evening air. A three-quarter moon hung low over the hills to the north. Everyone made their way to whatever sleeping space they laid claim to and began to settle down for the evening. Bea and Moshe passed a family of five, all kneeling and saying their bedtime prayers. Others throughout the camp were similarly engaged making her think of the old "no atheists in foxholes" saying.

She was fairly sure she believed in God as a benign, general force for good, but never really thought of specifically engaging Him in her life. When they reached their tent, they came upon Virginia and three children, hands clasped and heads lowered. Moshe joined them, settling comfortably into their circle, bowing his head. Bea waited, unsure how long it took to say prayers.

Not long. The little girl, who looked very much like Ian, finished for them all with "...forever and ever, Amen," after which she wrapped up in her blanket and demanded a story.

"Not tonight, Anna. I need to talk to Miss Beatrice tonight," Virginia explained.

"Two stories tomorrow then."

Virginia smiled, "Maybe. But I'm running out of ideas. Maybe we'll find some books tomorrow. That reminds me, Daniel, you and Anna need to finish the last chapter in your phonics workbook in the morning."

The children crawled into the tent and Virginia zipped the flap closed.

"Walk with me for a minute?" she asked Bea.

"Sure. Moshe, go ahead. Can you see if Brian is on his way back?"

Moshe nodded and left. They walked up the hillside a few feet and Virginia stopped.

"I can't go too far. It's not really safe here."

"You mean inside the camp? Why not?"

"Two nights ago one of the male refugees tried to get a six-year-old girl into his tent. Fortunately, she screamed her head off right before he gagged her with a sock. Her father was nearby and came running."

"That's terrible. What happened to the guy? Is he locked up?"

"Um, no. He wasn't locked up, but he *is* no longer with us." Virginia shuddered. "The father in this case acted as judge, jury, and executioner. I know how that sounds but we don't have the luxury of a trial process anymore. The incident changed the mood of the entire camp. Almost everyone is on guard and won't let their children out of their sight. It's completely understandable."

Bea said nothing but looked out over the campfires below and thought about monsters. The dead below were nakedly malignant but who knew what monstrous thoughts lurked in the minds of perfectly normal-seeming individuals?

Virginia was speaking again and Bea tuned back in. "… just hard to watch three children and be available for the colonel. I know this is a huge favor but would you mind?"

"Sorry,Virginia. Would you say that again?"

"Tomorrow. I'm on the roster to go on a foraging mission tomorrow and I need someone to help Ian watch the children for the day. I won't lie to you- it might be longer than that. The parties don't always make it back on schedule."

"Of course. Not a problem. What time do you leave?"

"Daybreak. It gives us as much time as possible. We're trying to get to the National Guard Amory and it's all the way over on Riverside. It's pretty far but they don't expect it will be too infested because it's more of an industrial area, not residential. They haven't told us exactly who else will be on the team but I know Ian won't be. We've agreed to never go on a mission together just in case something goes wrong, but the colonel expects him to be available on demand. I think the colonel's stated philosophy on families is, 'If we wanted you to have a wife, we would have issued you one.' But Ian and I know the risks we take affect more than just us. We want the children to have at least one living parent."

Bea nodded and said good night. Back at the tent she found Brian and Moshe lying on the ground, looking up at the stars.

"The stars are brighter out here. I never knew you could see so many," Brian said.

"It's because the lights are out. Light pollution kept you from seeing much of them," responded Moshe.

"I like it here. We had more trees at home, though. Do you think we'll ever go back, Bea?"

"I don't know. Maybe. I heard they might not have nuked D.C. so it's a possibility."

She joined them. The stars hung low in the sky, a brightly glowing tapestry that few in this country would have ever seen before now. Shivering, she found her blanket and wrapped up. The night was surprisingly cool after such a warm day. The moon set behind the hills and the stars seemed even brighter.

"Would you guys be interested in helping me watch the Dare's children tomorrow? Their mom has to go out on a mission."

"We're going out on that one!" Moshe exclaimed.

"Oh. Are you sure? How old are you, Moshe?"

"I'll be thirteen this summer."

She said nothing else but determined that tomorrow she would talk to whoever was making these decisions. She had no say in what Moshe was allowed to do but she wasn't at all sure she would let Brian go. Both boys seemed way too young to go out and scavenge a post-apocalyptic city.

The dead down the hillside kept up their guttural moaning and the sound blended with the calls of night birds to create a baleful lullaby in the night air.

~

Virginia woke to darkness and whispers. Ian crouched beside her, brushing her hair from her face.

"It's almost time. Are you sure you don't want me to go on this one for you?"

She sat up and rubbed her eyes. The children were still asleep, snug inside the little tent.

"Positive. I told you Bea agreed to help with them. You know Greg is going to attach himself to you, especially once he realizes I'm gone. So she'll mostly be dealing with Anna and Daniel."

He pulled her to her feet and held her close for a moment then slid his hands up her back, cradling her head before kissing her. She shivered with pleasure. His lips traveled down her neck then back up to her temple.

"Be careful out there. We want you back, safe and sound," he whispered into her hair.

Fifteen minutes later she stood at the gate, near a small campfire, with the rest of the team. Two men and Mei stood ready to go. To her surprise, David stood beside Cam, checking the clip in a pistol and stowing another in the pocket of some newly-acquired camo fatigues. The bandage on his head was gone but he still looked ill, with dark circles under his eyes.

"Are you ready for this? Another day in bed wouldn't hurt," said Virginia.

"I'm fine. I know exactly what we're looking for and have a pretty good idea where they would store it. We want to do this quickly, right?"

Bea stepped out of the darkness, blanket still wrapped around her shoulders. Brian and Moshe stood beside her, rifles slung across their backs, looking sleepy but excited.

"Are you sure the boys need to go?" she asked, voice still slightly raspy with sleep.

"Absolutely. I don't think we shall find large numbers of infected on this trip." It was Cam who spoke. "We're not going to a heavily populated area though the lads need field experience dealing with these dead bastards. They're a fact of life now, yeah? This is just as important as learning to drive, or swim, or look both ways before crossing the street." The big Celt continued to load shells into a shotgun as he spoke. Snapping the gun back into position and slinging the strap over his shoulder he looked down at Bea and said confidently. "We'll bring them back, not to worry." He picked up a large meat cleaver and held it loosely.

Virginia tucked a pistol into her belt and a large knife into her boot. She pulled her hair back into a long, sleek ponytail. "This will be a piece of cake compared to watching my three for a day. You have the rougher job. I'll watch the boys as if they were my own. Cam is right, don't worry." She turned to the boys, clear blue eyes sparkling, "What's the first rule of Zombie Fight Club?"

Brian and Moshe laughed, "First rule, avoid. Second rule, avoid. Third rule, headshots are best."

"Fine, I get it," Bea said.

David didn't speak but caught Bea's eye and nodded reassuringly while Brian looked at her pleadingly, not wanting her to embarrass him. She gave up and caught him in a fierce hug which he endured for a few seconds before breaking away.

The sun was barely above the hills to the east as they slipped quietly out the gate, stepping out onto a meandering series of urban bike trails that would lead them north.

Virginia matched her pace to Mei's. "Why are you going out on this, Mei-Mei? We need you back in the infirmary."

Mei shrugged. "Connie was supposed to go but she was killed last night. No one is willing to leave their children

143

anymore; not after what almost happened to the little girl. Then that attack last night. I can't say I blame them. If I had children I would feel the same."

Virginia reflected a moment. "I can't blame them either. If Ian weren't back there with them, I would never have come."

At first, progress was slow. The adults consciously flanked Brian and Moshe, keeping them protected against surprise encounters. All of them spoke as little as possible and when they had to, they whispered. The area here contained several luxury apartment complexes and the dead residents were numerous and mobile. Nail boutiques mixed with sushi restaurants dotted the lower floors street side. They encountered ambling corpses every block or so and Cam took them down with the heavy-duty meat cleaver. Every time he smashed it in a decaying skull the dead slumped to the ground like sacks of rotting meat. Wrecked cars littered the pavement, doors left open when they were abandoned, seats drenched in pools of now-dry blood. They passed by several gated communities with dead pressed against the elaborate, scrollwork gates, reaching out yearningly for fresh meat. They moaned and chittered as the team walked by.

Appalled by the sheer numbers of the dead, Virginia said quietly, "I hope those gates hold."

"They will. If not, we'll find another way back. This should be a short mission," David said.

"They all should be but sometimes things don't go as expected. I've been on some really long short missions." Cam tucked his cleaver in his belt loop and strode on.

Brian peppered David with questions about their escape from the city. He was especially interested in the flooded Mississippi.

"Were you in Memphis? Did you see that glass pyramid?"

"No. We made it to a little town above Memphis."

"Bea didn't drive, did she?"

David gave him a quick, amused glance. "Part of the way."

"You're lucky you're alive. She's a terrible driver."

David didn't comment.

Office buildings now predominated and soon these thinned out and became warehouses surrounded by razor-wire. They glimpsed a few dead in the distance, some still stumbling along, others lying heaped and rotting on the pavement. A strong wind swirled litter and plastic bags around and blew sand and grit into their eyes.

A building, single-storied and flying a large American flag, stood just beyond a block of self-storage units at the end of a dead-end lane. It backed up to a low, rocky series of hills. Though it was surrounded by razor-wire topped security fences, the gate stood open and two corpses, dressed in military fatigues, staggered about, performing a ghoulish sentry-duty even after death. They attacked immediately, careening toward them, blackened mouths dropping gobbets of flesh as they gnashed their teeth. After Cam took them down, David searched their pockets while Virginia and Mei slid the gate closed.

Two Humvees flanked the entrance and a tank rested halfway between the gate and building. The front entrance glass doors led to a lobby that ended in reinforced metal panels that looked capable of withstanding a bomb blast.

"There's no point in breaking through here. The noise would just draw more corpses and we still wouldn't get where we need to go," David said. "Let's look around."

A concrete walkway wound around the side of the building to a patio with a picnic table outside a narrow, side-entry door. Though they tried, none of them could do anything with the biometric reader which looked still functional, a soft, red light still glowing on the side.

"All these locks have their own battery back-up so I'm not surprised it's still functioning," David said.

"What about trying to get in through the roof? There are two AC units up there." Cam backed away from the building, trying to see more.

David replied, "I don't think we'll find a way in there. I'm sure it's hardened."

"I'll try to scout it if you like. Boost me up there." Virginia adjusted the .38 in her belt. Cam cupped his hands and practically tossed her up onto the flat roof.

"Sorry, love! You don't weigh enough," he called in a stage whisper. Virginia stood and dusted herself off before giving him a thumbs up and heading for the nearest roof vent. They heard her kicking then the clang of metal. Footsteps came back to the edge.

"I can't get in through the vent; it's too narrow. Did anyone bring tools? I might be able to remove a piece of the air unit and see how big that opening is," Virginia whispered, leaning down over the edge.

Moshe had a pocket Leathermen tool and Cam lifted him up, sending him sprawling on the asphalt roof surface. They managed to unscrew a large piece of sheet metal, peeling it away only to find a metal box unit recessed and screwed between rafters. Underneath that they found more riveted metal and a small electrical conduit. This was proving to be impossible.

"What we really need is some of the good stuff they have inside to blow this door to hell, yeah? But we don't so what shall we do?" Cam queried.

David replied, "We dig. The back of the building continues right into that hillside. They did it that way just in case of some sort of malfunction, the land itself will absorb and damper the force of any accidental explosions. Once we dig through we might be able to break through the wall."

Virginia and Moshe climbed back down. They all walked to the back of the building and surveyed the scrubby hillside. The rocky, clay soil was unyielding and painful to dig through. They made a search for any sort of landscaping tools but found nothing. David tried dislodging one of the bigger rocks stuck in the dirt, hoping to start a small avalanche that might reveal a wall.

Meanwhile, a growing horde of corpses gathered outside the fence. Searching hands and arms reached yearningly through the chain link. Even though they had been as quiet as possible, the dead, surrounded by buzzing, black clouds of flies, found them. To Virginia the moaning sounded as if they were in terrible pain, constant and driving.

She realized with a jolt that Brian was gone. Hurrying back around the building she saw him in the front parking area, crouched beside the soldiers' corpses. He had Cam's cleaver and was using it to hack at the bodies. He stood and walked back to her, holding something in the palm of his hand.

"Hey! I got something we can try. I got their index fingers. Let's go tell David and give it a shot."

Virginia nodded but headed back toward the Humvees. "You go ahead. I want to look for something."

Brian found David still digging in the back and showed him the fingers but David shook his head.

"Even if they haven't decayed too much for the reader to recognize, they'll still be too cold to work. It reads temperature as well as fingerprints."

"But can't we at least try?" Brian pleaded.

David shrugged and led the way back to the patio.

"Let me have them." Cam took the fingers and held them in his massive hands for a few minutes. "I have the warmest hands in Londonderry. Now give it a go." He handed them back then wiped his hands on his pants disgustedly.

The reader clicked and the light flickered to green briefly before changing back to red. Moshe whooped *sotto voice* and hit Brian on the shoulder.

"I told you it wouldn't work."

"Shut up. At least I tried," Brian countered.

Virginia walked around the corner, carrying a car jack. "Can we jack the door frame?"

Eventually they separated the frame enough that the door could be pushed aside. Stepping inside, they found the building only dimly lit by the small amount of light the narrow windows admitted. The power was out and whatever back-up lighting they might have had in the early days of the outbreak was long gone. David fished through several desks before finding a mini-mag flashlight. He flipped it on and the beam shone brightly. There were signs of a struggle. Overturned computers and smashed chairs lay scattered about the room. Beyond the office space/entrance area, dark shapes loomed in a room of indeterminate size.

"The ammo won't be stored with the weapons. Plastique will be in a section off by itself. Everybody keep an eye out. Although if any of *them* are in here, we'll probably smell them before we see them," David whispered.

Mei split off to the left with Cam, David stepped away on his own and Virginia kept the two boys with her. They moved deeper into the shadows of the room beyond. A few cubicles divided up the area at the front. A drinking fountain hugged the wall near the restrooms and before Virginia could stop him, Moshe darted over, pressed the handle and leaned down expectantly. The air-filled pipes in the walls banged in response.

"If they didn't know before, whoever is in here knows we're here now," said Brian.

Moshe returned sheepishly and they continued on, stepping around cables and other items that lay tangled on the floor, stopping every few moments to listen. This area felt colder and despite that- Virginia sniffed- something back here was rotting.

The boys pulled their shirts up over their noses and mouths and got a good grip on their rifles. This is what they had trained for. They kept a tight formation, the three of them carefully assessing the area front and back.

The thing came at them from behind a desk. Dragging itself forward along the floor with dead arms, it chomped down first on Virginia's boot then pulled her to the ground, knocking the breath out of her.

Gasping and fighting to inhale she kicked, snapping the corpse's head back and knocking several teeth to the floor. The woman wore a dark-stained white blouse with some sort of insignia on the sleeves, a skirt and low heels. Whitened eyes shone blindly in the rotting face and the cold, freakishly strong hands never let go of her leg, drawing her nearer to the insatiable, rancid mouth. She clung to a desk leg and kicked again but hit nothing. The knife in her boot slid out and clattered to the floor and she felt for it, barely drawing back in time to avoid a bite. She kicked again with no result.

"Be still! I've got it," Moshe spoke near her ear.

She froze in terror, sure she was going to lose a leg or worse. Just as she opened her mouth to tell him to stop, he fired.

Cold stinking chunks of flesh splashed on her as she closed her eyes and mouth tightly. She pulled her legs up to her chest, holding her knees and touching her shins. Still there.

Cam waded across the strewn floor and stood looking down at her. "What the bloody hell is this?"

She got off the floor and sat down on top of the desk. Drawing deep breaths, she kept her head down then pushed away and picked up her knife.

"We're fine. Moshe just saved my life. Let's go."

Everyone closed ranks again as they approached the very back of the building. So far they found nothing useful and they feared going home empty-handed when they came upon the entrance to a small room off to the right. A heavy, steel door stood ajar. The massive hinges moved easily and silently and they swung the door wide and stepped inside.

Chapter Ten

Empty shelves lined the walls. Spilled shells from open boxes were all over the floor and they took care not to step on them and slip. Clearly someone had taken everything they could before leaving in a hurry and not bothering to lock up.

David turned on the flashlight and moved amongst the mess, peering intently at the few labeled boxes on the floor. Mei exclaimed and picked up a pair of night vision goggles, wiping them off and stowing them in her pack. The rest of them filled their pockets with shells from the floor.

Virginia gathered what she could then went back to the door, watching and listening. Was that something moving over by one of the window slits? She kept watching but didn't see any more movement. She wanted to get out of here and was concerned about the dead clustering around the armory fence. Again, she was amazed at how the dead always found them and dismayed that there were still so many of them able to move around. They should have decomposed faster in the heat here.

Worry about the children consumed her. The incident with the child molester kept her awake for two nights, checking on the children to be sure they were still safe in the tent with her. But a tent was little real protection against a determined abductor with a gun, not to mention hundreds of thousands of ravenous dead. She and Ian desperately wanted to get back to their little mountain-top town but she wondered if they ever would.

She knew what was approaching from the east. The radiated dead were exactly what everyone who fought against Operation Clean-Up had feared. They were faster and better coordinated than any infected seen before. The few survivors who escaped them said their attacks appeared almost planned. One man, who later died of his injuries, said they were hunting in packs. And helicopter pilots confirmed that vast herds of them were headed west.

David growled, startling her. "There's nothing here. If we don't find a way to make those bastards stop shelling us, we'll never get the wall built. Without some sort of barrier in place those irradiated corpses will-"

He stopped talking and turned to go. If they didn't leave now they would be trapped here overnight. It was too dangerous to travel, especially on foot, in the dark.

"Let's go back and take a slightly different route, shall we? You never know, we might find a construction site with some interesting explosives. One always seems to find blokes working on the roads here," Cam said.

"Good idea. Let's go." David led the way and they all followed, jingling a little as they walked.

The day had warmed considerably while they were inside and the sun was high in the sky. Which made the crowd surrounding the compound easy to see and -she gagged- smell.

Dead in every imaginable state of decomposition waited for them outside the fence, moaning and shuffling, clawing at the chain-link. The metal groaned under the strain and bulges appeared at the weakest spots. Virginia stopped counting at seventy. More and more filed into the little street, no doubt attracted by the noise the rest were making.

There was no way they could get past a crowd that size. None of the team knew how to operate a tank and the batteries in both Humvees were dead. The only way out they could see was to climb the fence on the roof and try the area beyond the armory. Virginia went up first to take a look. The fence here too was topped with razor-wire and she climbed as high as she could without getting tangled in it. It looked like the hill ended in a block retaining-wall, also topped with razor-wire, a double barrier back here. The only thing visible past that was the top of a street sign that said *Cedar SW* and a dead traffic-light swaying in the breeze. She climbed down.

"We need a way to get over the razor-wire, pieces of carpet, heavy-duty floor mats, something like that. Once we're over we should be on southwest Cedar if that means anything to anyone," she called down.

The boys pulled the large floor-mats from the two Humvees and threw them across the razor-wire before climbing up and over. Soon they all stood surveying the street below the block wall. A commercial area, store-front windows smashed and doors open, lay below. A corner gas-station was a burned out shell and the fire had spread, engulfing one corner of an electronics store before it burned out. Purloined big-screen televisions lay abandoned as people perhaps realized they weren't going to be watching a whole lot of television in the near future. Scattered cars, abandoned as well, blocked the street, but they didn't see any infected.

Sliding down the slope to the street, they headed south. The sun was now well past the meridian and the shadows grew longer.

Mei said, "This will take us west until we turn left on Verity then we need to turn right on Sausalito to go back to the compound."

"How much farther do you think?" David asked, casting a worried glance at the sun.

"I'm terrible with guessing distances and I was always in a car before. Two, maybe three miles?"

They trudged on and took the left onto Verity. The buildings became less commercial and thinned out a little but they didn't see a sign for Sausalito. Once they encountered a snarling dog, legs splayed and shoulders hunched below its raised hackles. Mei thought it might be rabid but it didn't attack, just continued to growl until they edged their way past it. The sun began to dip in the western sky.

Distant *booms* sounded somewhere to the south. They stopped briefly and examined the horizon. Brian thought he saw smoke blowing out in the direction of the beach. They all shuddered at the thought of another artillery assault on the camp, but Virginia looked stricken and her shoulders slumped visibly.

They walked faster but the road was not taking them where they thought it would. The sun's rays were now slanted, creating deep shadows in alleyways which they avoided, never taking their eyes off them until they were several yards away. A dead dog, stiff-legged and belly bloated in decomposition, lay against the curb.

The road led them around the 700 block of Verity then ended abruptly. Orange barrels and caution tape marked the beginning of a road project that would never be completed. They stopped and contemplated the scene.

Mei spoke, "Sorry, everyone. I was wrong about where this would take us."

"Don't worry about it. The street sign for Sausalito could be down for all we know. We need to start scouting a place to spend the night. It'll be dark soon and though it doesn't bother the corpses much, *we* are definitely at a disadvantage," David said.

Virginia still had a haunted look in her eyes. "I'd like to go back tonight if we could."

Cam said gently, "I would like to go back tonight, too, but we are out of time. Your babies are safe with their dad. Don't worry, little mum."

Virginia nodded but she lowered her eyes as they turned to retrace their steps. Cam had noticed a bank a short distance back that looked secure if they could just break in somehow.

"A bank though, Cam. They're going to have that pretty locked-up. I don't like our chances of getting in," David said.

153

"Yes, but if we do we're safe for a bit. There are other shops in the building. Maybe those entrances won't be quite so difficult."

"Okay, I've got nothing better," David conceded. He looked tired and the dark circles beneath his eyes were more pronounced than before.

The Third National Bank and Trust building stood just across the four-lane. A few of the dead from the armory followed them and were less than fifty yards away. Experience told them that where a few corpses gathered, many more would soon follow. They had to get inside somewhere before nightfall.

The bank's main entrance at ground level had thick, plate-glass revolving doors. Breaking through that would be noisy and they wouldn't have a way to secure the building afterwards. The bank's parking garage next door should have less conspicuous entrance doors off of the various levels leading to the other businesses the building housed.

They entered the garage with weapons drawn. Several cars remained parked, encrusted with dust and sand that must have blown in from the shore, almost a mile away. Menacing shadows lay between the cars and they hugged the walls until they found the parking garage stairs. The wind increased in the partially open stairwell and bills in twenty, fifty, and one-hundred dollar denominations blew around, trapped in the air currents. Delighted, both boys grabbed and stuffed them into their pockets until Cam caught their eyes and frowned.

The first door they reached had bullet damage but was still closed tightly and wouldn't open. One more level up, they found a strongly secured, metal door standing partially ajar.

Cam put a finger to his lips and eased the door open revealing nothing but an inky blackness. Nodding to David he moved aside and David went in front, holding the mag-lite high. Virginia tried to pull the door closed once they were all inside but a protruding deadbolt wouldn't allow it. Cam tried but the bolt wouldn't budge. Giving up, they left it and moved on.

They were in a tiled hallway with a multitude of doors on either side. The area smelled clean with no tell-tale odor of decay. Passing by an open office door they caught the ghost of a whiff of coffee. Virginia inhaled deeply. She hadn't realized until now just how much she missed coffee.

The rooms down here were devoted to storing office and cleaning supplies. There was also what appeared to have been a company daycare. Construction paper, crayons and markers were scattered on the miniature tables. Toys were neatly stored in labeled bins. The whole floor seemed untouched by the disaster that had overtaken the city.

At the end of the hallway, they found the stairs next to the elevators. David stopped. "We can hole-up here if we want and keep a watch on that door. I'd prefer to look a little more; it's always a good idea to have another way out if needed. What do you think?"

Everyone agreed to push on. The stairwell was pitch-black and their footsteps echoed alarmingly. Virginia took the rear and held tightly onto the rail, behind Brian and Moshe. At each landing they stopped and listened before trying the door. The first one was firmly locked but on the second landing they found another open door. Someone had wedged it with a rubber door stop. They stepped inside.

The hair on Virginia's neck prickled. The smell was faint but something or someone had died in here. David's mag-lite illuminated a lobby area with dead, wilted plants, a row of chairs, and two candy machines. They were looted but candy still lay on the floor. They sorted through and found a few intact goodies. The mag-lite went out and they all froze in place. David shook it and the light flickered back on.

Underneath a desk Moshe found a shopping bag from The Archery Outpost containing a bow and several arrows,

155

still in their plastic packaging. He exclaimed and tore into the package, shrugging the bow onto his shoulder and securing the arrows in the snap-on quiver. Whoever was the intended recipient was probably not counting on getting it anymore.

Two training rooms led off the lobby. In one they found the decomposing body of a woman, propped against a wall. Her wrists were slashed and her blood had pooled and dried on the tiled floor. Her skirt must have hiked up in her death throes and Virginia pulled it back down, re-arranging it more modestly, trying to give her dead body a semblance of dignity.

Suddenly the woman's eyes opened, milky-white and blind. She hissed and jerked forward, teeth clicking together as she just missed tearing into Virginia's arm.

Startled, Virginia jumped back and Cam split the woman's head with his cleaver. She slumped to the floor, this time really dead. Black gobbets of brain matter fell with to the floor with a wet *splat*.

"What's the first rule of Zombie Fight Club, sweetheart?" Cam asked, wiping his cleaver on the woman's skirt.

"I know. It's just that I know she wouldn't have wanted anyone to see her like- never mind."

Another staircase took them down a level to a hallway that led to the bank lobby. The area was vast with teller windows, a fountain which now contained only green scum, and deeply-tufted, leather sofas.

It was brighter in here with the last of the daylight. The entire front was of glass with glass revolving doors facing west. Several dead roamed outside.

"I say we stay here but near the back. I don't want those things to hear us and begin to congregate. We can leave tomorrow the same way we came in or, if we have to, we can shoot out the glass here and run for it. There will be a fire door leading back to the garage stair, too," said David.

They sat, eating the candy and watching the fading light. The sunset was incredibly vivid. Brian said it was so colorful because of all the smoke in the air.

"Never thought about pollution being pretty before. There've been so many fires I wonder if they'll have an effect on the weather. If it's smoky or cloudy enough it could block the sun and cool the entire planet down. It happens sometimes after a really big volcano eruption."

"Mount Tambora did that. After that one blew up, it snowed in July. There were massive crop failures, too," added Moshe.

"Mates, let's take it one step at a time. It's all I can do to handle surviving the living dead; don't throw climate disaster at me as well. I came to America for the sunshine. Don't take it away," Cam pleaded.

"Really? You moved here for the weather? That's a long way to go for a little sunshine," David remarked.

"Ah, but you don't know how the damp and cold freeze the heart out of a man. When the plane left Heathrow it was 8 degrees," he lamented.

"That's not that bad. Celsius, right? That's 43 Fahrenheit," Brian calculated quickly.

"Sure it is, but that was in July," Cam said dolorously, shaking his head

"So Cam gets the trophy for greatest distance traveled to experience the apocalypse, American style. Who traveled the least?" asked Virginia.

Mei raised her hand. "Probably me. I'm about 45 minutes up the coast."

"No, I was closer." Moshe's voice was solemn. "My sister and I have savings accounts in this bank. We used to come here with my mom."

His voice wavered a little as he continued, "We came here and withdrew a bunch of cash once my mom realized what was happening. Then she opened up a safe-deposit box and stuffed little gold and silver ingots in her purse and in our backpacks. I'd never seen those before but they were heavy! I'm not sure I really believed what we were hearing but when mom did that, I knew something was up. Mom usually uses her debit card for everything."

They all sat quietly while the words spilled out of Moshe in a torrent. They had each seen this before, experienced it themselves. This need to recount, to explain, to try to make some sense out of what had happened to them.

"I'm not even sure when it all started. I remember my mom turning the television off when we came in the living room a couple of times and not listening to the radio in the car on the way to school. We were only allowed on the internet if we had permission but I got texts from my friends telling me that some kind of flu was killing a lot of people and making other people crazy, but it was on the other side of the country. We thought it was creepy but it was too far away to get scared about. Mom just said to avoid people who looked sick or odd in any way.

Pretty soon we started seeing *Closed* signs on stores and stuff. Empty Metro buses were parked alongside the roads. Even the homeless were pushing their carts alongside the roads and heading north.

We live, *lived*, in the Palisades. It's north of here and we had our own swimming pool and tennis courts. I took lessons but I *hate* tennis. I'm better at archery, those lessons were fun. We had gates and a security guard, too. The guard didn't have a gun. I know because I asked to see it once when I was little. He laughed and said the gates would keep the bad guys out.

Hardly anyone was in school that last day. Mom came and picked us up before lunch. I remember there was barely room in the car for us because of all the groceries and bottled water. Everyone we saw looked scared. We heard gunshots on the way home and saw some people lying on the ground. My sister started crying and begged her to stop but Mom just kept driving. We hit something then rolled over what felt like a huge speed bump. Mom cried but she still kept going.

When we got home the gates were open and there was no guard in the little booth. Someone left their car parked in the street and we drove on the grass to get around it. Front doors and garage doors on houses along the street stood open, making them look like someone had broken in. Our house looked the same as it always did and we pulled into the garage and lowered the door. I looked at the front of the car and I'm pretty sure there was blood on the grill and three teeth and some hair stuck in the tire treads. Then Mom turned that little bar that locked the garage doors manually and we went inside.

Sara, that's my sister, went to her bedroom and came back with her blanket, that disgusting one she's had ever since she was a baby. She turned the television to the Disney channel first thing but they weren't showing anything, just a blue screen. She started yelling like she always does and went to find Mom.

I channeled up and down but most other stations weren't broadcasting either. KSEE was showing the interstates all around the city. The only people moving were the ones on motorcycles or bikes and even they had to stop and walk them around blockages or across the median to keep going. Most of them wore backpacks and were pulling babies in little wagons hooked up to the bikes.

On another channel they were showing the crowds around the hospitals. Hundreds of people were there, waiting in line or sitting on the hoods of their cars in the parking lot. Some bodies were on the pavement, not moving, but you couldn't tell if they were dead or alive. The news guy kept saying everyone should stay home and not go to the hospitals.

In California we're always getting ready for an emergency but it's usually earthquakes, flash floods or fires. We did the usual stuff: filled all the tubs with water, went through our bug-out backpacks, made sure our clothes and good boots were by our beds. This time though, Mom unlocked the chest in her closet and got out three guns and put them on the bed. One was a shotgun and she called one a .22 and the handgun was a Beretta. I didn't even know we had them. Mom said to be sure Sara didn't go near them.

My dad is a doctor so we barely saw him the past few days but that was nothing new. We hardly ever saw him during the school year. Every August, before school starts, we go to Mexico on vacation and Dad plays golf in the morning then we all swim and snorkel in the afternoon. That's really the only time we see him.

Mom worked from home most of the time. That last day she went into her office and partially shut the door and called Dad. So of course we sat outside in the hall and listened.

Dad said something then Mom said, "Everything's ready; I loaded the guns. We can come down to the hospital and pick you up there."

Dad shouted so loud we heard him in the hallway, "The roads are blocked. Have you seen the crowds around the hospital? Don't come anywhere near here! We're getting ready to evacuate the uninfected patients up to the top ward. The whole place is infested. Our only shot now is evacuating from the helipad but we'll be lucky if that happens."

Mom said, "Don't shout at me, Benjamin. (I'd never heard her call him Benjamin before. It was usually just 'Ben'). We'll go on foot if we have to-"

Dad yelled something else but I stopped listening because somebody was knocking on the garage doors. More than just knocking, it sounded like someone was trying to knock the house down. I went down to look out the kitchen window but I couldn't see anything. Sara came halfway down the stairs and sat there, holding her blanket and with her thumb in her mouth like when she was a baby.

Mom came out of the bedroom, carrying one of the guns. I think she'd been crying. She motioned for us to come upstairs and we followed her to the media room that looks out over the garage.

Mrs. Sutton from next door stood in our driveway hitting the garage door with her fist. She didn't look angry, she just had looked, I guess, dead. Her eyes were white and her face kind of gray. She was wearing her bathrobe and still had one slipper on. All the skin was gone from her legs and you could see the bones.

Sara screamed and Mom put her hand over her mouth and pulled her out of the room. Mrs. Sutton stopped hitting the door and looked up, turning her head jerkily like a bird, as if she were listening. Then she began clawing and pounding on the door, harder than before.

We closed all the blinds and huddled in the living room, watching more news and trying to ignore the hammering on the garage door. The television showed the Tower in London completely surrounded by crowds of infected spilling out into the Thames. They broke through the paling fence and were starting to stack up against the Tower walls. You could see the Tower Bridge and we watched an airplane crash into it and hit the water. The news lady said the whole island of Great Britain was under voluntary quarantine. Ireland, too.

They said they shut down the Chunnel but it didn't make any difference. The virus was already on the European mainland. Iceland was supposed to be a clean-zone and they had shore patrols out and anti-aircraft guns set up, shooting planes out of the sky if they flew too low.

Mom kept trying to call my dad but the phone circuits were overloaded. She couldn't get through even to 9-1-1. Sara was on the sofa with her thumb in her mouth and still holding that blanket. It was like she was two again. Mom was in the kitchen, making sandwiches when we heard a gun fire, right outside our house.

161

The pounding on the garage stopped. Then somebody rang the doorbell.

It was Mr. Becker from down the street. He was trying to look in through the side windows. He didn't look crazy, just worried, so I opened the door.

Mom kind of lost it when she heard the door open and she came running out from the kitchen holding a gun. Mr. Becker put his hands up even though he had a big rifle over one shoulder, and stood there trying to talk to her. She finally believed him when he said he wasn't infected and just wanted to be sure we were okay. He said that he was sorry but he had "put Mrs. Sutton down" and didn't have time to dispose of the body.

They were leaving. He said he and Mrs. Becker were taking their kids and going to a cabin in Montana. A plane was supposed to be waiting for them at the airfield. He wanted to know if we wanted to go with them. He said things were bad and it wasn't going to get any better. I looked out and saw Justin and Jason looking out the windows of their SUV.

Mom asked how he knew that and that was the first time I heard of "Operation Urban Shield." Mr. Becker worked for a defense contractor on "logistics and deployment of resources." He said it was all top secret but that didn't matter anymore. The city and everyone in it was going to be sealed off. Even now it was risky to leave but a small plane was our best chance to get out.

Mom said we couldn't leave without Dad and asked if they could wait. He said they couldn't. Mom thanked him and said goodbye. I don't know if they made it out or not. The news that night said a number of light aircraft were shot down by "persons unknown."

That night we all slept in the same room. Mom sat by the window with the shotgun. I don't think she slept much. I kept waking up and each time she was by the window, looking down.

I think it was the next day I realized we were never going to see my dad again. It was right after that earthquake off the coast, the big one. We didn't really feel it but we saw pictures of the tsunami on the news. Only the one television station was still broadcasting and they started showing pictures of downtown too. It was on fire. You could see people moving around in the smoke. They were walking; even the ones on fire were just kind of shuffling along. They were zombies! How obvious is that? The news kept calling them victims but- good grief! How stupid do you have to be not to know they were zombies? I never told Mom this but I think I saw Dad in that crowd.

After that the news lady started crying. She just sat there and cried on camera. Finally someone pointed the camera at the wall but you could still hear her crying.

Some of my mom's friends told her that the military was sending in ships to the wharf to take survivors to a secure facility. I know a lot of them packed up and went down there but we never got any more information about it.

Mrs. Sutton's body was still in our driveway and Mom kept saying she had to do something about it, for health reasons. It had swollen up like a balloon and there was a smell- a pretty bad smell. Mom paced the house, trying to call Dad, then my grandparents, then checking to see if anyone was outside in the street. Sometimes we heard car alarms and saw smoke in the distance but everything was mostly pretty normal except for the dead body in the driveway. A few more of our neighbors left, cars stuffed full of sleeping bags and boxes, driving past our house and slowing down to look at the driveway, then speeding up.

By the third day the electricity was going off and on. Mom cooked all the frozen food and put it in the basement where it was cooler. She kept making us eat even though we weren't really hungry. She said if we didn't eat it, it would all be wasted. We were sitting at the kitchen table, eating these huge steaks when weird moans drifted in through the window. Mom looked out then closed it very quietly. We all stood there looking down at the street.

There were five of them, two men, one woman, and two kids. They wandered along the street, looking really dazed. Every now and then they bumped into each other and went staggering off in a different direction for a while then drifted back to the group. The woman was missing an arm but they weren't all that scary except for their eyes. They were that dead-looking white, like Mrs. Sutton's.

A cat darted across the road in front of them, hissing as it scrambled up and over our gate leading to the back yard. They turned and staggered over toward our house. The woman tripped over the body in the driveway and couldn't get back up. The others ignored her and began to bang on the gate.

They stayed there all day. Another one came and joined them. Mom was afraid they would draw even more so she got the shotgun and went outside. She told us not to watch but we did.

The shots exploded their heads and that black mush went everywhere. Soon they were all down and not moving anymore. We went out and the three of us dragged them over to Mrs. Sutton's back yard and dumped them in the swimming pool. Mrs. Sutton came apart and we had to drag her in pieces. That part was really bad and Mom couldn't stop crying. We were fast and I think pretty quiet but I guess the sound of the shots attracted attention.

We had just dumped the last corpse when we heard Sara screaming. Mom ran back to the driveway but she forgot the shotgun and-"

Moshe lowered his head and spoke in a choked voice, "Before Mom could get to her, *they* got my sister. They pulled her to pieces. She was so small it didn't take long. I picked up the gun and ran but it was too late. Mom had a really bad bite on her hand. After she shot them she stomped

164

their heads into shards. Then she fell down in the driveway and just screamed."

His voice was low and fading but he continued, "The next morning, Mom was really sick and throwing up. The wound on her hand turned black and stank even though she kept cleaning it and changing the bandage. She packed everything she could into my pack and made me practice loading and unloading the guns and dry-firing them. Then she made me tie her hands together and lock her in the attic and told me to go find my dad. She made me promise not to stay in the house."

He finished, "I stayed. I couldn't tell her I was pretty sure Dad was dead. She was so cold; I gave her all the blankets but she couldn't stop shivering. I heard her in the attic, moving around a little then everything was quiet. I was sitting at the bottom of the attic stairs and I guess I fell asleep. When I woke up, I heard scratching on the door and then the sounds started. It sounded like she was in so much pain. I almost opened the door before I remembered."

Everyone was silent. Virginia ached at the look of loss and despair on his face. No child should look like that.

Mei asked gently, "How did you get to the camp?"

"After a few days, I left to try to get downtown just in case my dad was still alive. I mean, I didn't know for sure that he was- one of *them*. Cam was out on a raid and he found me."

"Nearly shot the little bloke. I broke into a chemist's shop and I was in back, loading up on all the meds and supplies I could find, when this one comes in and starts stuffing his pockets full of sweets and vitamin tablets!" Cam said.

Moshe looked abashed. "I hate vegetables and I love candy, so..." He trailed off.

"It makes sense to me," said Virginia, thinking of what it must have been like trapped in a house with your infected, dead mother. She put an arm around Moshe briefly before standing.

"I'm taking first watch. Get as much rest as you can. Mei, I'll wake you around midnight?"

They claimed their spots for the night and settled in after placing their weapons within easy reach. A growing number of dead continued to patrol the area near the doors. They weren't focused on the building or anything really, as far as anyone could tell but their mere presence was sinister and unsettling.

Nevertheless, most of the party soon found themselves in the peaceful, twilight world between dozing and actual sleep. Virginia perched on the arm of a deep, club chair and pulled her knife from her boot, balancing it on her palm and looking out at the night.

Then the electricity came back on.

Chapter Eleven

Great, crystal chandeliers blazed to life, blinding them momentarily and bringing them to their feet, fumbling for their weapons. Alarms blared, agonizing peals of sound echoing all around them. They had no idea how to shut it all off.

Worst of all, the ponderous brass-framed, revolving glass doors began to turn automatically. Each revolution disgorged clumps of stinking, shambling dead into the room.

The alarms excited them. A hugely fat man, shaved head covered in tattoos, pushed a slower ghoul to the ground and waddled forward eagerly. Virginia waited, standing on the arms of the chair until he was close, then jumped on his back and sank her knife into his rotten skull. It was like cracking the shell on a soft-boiled egg. He teetered and fell. She rode him to the floor, banging her knees, and then sprang back up in time to drive the knife up into the soft, rotten flesh under the chin of the dead woman following him.

Cam buried his cleaver between the eyes of a teenaged girl wearing a stained blouse, pleated skirt and knee socks. She was so decayed the cleaver sliced down through her head, neck and collarbone, only stopping at her sternum. She collapsed to the ground in a black, wet heap of flesh.

They were all so decomposed that it took very little to bring them down. Even so, they kept growing in number as more and more emerged from the endlessly revolving doors. The group had to retreat.

The fire exit door sign glowed red just beyond a cluster of desks and they ran for it only to find it chained and locked. Someone must have tried to barricade themselves in here previously. Virginia cursed mentally that she hadn't checked it before.

David must have had a similar thought though his cursing wasn't just mental. "Back out the way we came, ladies and gentlemen. Follow me."

They fought their way back through the ever increasing throng. They kept the boys in the middle and ran, Cam swinging his cleaver and slicing off reaching, dead hands.

Gaining the staircase they closed the door behind them and made their way back to the hallway through which they had entered. The exit door was still ajar but, blinded by the bright light in the hallway, they couldn't see anything in the darker parking garage. Virginia located a panel of switches on the wall and pressed and flipped them at random until the lights went out. She felt her way back to the exit door and they stood waiting for their eyes to adjust again to the darkness. Down the hallway they heard a bell chime. It was a familiar tone but it still took a few seconds to identify it.

An elevator. They heard a slight metallic squeak and rumble as the doors opened. Dark shapes staggered out. The smell roiling down the hallway was suffocating.

"They must have been trapped in there for days, poor bastards," Cam whispered.

"And I let them out. Sorry, everyone, but it's time to go," Virginia said quietly, already shepherding the boys toward the door. They made it out and down the stairs before the dead reached the door. They heard a dull thud of bodies falling down the steps behind them and they walked faster.

They entered an eerie landscape. Lights illuminated some streets while others remained dark. Traffic lights blinked a yellow warning. A few stores were lit but most were not.

Cam said, "Okay, mates, we have no idea how long the lights will be on so we'd better make the most of it."

"This time I say we go up a street then try to find the bike trails. The only thing is, I don't know how to find south in the dark," Mei said.

"I can't see the stars at the moment but let's get away from the street lights and maybe I can figure it out," said Cam.

They eventually arrived at the same construction sight they turned back from before but this time they trudged on past the barrels and turned the corner. In the midst of an area littered with concrete barriers and stacks of rebar, they found a construction trailer. David called for a halt.

"I'm breaking into that trailer. We still need explosives," he said. His voice was tired but determined.

"David, do you really think they would have left explosives inside a trailer?" Mei was a little skeptical.

"Circumstances being what they are, it's worth a try."

Halogen lights attached to utility poles lit the site almost as brightly as daylight. Inside that zone they would be blind to whatever might come along in the dark so only David approached the trailer while the rest of the team kept watch in the shadows. He used Cam's cleaver and made short work of the flimsy door frame, then disappeared inside. A light came on and they saw him moving around, searching.

Virginia thought she saw movement on the overpass above. She stared hard at the guard rails but decided it was probably the myrtles planted alongside the road when she was startled by a heavy thud. She turned and saw a struggling body impaled on the rebar. Arms and legs waved frantically trying to get up. Another body hit the ground, a few feet away from Brian and dragged itself toward him. Brian stomped the skull only to have another land on top of the one he just killed.

Corpses plummeted all around them; some so rotten they were virtually exploding bags of pus and rot. Those still mobile attacked immediately, dragging their broken, decaying bodies along with claw-like hands. The team was overwhelmed.

Cam shouted, "David!" There was no response.

"David! Get out. Now!"

David appeared at the door of the trailer, his rifle over one shoulder.

"Go! I'll catch up!" David shouted over the noise of the infected.

As soon as he spoke, the dead turned, closing in on him at the steps leading down from the trailer. Using the butt of his rifle he brained two of them and ran, stumbling and almost falling over a body. Out of the lighted area he was temporarily blind. A hand closed on his leg and another on his arm. A gun cracked somewhere in the darkness and the dead woman holding his arm dropped off. He stomped the dead creature on the ground until he heard bones crack and the hand fell away. He felt a hand on his arm and raised his rifle again, only just recognizing Brian in time.

"This way."

He let Brian lead him until his eyes adjusted to the night. They regrouped on a sidewalk next to a steep embankment.

"Everything ok? Good. I'm thinking up is the best direction for us. Maybe we can get our bearings if we can see a little more," Cam said.

The embankment above was sandy and landscaped with little mesquite bushes and painfully prickly barberry plants. The dead followed and they could only hope they were too clumsy or stupid to climb the bank.

Scrambling up the steeply sloping hillside, losing their footing and grasping the thorny shrubs to keep from sliding back down to the creatures now mobbing the sidewalk, they struggled on. Cam took the lead and Virginia brought up the rear, closing her eyes and mouth against the grit kicked loose above her. She began to slide backwards and grabbed a bush, gasping with pain as the thorns pierced her flesh. Pulling herself slowly upward buried the thorns even deeper. Finally she reached the top. A warm hand came over the side and Cam pulled her up the rest of the way. Her hands throbbed.

They were in a parking lot, dimly lit and deserted. Leaning against one of the lamp poles, Virginia extracted thorns from her palms with her teeth while looking out over the valley below.

Lights glittered everywhere like a fairy land. She had forgotten how beautiful a night skyline could be. The enormous bridge looked star-spangled and almost magically bright.

Mei stood beside her, looking down with her newly-acquired NVGs. She made a low sound in her throat and handed them over to Virginia.

Creatures indifferent to the light swarmed the bridge, moving amongst the abandoned traffic. There were more in the water below, thrashing about and then sinking. She turned round slowly, scanning 360 degrees, hoping to recognize something, *anything* that would point them toward the camp.

A deep hum in the distance made them all freeze, looking for the source of the sound. The beating blades of a helicopter grew louder in the night air. The low-flying bird, lights searching the ground, flew over the beach then approached an area in the far distance to their left. It circled once before landing.

"That's it!" David exclaimed. "I can see it. Let's try to make it back before the power goes out again."

~

David woke to the sound of a child's laughter. It sounded strangely out of place even before he remembered where he was. The air was fresh, early morning fresh and the sun beating against his still-closed eyelids was just light, not

171

yet heat. Light footsteps on the ground faded as the child ran by on her way to who knows where.

Something was wrong with his back. A dull ache radiated out from a spot near the base of his spine and he groaned and rolled over. The pain ceased. He opened his eyes now and sitting up he picked up the rock he had apparently lain on all night and flung it over the fence.

Very late last night they arrived at the compound gates, together and unhurt, but having failed to secure the explosives. They were admitted but had to pass by the dogs and then spend the night on the ground in quarantine, outside now as the former quarantine space had been destroyed in the last barrage of mortar fire from the ship.

Brian and Moshe were asleep on the ground a couple of yards away. Cam, Mei, and Virginia were nowhere in sight. It was still so early that a light mist hovered a couple of feet above the ground, giving a dream-like appearance to the entire camp.

He stood and folded up the blanket the guard had given him last night and went to look for something to eat.

Cam and Mei were assembling the communal breakfast table, talking in low voices. David helped them wrestle the heavy planks onto the saw horses. Wonderful smells were coming from what he assumed was the kitchen. He sniffed and thought he detected pancakes possibly accompanied by maple syrup. He looked at Mei who shrugged and grinned.

"The electricity is still on. We're getting a real breakfast today."

The line for breakfast formed early and it was a while before everyone was served but David never got a chance to enjoy the "real" breakfast. He was summoned for an early morning meeting with Colonel Hamilton. Ian was there, along with the two officers who arrived last night by helicopter. They exchanged information gleaned from various sources about the confirmed fall of the government and the threat from hostiles outside the nation. For the most part, the rest of the world was too busy dealing with their own disasters to bother with plans of conquest. Eventually they got around to discussing their own situations.

"The landscape has changed. We think we're dealing with just the one ship now and this makes it easier to handle," Colonel Hamilton said.

David asked, "Has anyone been able to monitor their communications?"

"Again, it's more what we're *not* hearing. We have known for several days that one of the ships carries infected crew, now we've had no communication between *any* of the ships for at least two days. We can't tell yet which one has fallen but we are reasonably sure that at least one more has," said Ian.

Colonel Hamilton ran a hand through a buzz cut of gray hair. "As you know we've made every effort to secure some way to destroy the ship but we have been unsuccessful. Of course, now that we've reestablished communications with Midwest we expect you have far greater resources than we have been able to secure. We have tried but we've been unable to contact any of the Pacific Fleet. If just one ship could come in we could conceivably be gone before the expected hostiles get here and live to fight another day. We're trying to survive but we're close to the stone-age in resources now."

The older officer barked a short, incredulous laugh, "You think *we* have resources? We came here to see what you could send *our* way. We haven't heard from any of our fleet for days."

"Could they be running silent?"

"Some are but I don't think that's what happened to all of them. Immediately after the first quake we flew victims directly to our carriers that in turn sent them to other ships or land hospitals. We lost contact with all of them less

173

than 48 hours later. If we have anything left it would be subs or battle ships and they are under direct orders not to dock."

He paused then continued, "Midwest Command is under siege, gentlemen. We have over 200 people left in our camp since the typhoid fever outbreak. We have limited food, almost no medicine, and no way to evacuate more than a few. All we can do is hope to survive until the dead are no longer a threat. Flying over we spotted roving bands of dead, faster than any we've seen before, spreading out from the southwest and some appeared to be heading our way. This chopper ride was our last. We are out of fuel.

Eastern Command has been quiet for several days and we have no idea what is going on there. All of our carriers were called home several days ago but as I said before we have no contact with them. They could stay out a long time if they wanted to wait and see if the infection burned out.

I pray that there are other pockets of survivors here and worldwide but we may never know. We're a balkanized country now. We won't recover from this in our lifetime, if at all."

Everyone's cards were on the table. No help would be given or received. Colonel Hamilton opened a drawer in his desk and pulled out a bottle.

"Gentlemen, this is Glenfiddich Rare. My father gave me this years ago and I was saving it for my daughter's wedding. I haven't heard from my daughter or my wife for several days now. I have a feeling there won't be a wedding anytime soon so-

He gathered some semi-clean shot glasses and poured each of them a dram. "May the Lord bless you and keep you. May He make His face shine upon-"

David drank his glass then slipped away. It was close to noon and the whiskey on an empty stomach was making his head spin a little. He needed food.

Laughter rang out somewhere ahead of him, delighted childish laughter that again seemed so out of place here. He left the shady colonnade and turned a corner toward the rock pool and stopped.

Children were splashing in the pool. A woman stood holding a toddler in her arms, dunking him in and out of the water as he screamed with delight. After a second or two David recognized Beatrice.

Sleek, bare arms and legs were now a light, golden shade that contrasted beautifully with a white bikini. Lighter streaks of blonde shone in her hair she had casually knotted in a loose bun. She saw David and, holding the toddler on her hip, beckoned him over,

"I'm glad you're back! Brian told me you guys didn't find the explosives?"

Droplets of water clung to her skin, making her appear to shimmer in the sunlight. The little boy demanded, "More!" She dunked him again.

David had a little trouble finding his voice. "True. It looks like there isn't going to be a rescue by sea either so we're brainstorming again."

"We weren't really counting on a sea rescue, were we? I mean, we have a pretty decent plan already, right?" Her eyes were anxious and her voice shook a little.

"Bea, I really need to get something to eat right now. Can we talk later?"

"Oh, sorry. Of course. I need to get Greg back to his mom anyway. See you at dinner, maybe."

He agreed and finally made it to the kitchen, where a sympathetic volunteer offered him a bowl of rather tasteless bean soup accompanied by stale cornbread.

"We used all the eggs for the pancakes," the cook said apologetically. "The cornbread is so much better if you use eggs. What we really need are some chickens."

"Maybe we'll find some next trip." He took the food outside and sat down on a mound of ribbon grass next to the statue of Venus.

A commotion broke out near the entrance gate. He heard a metallic rattle and then a *screech* as the salt-air corroded gate hinges swung wide. A group entered, four people carrying a body on a stretcher. The dogs went nuts and started barking. A guard motioned the group in but kept the rifle trained on all of them. The stretcher was placed on the ground and the bearers passed by the dogs who were quiet this time. Their handler led them by the stretcher where they once again howled. The patient was handcuffed and a thick cloth gag stuffed into his mouth then tied around his head. They went straight to the infirmary. Poor bastard, whoever he was.

The cornbread descended to his stomach and sat there in a cold lump. He didn't feel full, just less hungry. Surveying the camp he saw just how tired, how dirty everyone was. Almost all of them could use a haircut and most of the men sported ragged beards. The smell of the latrines competed with that of the dead. Sometimes he thought that smell would never go away.

A part of him hoped his brother would be here or he would at least get word of him. Continued attempts to reach the rest of his family failed too. More and more he thought of striking out and heading up the coast to find them. He had reunited Bea with her brother but he still felt reluctant to leave her. She aroused a protectiveness in him he wasn't completely comfortable with. Sometimes he thought of introducing her to his parents, wondering if they would approve, then laughed at himself. Civilization had fallen, the living dead had risen and he was nervous about bringing a woman home to meet his parents.

He glanced back at the rock pool where Beatrice was fending off a splash attack by Ian's little boy. Realizing he was staring, he lay back in the grass, concentrating on the blue sky, not wanting to look like a creep. A door slammed.

Mei hurried down the steps from the main house, heading his way. He stood and shaded his eyes against the now hot sun. Suddenly he felt dizzy and put one hand against the statue.

"David! You're swaying on your feet. Let me see your eyes." She took his head in her hands and looked at his eyes.

"Your pupils look fine. Have you been drinking?"

He explained and she laughed. "Sober up now. Ian wanted me to find you and bring you to a meeting immediately."

"Again?"

"We have one of the enemy."

"The enemy. You mean the Chinese?"

"Yes."

"How?"

"A team of foragers found him on the beach this morning. He was trying to get back to a dinghy he'd hidden amongst some rocks."

"What's he like?"

"Young. Scared to death. Infected."

"I think I saw them bring him in. What was he doing?"

"He was apparently part of a team sent ashore looking for medicine. Only one of the ships had medical supplies and facilities and that one was supposed to serve both of the others. Probably to try to contain the virus on one ship in case something went wrong. That ship is one that went dark. We have him under restraint but he's still very coherent and I've been talking to him in the infirmary. We don't know how much of what he's telling us is true but we're trying to get as much info as we can before we lose him."

"Let's go."

Chapter Twelve

Bea, still fending off Greg who seemed determined to drown her, watched as Mei and David talked. When she saw Mei touch his face she again felt that stab of jealousy though she knew she was being ridiculous.

"More!" Greg shouted.

She scooped him up and blew raspberries on his belly. He chuckled in delight.

"More!"

"No, I think a nap is what you need right now, little guy. Let's go find your mom." She pulled on a worn, faded, Silver Chair tee shirt and flip flops. Holding on to a tired, wet, and slippery toddler was more of a challenge than she had anticipated and it was with a feeling of real relief that she handed him over to Virginia.

"Thanks, Bea." She took him in her arms and wrapped him in a well-worn blanket. His eyelids were already heavy with sleep and he lay against his mother's shoulder, suddenly quiet. Virginia smiled.

"I never get tired of this feeling. Just to have them in my arms is heaven. For a while I thought- never mind what I thought. I have them back now. I just have to find a safe place for them, for all of us."

Bea wandered back up the hill and found Fitz reclining in an old Adirondack chair, a bottle of beer in one hand and a shotgun across his lap. An open laptop rested on the grass beside him.

"Fitz! Can I use that for a few minutes?"

He grunted, "Go nuts. A lot of sites are down. Some haven't been updated in a week."

"That's okay. I'll take what I can get," she said.

"How do you feel? I heard they had typhoid fever at the camp in the Midwest."

"I feel fine. Just a little tired."

"They say that's the first symptom," he said with gloomy satisfaction. "We're living on borrowed time, all of us. Even- *especially* the one we just caught."

"What did we just catch?"

"A comrade of the People's Republic of China, that's what. An infected one if the rumor is right. Found him on the beach about an hour ago. I'll be happy to put him out of his misery." He patted his shotgun and took another swig of warm beer.

Bea opened the browser. It took a few tries to get connected but she finally logged on and pulled up her email, hoping against all rationality to hear something from her mom, dad or even Evan but there was nothing.

She clicked to the World Health Organization website searching for updates.

World Health Organization
Update-Z-virus from acting Director General, Keiji Jama

(Revised version. Please disregard earlier communiques.)

Since March 20__, the so-called 'Z-virus' has taken the lives of roughly 90% of the world's population. To say that we were caught napping with regard to this disease is no exaggeration. Over the last few weeks health officials have sorted through vast amounts of data from around the world. We have authorized the release of the following information:

Diagnosis and symptoms
Chilling and vomiting are often the first symptoms if the victim survives the initial attack. Caution must be used not to confuse the bacteria-caused bubonic type illness with full-blown Z-virus. It is best to restrain all victims, especially when in doubt.

179

Transmission

The vast majority of infections have been transmitted directly by bites, human-to-human. There have been cases reported that may have resulted from deep puncture wounds inflicted by the infected. The bubonic-type comes from contact with the bacteria that develop in the decay process of Z-virus victims.

The incubation period varies considerably from case to case. The time from first infection to full-blown disease can depend on location of bite, overall health of the victim, or other factors we have yet to confirm such as weight or age.

Treatment

The rapid progress of the disease makes treating it somewhat problematic. Amputation has been attempted when the bite is in an extremity but victims usually succumb to blood loss or secondary infection in the cases reported.

Prevention

Avoid any contact with the infected.

Mortality Rate

100% in all known Z-virus cases. Numbers for the bubonic-type illness are unknown but we do know it is survivable. There is no data on the long-term effects of the bubonic-type due to lack of any opportunity for long-term studies.

No new information there and she clicked back to her email. The docs that Sylvie sent were still there. She wondered if anyone else would ever read them, if there was any way they would be used in the future. She opened a document titled *Hythe Incident Report.*

An unfortunate peculiarity of the Kentish coast in southern England is that, due to its terrain, it cannot be easily defended against an enemy force. The invading Jutes, Saxons, and Romans were aware of this and used it to their advantage. Winston Churchill, whose home occupied several acres of that lovely region, was cognizant of the area's weakness. So too was Adolf Hitler.

When the aerial horrors of the Blitz that destroyed over a million houses as well as factories, docks and killed over 20,000 people failed to break the spirit of the British people, Hitler made the decision to inflict schrecklichkeit (frightfulness) by invasion, but not of the traditional kind. He did so with biological "weapons" first encountered by Rommel's troops in the deserts of Egypt. What follows is a survivor's highly classified account of an unusual land assault that occurred in May of 1941 upon the beaches near Hythe in Kent. This brief recounting was expunged by the MI5 from the BBC's "As We Saw It" project, a compilation of first-hand accounts of the war told or written by the men and women who survived it.

"The weeks leading up to the Blitz were ones of preparation and I must say, excitement, for me and for my brother. Trenches were dug in all the parks, gas masks issued and most of our garden dug up and an Anderson shelter placed in the ground there. Dad parked the old Austin Seven in the shed and removed the tires before covering it with a tarp. There would be very little petrol for anyone but the military for several years. We all walked a lot or rode bicycles if we had to go far.

Dad sealed all the windows in the front room and Peter and I stuffed paper up the chimney. We were meant to keep a blanket and bowl of water in there at all times so that we could soak the blanket and hang it in the doorway and this became our "safe room" in case of a gas attack. I did not like wearing the gas mask and felt I would suffocate if ever I had to use it. Nevertheless we were meant to keep them handy at all times and usually wore them around our necks and shoulders somewhat like a rucksack. If a policeman or warden saw us out without ours we would be ordered home to fetch it.

When the first silvery, sausage-shaped barrage balloon went up we spent some time admiring it and felt quite safe thinking that enemy planes would get entangled in it and crash. I suppose we should have thought about what that plane and its cargo of bombs would do when it came down.

The beaches were out of bounds as they were barricaded with concertina wire as well as mined in places. At night we listened to Mr. Churchill speak on the wireless and his speeches were somber yet thrilling and filled us all with hope that we would prevail in resisting the Hun.

The Blitz, when it came, was the most frightening time ever in my life. The air raid sirens shrieked their shrill warnings and we would evacuate to the Anderson and sit waiting for the all clear. Soon we spent most nights out there and moved a mattress and tins of food into the hut as well. We even moved a cot in for Baby Eileen but she usually slept with all of us on the mattress.

Being outside London and in a small town we thought our biggest danger would be from a sea invasion but we failed to reckon with the German planes flying over us on their way to London. They would often drop some of their bombs to lighten their planes and gain altitude and we suffered several hits. One night, Mr. Bloom, the air warden on duty, settled his wife and their infant twins into their Anderson before heading out to his post, only to see the shelter suffer a direct hit before he left the block. Everyone inside was blown to bits. Mr. Bloom moved away after that and we never saw him again.

I think none of us were the same people we had been before. Many of our friends were sent away to stay with family in the rural counties and the schoolrooms were at times almost empty. After the Germans started sending the doodle bugs* every night Mum and Dad began to look for some place to send us but I'm afraid Peter and I threw tantrums until they gave up, saying no one would take us for very long anyway. At times Mum would grab us and hold us so tightly that it hurt.

One Sunday evening Peter and I were up in the Wendy house in the oak that looked out over the lane. A strong wind blew in from the sea and the old planks groaned as the tree branches swayed. There hadn't been any bombers for two nights and we thought maybe the Blitz was over for good. From up high we could look out over the neighborhood and to the sea. Peter had Dad's field glasses trained on the beach. He said a lot of people were heading from the beach into town. I told him he was fibbing and made him let me look through the glasses.

He hadn't made it up. Shambling along the streets, water-bloated figures invaded our little town and spread out. Two men with no clothes on at all, came down our street. I remember being embarrassed that they wore no clothes and thought they must be really ill as their skin was so mottled and gray. Then I saw that they had no eyes, only sockets out of which crabs were busy crawling and feeding on the flesh. Peter screamed and Mum came outside, looking round and calling for us.

Those people in the street stopped when they heard all the noise we were making and they started clawing at the hedge. Our hedge was the old-fashioned kind, tightly woven ash and hawthorn so of course they couldn't get through but they kept at it. The hens squawked and clacked to high heaven and retreated to their coop.

One of the men got his hand stuck in the hedge then slipped and fell down. His arm pulled away at the shoulder socket and hung there in the branches whilst he struggled to get back up. There was no blood just some sort of black goo dripping from the socket. He didn't seem to notice that he had just lost an arm.

Mum saw us in the tree and called for us to come down. Dad came outside, saw the two men and his face went white before he ran back into the house and came out with Granddad's ancient shotgun. He yelled at us to go inside but by then Mr. Ollie from next door was out there too, wielding the curved scimitar that usually hung on the wall over his fireplace. I recall that it had silk tassels dangling from the hilt and he held it with both hands out in front of him, knees slightly bent and looking round frantically for the source of the trouble.

Dad went out the garden gate and fired the shotgun, hitting one of the men in the knees. He went down but, incredibly, was soon back up and now coming after Dad. Mr. Ollie then moved in with his scimitar and slashed the man in the belly but that barely slowed him down. Mr. Ollie's eyes went wide and he swung the blade again. This time the man's head rolled in the gutter.

To our fright the mouth continued to move and Dad, looking more disgusted than anything, stomped it. I remember a cracking sound and then seeing black fluid running in the cobbles. Then Mr. Ollie screamed.

The one-armed man hadn't got back up but he was still moving and he got close enough to bite Mr. Ollie on the leg. He continued to scream whilst trying to shake the man off.

Gunfire, rapid and loud, rang out and a company of the Home Guard came down the lane. Struck, Mr. Ollie sagged to the ground, his attacker still firmly biting his leg. Though riddled with bullets, the one-armed man pulled away a mouthful of flesh and chewed noisily.

No one seemed to know what to do. Poor Mr. Ollie was quite dead, shot down by his own neighbors who stood over the unbelievable scene, aghast.

With a roar of engines and the screech of brakes a company of regulars arrived. They took immediate command, gathering all of us in our garden whilst they used

184

flamethrowers to burn the bodies, including Mr. Ollie, in the streets. I shall never forget the smell of the roasted flesh nor how sick I was from the ghastly, oily smoke that soon filled the village. Contained fires burned throughout the lanes.

We were all checked for bites and scratches and were told to never speak of what we had seen that day. We were told the war effort hinged on our silence but they never gave us any further explanation. We all gave our word and I don't know that anyone ever broke the silence. I am breaking it now as an old woman as I want my grandchildren to understand some of what their ancestors went through during a war that is only a dull spot of history in a book to them."

Researcher's note: This extremely small-scale invasion did not bring about the mass panic intended but rumours did circulate for a time. This researcher likes to think that it merely strengthened Britain's resolve to prevail. For additional information from this timeframe see vault # 32, Whitehall sub-basement 4.

*doodle bugs-unmanned flying bombs that dropped once they ran out of fuel.

Bea read the account with growing frustration and then read it again looking for tips, a clue, anything to help her deal with this nightmare ravaging her world. Again it brought home to her that the virus must be contained quickly and ruthlessly if needed. Draconian tactics must be used as soon as it appeared or it would simply be too late. Then she remembered.

Shutting down the laptop she placed it next to a now slumbering Fitz and ran down the path to the main house. Passing underneath a loggia entwined with grape vines she went inside.

She hadn't been in this part of the house before. Graceful, arched doorways gave an Alhambra air to the atrium. Water splashed in the stream bed before running outside. If it weren't for the blankets everywhere, the cots stacked up against the wall, and cases of bottled water this would have looked like a setting for a tale from *A Thousand and One Nights*. It seemed quiet after the hubbub of the rest of the camp and she listened for voices in vain until she came to a set of double, beautifully carved wooden doors. Someone was talking in the room but she couldn't make out the words. She moved in closer when the doors suddenly opened and two men brought out a stretcher bearing an Asian man in a filthy, blue uniform. Bea ducked behind a column and peered out.

Mei walked alongside the stretcher, holding a bottle of water and tucking a blanket around the soldier's shoulders. He had a shock of dark, coarse hair, pale skin and bad teeth. He looked very young. Someone had gagged him with a cloth and his hands were bound. Terror-stricken eyes searched the atrium as the men paused to open the door, bright light momentarily filled the space and then they were gone. Bea moved back to the doors now partially ajar.

Colonel Hamilton spoke, "That's it, gentlemen. We know they were supposed to be the advance guard of a much larger invading force but they have completely lost contact with the PRC. Their captain was injured in an onboard fire. There has also been some sort of power struggle in the chain of command.

If they can't find what they want here, they can lift anchor and move on. Of course they can bomb us even closer to the stone-age than we already are before they go. They knew there were survivors but didn't have a clear indication of location because their equipment is malfunctioning.

I ask you to consider the opportunity this situation gives us. We have a living weapon in our hands, if we act quickly. We can release him and let him go back to his ship. If he makes it on board and spreads the virus, all the better for us."

There were murmurs of agreement and then scattered conversations began. Bea thought of the look of terror on the prisoner's face and was dismayed. She looked in and saw David seated near a stone fireplace. He was frowning and nodding his head in response to something Ian was telling him.

She knocked lightly on the door and pushed it open, stepping into the room. David looked up and raised his eyebrows. She was suddenly conscious that she wore little more than an oversized tee shirt and flip flops but she cleared her throat anyway and waited until she had everyone's attention.

"Hi. I'm new here and I haven't met most of you. I'm Beatrice Kelly and I have a suggestion. What if you cured, or at least attempted to cure, this soldier? What would it hurt? We could then send him back and he will let them know we have a cure, well a possible cure anyway. Maybe they would let us board and get away. Letting him die seems wrong. There are so few of us left now, the living I mean. Every new person we can save feels like a gift from God."

There were a few smiles around the room, some annoyed, some condescending. Colonel Hamilton spoke first and to his credit, his tone was business-like and genuinely interested.

"How do you propose to cure this soldier? Has something new been discovered that I should know about?"

"Malaria. It is possible to cure the early-stage virus with a malaria inoculation. It's been done."

"Young woman, I don't know where you got this idea but do you have any proof? Do we even have the means to try something like this?"

David spoke up. "Sir, scientists in D.C. attempted this cure with a degree of success. It is not guaranteed in any event and we lack the means to try it here. I'm sure Beatrice means well but-"

She interrupted, "We do have the means to try it here. The CDC sent malaria samples that should still be in storage but it has to be done now. As soon as possible."

"Why was I not told?" the colonel asked.

Ian said, "I think I can speak for all of us, sir. We didn't know the samples existed until now."

The colonel said, "We still have to make a decision. This soldier represents a chance to take out the last ship. I can wait a few hours more but not much longer. Ian, you are responsible for overseeing this 'cure' attempt. Report back to me as soon as there is something to report. That will be all today, gentlemen."

Ian took Bea's arm, frowned at her and began to walk out of the room then paused as the colonel motioned him over. Bea waited.

The colonel lowered his voice but Bea still heard him. "Find that young woman some clothes. Tell Fitz that I expect better than this from him. We ought to be able to clothe our refugees decently."

"I will, sir."

Bea opened her mouth to say her outfit had nothing to do with Fitz but Ian pulled her along, still frowning. Once they were outside he spoke.

"Where are the samples?"

"Barry stored them in the spring house."

"I never heard anything about them."

"Well, we were shelled while we were opening them. I didn't even think about them until a few minutes ago. They sent two different strains. Do you remember which strain they used on Virginia?"

Ian said nothing, just kept walking. He looked off into the distance and his mouth was compressed in a thin line. Finally he said, "I've never told anyone else about Virginia getting infected. You and your brother know. So does David, of course, but it's not general knowledge. I don't want my wife to be experimented on or dissected. If I had known we had the samples I certainly would have spoken up. I don't want anyone to die if we can save them but I don't want Virginia's name brought into this. Do you understand?"

Bea was somewhat taken aback. His tone was just short of threatening. "I understand completely, Ian. I would never do anything that would hurt Virginia. I'm disappointed that you think I would."

His shoulders fell and he seemed to relax a little. "I didn't think you would do it on purpose. It's just that some things are dangerous to talk about in desperate times. People are often considered expendable. And no, I don't know which strain they used on Virginia."

They found Barry in the infirmary and they had a quiet talk in the hallway with both him and Mei.

"Do not under any circumstances tell him what we are using to treat him. We don't hold a lot of cards in this poker game so we have to play the few we do have very close to our chests."

They agreed but had one condition of their own. Neither of the nurses would inject the prisoner unless he agreed to the treatment. After a brief question and answer session with Mei, he consented.

"One more thing, Bea," Ian said.

"What?"

"Get dressed. You've upset Colonel Hamilton."

She stuck her tongue out at him and walked away, smiling. She hoped she had just saved a life. Then she had another thought. She might have just taken away the only effective weapon they had against the hostile ship. A ship that could easily destroy them all.

~

Bea leaned against the wall and slowly slid to a sitting position on the cool tile. It was sometime in the early hours of the morning and she was exhausted. She knew she wasn't helping anyone by being here but she felt responsible for what the prisoner was going through now, for better or for worse.

The family living in a large supply closet had been sent elsewhere and the prisoner moved in. He had been injected and within hours developed a high fever that left him alternately sweating and chilling. Mei barely left his side and a worried frown creased her brow. When the prisoner's temperature reached 104 degrees she started to unwrap some of the blankets but Ian, also hovering closely, stopped her.

"We need to maintain a high temperature for as long as we can. It's best if it spikes at around 105."

Mei raised an eyebrow. "I didn't know you had a medical background."

"I don't but I do know a little about the process. Malaria therapy has been tried before, most notably with syphilis."

"Where did you get that information?" Mei asked.

Ian grinned. "Wikipedia. I had to learn something about the treatment since this is my assignment. But really, if we can keep the temperature at around 105, that's best."

Mei sighed, "Brain damage can occur after 103. We have zero medical history with this patient. I can't even type his blood! I'm not comfortable with this at all."

"Just picture the fever burning away all those nasty little bugs. Take a break, Mei. I'll wake Barry for his shift in a few minutes and I'll stay here as well."

Mei nodded and, stretching her back until she heard a crack, wandered out into the hallway and saw Bea, slumped to one side, eyes closed.

She poked her and Bea jumped. "Mei! How is he?"

Mei sat down beside her. "Stable. The fever is higher than I like but scorching this s.o.b. virus to death is what it's all about. I hate experimental medicine. Ian is pretty sanguine about it. I feel like he knows something that I don't."

Bea shrugged, "Maybe. Or maybe he's just an optimist."

"I don't know. I love what I do because it almost always ends positively. Human beings are incredibly resilient but I wonder if we can overcome this. I wanted to have children someday but now? What a horrible world to bring a child into. Scratching out a place to hide, foraging for food, inadequate medical care. I can't see a path forward at the moment. Maybe I'm just tired. I miss my family."

Bea asked, "Did they make it? I mean, are they still alive?"

Mei said, "I don't know. I was called in to work when this all started and you probably know what the hospitals were like. Lines for the E.R. stretched around the block. The infected outside died and reanimated of course. We were completely mobbed. Once we realized what was going on it was way too late. I was trundling an expired patient to cold storage in the morgue when she sat up then rolled off into the floor. I thought I was losing my mind, you know? Just crazy tired. I tried to get her back up on the stretcher and that's when I knew something else was going on. That mouth fastened down on my shoe like a bear trap. I had to stomp her with my other foot before she would let go.

Finally I shoved the stretcher up against her and ran to the morgue for help. Bodies were up and moving there, too. The ones in body bags writhed and twisted along the floor. Others, naked with that blue mottled flesh turned as soon as I opened the door and lurched over, mouths wide. I shut the door and left. My dead patient was gone who knows where. I looked for security but there were too many for security to deal with and security didn't know how to deal with them anyway.

Eventually all we could do was try to escape. A few of us did get out but this was as far as I got. I got a text from my dad telling me how much he loved me but that was the last time I heard anything. I've been trying to call but I get nothing." Tears ran down her face and she wiped her eyes before continuing. "My parents were incredibly controlling to the point that at times I almost hated them. I hesitate to call them racists. I prefer to think of them as traditionalists. They didn't want me to marry anyone not Asian. My mother told me she didn't want 'blue-eyed mongrel' grandchildren."

"Ouch."

"I know. I was dating someone 'not Asian' at the time she said that and I think that's one reason we eventually grew apart, although I never told him what my parents felt. Who knows, maybe he sensed it."

"So I'm free to do what I want but I never wanted it this way. It seems so silly, doesn't it? Each and every life is precious and should be cherished. If I ever get another chance to love someone and pledge my life to theirs, I'm doing it. I like blue eyes."

Bea said nothing but felt a quiet despair. She told herself she had no right to feel this way but it didn't help.

Mei said, "I think I'm going to get that chance. Sometimes the most unexpected things occur, don't they? The end of the world as we know it and love is still possible."

Her face glowed softly as if lit from within and Bea felt that sharp twist of jealousy. Mei was so lovely. No wonder David looked at her like he did.

Harsh words rang out in the storage room. Words Bea didn't understand. "What did he say?"

Mei shushed her and listened then smiled wanly. "He wants his mother. It's amazing how often that happens."

Muffled voices erupted inside the storage room and they heard metal clank against metal. Mei left and didn't come back. The sounds ceased and the nighttime hush again descended.

Bea thought about what she missed the most. Her mom and dad had been gone for so long that missing them seemed like a normal part of life. She missed showers and clean clothes and her lumpy old futon mattress. She missed the musical clink of ice cubes in a glass and chicken sandwiches from Wendy's .99 cent menu. She missed Evan more than she thought she would and hoped he had somehow survived.

What would she do in the new world? Be an art historian again? That was laughable. What luxuries the old world had offered that someone could actually be paid for that kind of work. She had no particular skills needed now. If she were an engineer she could build something. A computer systems expert could try to repair the failing internet. A cobbler could make shoes. A gardener could grow crops. She, however, was just as useless as a life coach, professional organizer, or a color consultant.

A breeze blew in through the windows bringing a trace of salt and dead things with it. It also brought the sound of the dead, stumbling around the moonlit beach, endlessly hungry and endlessly searching.

Chapter Thirteen

A full moon shone coldly down on the creatures
thronging the beach. Waterlogged, mutilated bodies slogged
across the sandy surf, stepping on other undead bodies, spiky
nails thrusting up from shattered wooden planks, broken
glass, all with indifference. A mob of the creatures would be
a threat but not if there were room to run. These ghouls were
winding down, subject to decay in the moist heat and the
sucking tides that pulled them out into shark-filled, watery
hunting grounds. A group of dogs, almost but not quite feral,
trotted along on the firm, wet sand. They were hunting as a
pack tonight and didn't hesitate to attack the slow dead and
strip away chunks of stinking flesh to drag away and devour.

A hundred miles to the east the same moon lighted a
different scene. Moving across a rolling landscape, herds of
pronghorn antelope followed an ancient route their ancestors
have traveled for millennia. Leaving their winter valleys and
heading for springtime meadows on the coast, the nimble
Antilocapra americana make an incredible journey that is
epic in its length and difficulty. The female antelope are
pregnant and within weeks of giving birth. Despite this they
are able to ford rivers and outrun any predator on the
continent. Even the fawns, just a few days after birth, are
able to outpace that tireless predator, the coyote.

Hundreds of thousands of dead pursued them now and
though the antelope were in no immediate danger
themselves, they unwittingly led the dead along a path the
infected would have been unlikely to find alone. Fumbling
and lurching across the countryside, they had 'survived' the
nukes detonated over the southwest and were now a different
and hardier version of the living dead. The bacteria that
should have been rapidly eating their dead flesh had been
eradicated by the sterilizing effects of the radiation. Their

bodies were sinewy and tough, their movements more controlled and quick.

Some were washed away when they plunged into the fast-flowing, spring-melt swollen rivers, tumbling helplessly among the rocks and currents. Others, distracted by unwary fauna, wandered into the greening woods and valleys. Despite this, the seething core of dead remained vast, a dark, moving cancer on the landscape, a surging, tireless threat that drew ever closer to the western coast.

~

Private Tsou, hollow-eyed and pale, accepted a sip of water and leaned back, keeping a wary eye on the door. Tremors still shook his thin frame and Mei continued to monitor his temperature. Convulsions had racked his body throughout the night, leaving him sore and exhausted.

They had no way to culture the virus from his blood to see if it was still there, no way to check for a possible antibody response. Mei continued to grind her teeth in frustration and mutter about "medieval" medical treatments and "stone age" facilities.

Despite this, by late afternoon the prisoner managed to keep down a thin broth with crackers and take a few shuffling steps, constrained by shackles and watched by armed guards. He showed no Z-virus symptoms and even had the beginnings of a scab covering the bite mark on his shoulder. Mei and Barry declared him ambulatory and prepared to remove his restraints before they were overruled by Ian.

"Sorry, guys. No way are we letting a member of a hostile, attacking force roam our facility. We'll release him when it is appropriate and not a moment before."

Ian was running on fumes. He kept a near-constant watch on the prisoner while doing his best to sell the brass on an idea that he and David had hatched, with Virginia's help, in low-voiced meetings throughout the night.

Now that they knew no ships would be showing up to evacuate them, the work on the barrier wall commenced again at a frantic pace. With electricity still flowing they rigged lights and worked throughout the night, repairing the damage from the shelling and moving more of the concrete and steel forms into place. The wall rose slowly but solidly. Originally intended as a barrier to keep illegals out, it would now serve a different purpose. No one knew exactly when the dead would arrive or how many there would be but pilots had seen enough over the last few days to know that if they didn't have a strong wall soon, their little encampment would be overwhelmed. No matter how spirited their defense, how noble their sacrifice there would be no one to write their story if they didn't survive.

Even if they did survive, they were still nothing more than a beleaguered outpost of a dying civilization. They needed to find a way to escape. The lush agricultural valley that was California was entirely dependent on a complex dam system that diverted water from other states. Unless that system was maintained, California would soon revert to a semi-desert environment, no longer suitable for growing crops.

Ian and David's plan involved returning the cured prisoner to his ship and having him present the advantages of an alliance. With Mei's help they questioned him at length and they now knew the one remaining ship was vastly undermanned and in desperate need of medical supplies. An early outbreak of the virus had been ruthlessly contained with the infected soldiers either executed or allowed to commit suicide. More had been killed in the onboard fire that injured the captain and several others. There was plenty of room on board for the refugees.

They planned to send a personal appeal in a letter dictated by Colonel Hamilton and written by Mei. A letter offering food and medical care and supplies in exchange for evacuation. The plan then was for the ship to take them up the coast in an attempt to find an area free of the dead. If such a place existed.

If they could get the go ahead. The colonel had yet to agree but in truth, now that the prisoner was (possibly) cured he was no longer a weapon. Ian had taken a lot of flak over that in private but held on doggedly to his proposal. The strain was visible on his face and now, having been awake for nearly 24 hours, he prepared to meet with the colonel. It didn't begin well.

"We've just gotten word that the East Coast Command Center is gone. After several days of communications blackout Midwest Command did a flyover and found the facility on fire. No survivors were visible from the air. Gentlemen, our world is going dark. Now, to our present business. I understand we have lost our weapon." The colonel looked at Ian.

"No, sir. I believe that we still have our weapon and by curing him we've given that weapon even more reason to want to make our case. According to Private Tsou, ship's command lost contact with Beijing days ago. Before that there were indications that their government employed tactical nukes in Guangdong and Sichuan provinces and possibly others. They probably don't even have a country to sail back to if they could. If he is able to persuade his command to help us evacuate, we may live to fight another day. We have a cure, sir. Somewhat limited to early-stage at this point but as far as we know, no one else has achieved this. Dangling something like that out there could win us a lot of friends. And we need friends.

If we had sent him back to infect his people, we would have had to clear every nook and cranny of that ship before we could use it and who knows how many of our own people we would have lost in the process.

The virus has destroyed our world. We have to build it again. I propose that we start off the right way, with mercy and kindness." He stopped, mouth suddenly dry, and took a drink of water.

The colonel laughed incredulously but he looked at Ian with compassion. "Son, how long do you think we'd last if we dealt like that with the enemy?"

David said, "This might be a way to neutralize this enemy. The prisoner should be returned to his ship as soon as possible. Even if they don't allow us to board their ship, perhaps they won't fire on us this time if we try to board the ship that is still afloat and clear it out. We have the inflatables still in storage. Enough to get us out there.

Ian is right. We *are* building a new world and this is the right way to do it. The infected from the strike zones are approaching rapidly; they'll be here in a few days. Our defensive wall is as strong as we could make it but I doubt that it will give us more than a brief respite. If we can't find a way to evacuate, ultimately we're lost."

Colonel Hamilton made a steeple with his fingers. He looked like a man wrestling with a problem he couldn't resolve and it had exhausted him. Finally he spoke.

"Return the prisoner. If this fails we can still try to take the drifting ship. It's going to be hell getting out there if they decide to shell us again. May God protect us."

The meeting broke up and moments later Moshe shot a string of lit firecrackers tied to an arrow to the north side of the beach. The sharp pops drew the attention of the roaming dead who began a slow shuffle up the shore.

A small armed patrol slipped quietly out the gate and picked their way down the hillside to the rocks where the private had hidden his small boat. He made it into the surf without incident and paddled out to sea. He seemed ludicrously cheerful and even waved as a strong offshore wind sent him racing through the waves.

198

The team were up the hill and inside the gate before the dead were really aware of their presence. All they could do now was continue to work on the wall and wait.

~

An Australian soldier penned the following narrative in late 1972 or early 1973 then put it away for twenty years. It was discovered after his death by his grandchildren whose attempts to publish it brought it the attention of H. M.'s government. The Ministry was unsuccessful in purchasing the work and it was eventually published, but as fiction, in a tabloid popular in America where it spawned a short-lived spin-off of apocalyptic/combat, comic books.

Da Nang 1968

They called it war crimes. Didn't feel that way at the time. It felt like survival. What else could we have done? I've asked myself that a million times since they pulled us out. We're not supposed to talk about it. That was one order that was easy to carry out. It's hard to find the right words.

It was my first deployment. We trained for weeks back home, trained until we were so knackered we nearly dropped dead every night. By the time we finished basic, some of us actually looked forward to the combat zone. We didn't think it could be any worse than what we had just been through.

The ship that took us from Brisbane Bay to Da Nang was enormous. This was Sergeant Wall's second deployment and he had a thick, red scar on his neck that went up the side of his mouth then into his scalp. I never knew what caused that but he was lucky it missed his eye. He kept us busy with calisthenics every morning and every evening we had target practice off the bow, shooting at clay targets. I guess they wanted us busy so we wouldn't have a lot of time to think about what we were sailing into. The food was good, too.

Once we got off the ship we saw Vietnamese everywhere wearing white pajamas. There were more out in the fields wearing those black, conical hats. It was confusing. Were these the enemy? They didn't even look up when we walked by, like they weren't interested in us at all. The whole place was green and lush with trees and vines everywhere except in the water-logged fields those people were wading through. I reckoned they knew what they were doing but I would have been worried about crocs lurking in there.

After we disembarked the first thing they had us do was load a bunch of trucks with supplies. It was hot and you could almost see the moisture in the air. I remember feeling like I would die if I didn't get some water soon. Just when I reckoned I was going to keel over, the water trucks showed up. It tasted a little off and wasn't cold but we gulped it down anyway.

The supply trucks took off and the transport trucks rolled in and we were loaded this time. Before we left, Sergeant Wall gave each of us forty, live rounds. I attached one magazine to my SLR and stowed the other in my belt, wondering if I had enough ammo to stay alive. I felt like a sitting duck in that transport and I stared hard at all that greenery flashing by, expecting snipers in the trees.

The smell was something I wasn't prepared for. Mold mixed with the oil they poured on the roads to keep the dust down mixed with sewage gave off an unforgettable odor. It got in your nostrils and stayed there. I've never smelled anything quite like it anywhere. Sometimes it shows up in my dreams.

We went by more fields and again saw those little people in their pajamas and hats, never looking up. We could have been ghosts they ignored in the hope that we would just go away. We would have happily gone away but all of us were committed for a year.

The road began to wind up a mountain and that's when we got to see the top canopy of the jungle that dominated the area. The sight was breathtaking with more mountains visible in the distance, near the coast. Silvery waterfalls cascaded down the sheer, rock cliffs. The sergeant said he had seen panthers, monkeys, and even the occasional elephant in the early morning. For a few minutes I forgot why I was there and I just enjoyed the beauty of it all. The truck continued up until we reached a plateau with good visibility all around.

Camp was primitive. Latrines were out in the open and the most personal bodily functions were on fairly public display. We had tanks of water for drinking but most everyone bathed in the stream on the edge of camp, if we bathed at all. They passed packs of cigarettes out like candy and the tobacco aroma helped mask the body odor. Most meals were eaten cold even though we had cans of sterno. Private Dalton showed us around and made sure we had our rations and ammo.

We were waiting for intel and orders. A patrol had gone out a few days ago and never returned. The jungle is full of little villages that were practically invisible from the sky. Most of the occupants were just non-combatants and farmers trying to hide out and live their lives but occasionally VC soldiers holed up there and used them as a base of operations and we had to clear them out. The troops conducting the mission were familiar with the territory and had completed a dozen similar raids before this one. Sergeant Wall said he didn't know if they were dead or captured but they were our mates and we couldn't leave them behind.

On the evening of September 20th we got the order to move out the next day. Air reconnaissance found evidence of human habitation in the jungle about nine klicks due north. Not far at all.

We left before dawn. The route took us slightly down onto a cleared plain we would have to cross before we entered the jungle again. I felt exposed without the canopy overhead and I knew we were tempting targets for anyone watching from the trees. Crossing quickly we gained the jungle cover and soon found a game trail leading up toward our destination. We kept a constant watch for hidden guard outposts but the two we saw were abandoned. Still, we knew we were getting close.

The trail ended abruptly and we came to a sudden halt. Just past a tall clump of jambu, a clearing revealed seven or eight huts clustered along the fringe of the jungle surrounding neatly-tended, square fields. We saw no one except for a child, naked and covered with dark blood, standing outside one of the huts. He appeared to be in shock and swayed on bare feet, blank eyes unfocused and wide, with a stained bandage taped to his side. The VC often used children as living bombs and we approached carefully but the boy carried no explosives or other weapons that we could see. He did, however, have several bite marks on him that looked oddly human.

We skirted the child and cleared each hut. All were empty but we found helmets and several folding shovels. That was proof enough that our men had been here at some point and gave us hope they were still alive. I paused inside the last hut, thinking something smelled wrong here. A stench of rot lingered in the still air. I checked the dirt floor to see if anything had been buried but the dirt was solidly packed and undisturbed.

I heard a disturbance outside and emerged to see Sergeant Wall trying to pull the bloodied child off of a furious Dalton. The soldier held his bleeding wrist in front of him and glared at the boy who growled and twisted in the sergeant's grip. He twisted about and his dripping mouth clamped down on Wall's arm. Fortunately the sergeant had his jacket on and all the child bit was a mouthful of canvas.

The sergeant flung him away, sending him sprawling in the dust but the child immediately began to crawl back. Sarge backed away but the boy never stopped attacking until the sergeant picked him up and threw him into the trees, hitting his head against a mangrove. His skull cracked and covered the tree with a dark ichor. He didn't get back up. The body stank as if the child had been dead for weeks.

"We've lost too much time. I want everyone to spread out. Use the walkies to stay in touch, and everyone meet back here at 1200 hours. We need to wrap this up today." Wall gestured and we split but none of us got very far.

Two VC, dirty and exhausted, emerged from a camouflaged pit less than thirty meters into the jungle and, hands held high, surrendered. We disarmed them before the sergeant questioned them. Both claimed to know nothing about our missing guys but one of them had a Zippo lighter and a pack of Winfields.

"You know where they are and you're going to tell me!" The sergeant shook him like a dog shakes a rat. The soldier's shoulders slumped and he stood and nodded, seeming resigned. His compatriot was silent.

They led us a short distance into the jungle to a pit the top of which was overlaid with fern and bamboo branches. I suspected a trap and kept my eyes on the trees around us. The smell of death was overwhelming. Angry, Sgt. Wall shoved one of the VC toward the pit.

He screamed something like "Bo doi!" and tried to run but Sarge shot his knee out. He fell to the ground and rolled in agony.

A pulley was rigged to a platform that could be lowered and raised to get the prisoners out. The rope was wrapped around a tree. I was closest to the pit, dreading what we were going to see when a faint rustling and then a moan arose from the hole. Someone down there was still alive. I reached around and unwrapped the pulley rope.

The VC started to holler again when he saw us start to pull that rope. I've never seen anyone more terrified. The bloody bugger kept yelling "Bo doi!" and tried to stand on that shattered knee, falling down in agony but still pulling himself away, fingers hooked into claws that dug into the jungle floor.

The moaning grew louder and the smell of rot and death was suffocating in the close, moist air. Just from the odor I knew we would be dealing with dead bodies or at least a lot of gangrene. The groaning sounded agonized. I knew the VC used torture but I had hoped I would never see it close-up.

The platform stopped and we pulled it over to level ground. We were surprised that as well as a few of our men there were non-combatants on there. Women and children crawled over each other in their eagerness to escape and all of them were wounded in some way.

Two children stumbled clumsily off the platform and, to our amazement, attacked the wounded VC soldier, latching on to him and burrowing into his exposed flesh with their teeth and hands. Shocked, we didn't understand what was happening and I think we all just froze for a few seconds, watching until the little girl bit into his throat and blood fountained out in a dark, red arc. The soldier's screams turned to choked gurgles and then he wasn't moving anymore.

Something grabbed me by the shoulder and jerked me back hard. I turned to face one of our guys. He reeked of rot and his flesh was a sickly, gray-white. He opened his mouth wide and I saw beetles and worms crawling about the blackened tongue just before he tried to take a bite out of my face. Luckily I flinched and that mouth hit my helmet, knocking me backwards so hard I thought my neck had snapped. I sprawled on the ground and he fell on top of me, *that hideously searching mouth still biting. Instinctively, I pulled my knife and thrust it up, driving it into his eye. I swear he didn't even bleed, just twitched a little then collapsed. Rolling him off of me I retrieved my knife. There was no blood on the blade, just black goo that stank like you wouldn't believe.*

All about me we were fighting the wounded, both the villagers and our guys. The other VC soldier was screaming something. Sergeant Wall paused to listen then shouted, "Shoot them in the HEAD, the HEAD!"

We did. Even now it's hard to recollect the horror of deliberately shooting women and children, not to mention our own guys. I don't know what the VC did to them but all of them had serious wounds and advanced gangrene. I honestly don't know how they were able to move. We threw the bodies in the pit and torched them. The rising column of smoke was like a billboard alerting anyone to our location so we did double-time back to base camp.

Sergeant Wall made sure we kept radio silence all the way back and told us not to speak of the mission to anyone on the radio until he filed his report. He spent a good deal of the evening questioning the prisoner. Apparently "bo doi" means "devil" in Vietnamese and, according to our prisoner, that is what those villagers and soldiers were, or had become. He said the only way to kill them is to burn or behead them, preferably both. He claimed to have no idea what had happened to the rest of the platoon and though we searched, we never found any more information on their whereabouts.

Private Dalton grew worse overnight and the sergeant reckoned he had blood poisoning. The bite on his arm turned black and gangrenous. The next day a chopper landed at camp and medics loaded him on board along with the captured VC.

The secrecy of our location was now compromised with all the activity so we broke camp and took up a new position, further north. The reports the North Vietcong and our own press put out later about the incident were incomplete and biased. Those creatures were not innocent women and children, slaughtered indiscriminately. I don't think there was a soldier in our platoon who didn't have nightmares about that day. I know I still do.

Bea closed the laptop and rolled over onto her back in the velvet mound of emerald moss. She had found this secluded little alcove this morning and begged Fitz to let her use his laptop again. Checking her email proved as fruitless as usual so she was once again going through the British files. The last three days had been quiet as they waited for some sign or communique from the Chinese ship. So far they had heard nothing.

Brian and Moshe spent their time shooting at an improvised target with the bow and arrow set Moshe had found. Moshe was quite a good archer and before long Brian wasn't bad either.

The wall was complete. Unless the coming dead were able to climb the sheer, steel plates, scale the scree then the cliff, they should be okay.

She had been helping with meals and training with weapons. She had cleaned, disassembled, and loaded almost every type of firearm they had. After this she was issued a Glock, almost identical to the one she lost in the river. Lacking a holster, she stashed the gun in one of the front pockets of her cargo pants for easy access.

They were all on high alert. Mei had packaged their medical supplies for easy transport. Fitz issued everyone a backpack containing water, a knife, and two MREs. Stacks of inflatable boats, grappling rope ladders inside, were tied close to the gate.

It was almost time to set up for supper. The electricity had been on now for close to a week and the meals were consequently been much improved. A foraging group found

206

three hens yesterday and triumphantly carried them back, holding them upside down as they squawked. This morning a bedraggled rooster showed up, no doubt looking for his lost harem. All four now scratched contentedly at the bottom of the garden.

A hot, dry wind started blowing in from the east two days ago. If they slept with the tent flaps open they woke up in the mornings covered with a fine grit. After sleeping in the heat of the sealed tent for one night they decided they preferred the grit.

Bea returned the little laptop to Fitz and just as she started down the path to the kitchen she heard a sound, a deep sigh that escalated into a moan but like the moans from a thousand people in ghastly agony. Sentries at the top of the hill were signaling frantically. At the same time the growing breeze brought a scent of mold and decay, like meat turning, but not quite rotten yet. She ran back up to the hill overlooking the scree. They were here.

Chapter Fourteen

At first just a few clustered around the base of the wall. Over the past week Bea had gotten used to the slow, shambling pace of the local dead. These were different. Their movements were faster and much more coordinated. They didn't just run stupidly into the barriers, they seemed to be testing them for openings or weak spots. When they came to the spot where the barriers met the rock cliffs, they continued to dig and grope for handholds. Bea caught her breath when one of them clawed away a loose section of rock.

Brian, Moshe and most of the camp soon joined her. Despite all the training over the past few days, hardly anyone carried their evacuation packs. A few even brought snacks and continued to munch as if they were watching a movie.

Some, though, brought their weapons and were starting to aim them down at the dead before Colonel Hamilton showed up and told them to put them away. He moved through the crowd, repeating the same speech at intervals, speaking quietly but with urgency.

"That's useless, people. We can't kill them all. Get your gear together and remember the drill."

The dead continued to flow into the narrow canyon and spread out along the wall. Their numbers seemed limitless as more and more of them continued to press into the confined space. That musty, moldy scent grew stronger mixed with a faint whiff of decay. Many, many of them were featureless with raw, charred-looking skin.

More rocks from the lower section of the cliff that seemed so solid tumbled to the floor of the canyon leaving a gap large enough to crawl *behind* the barrier. As they climbed on the rocks that made up the slope, the rocks began to fall and scatter and the dead slid down to the base. The builders had planned for this even though none of them thought the dead would ever make it past the steel and concrete forms. The scree was the second line of defense if for some reason the barriers failed. They knew the slope was unstable, too unstable to climb.

What they *hadn't* anticipated was that the sheer weight of the dead would press down and stabilize the rocks eventually giving them a climbable slope all the way up to the cliffs. The cliffs stopped them for now, but the corpses on top were already picking and hammering at the rock, causing it to collapse and rain down upon them. Some were taken out when the heavy debris trapped or crushed them. Their fellows simply stepped on top of them and continued to claw their way up.

The camp prepared to flee. Bea came upon Virginia helping Daniel and Anna put their packs on. She hoisted Greg up on her hip before picking up her own pack. All three children were calm, possibly because Virginia was so matter-of-fact about what was going on.

"Okay, guys, here's what's going to happen. Remember the boats we inflated? Probably in a few minutes we're taking them down to the beach where we'll float out to another boat, a really big one. We'll probably get our own room there after we clear the sick people out."

"Can we go swimming?" Daniel wanted to know.

"Probably not but we might do a little fishing in a few days."

"What about the chickens?" Anna asked. All of the children had been excited about the chickens.

Virginia paused. "I hadn't thought about that. Come with me and let's look for them." She turned. "Bea, see you in a minute? Nothing has changed. Men are going in the advance boats to start clearing out any hostiles. We follow with the children."

"Virginia, I'm going with the advance party. Brian and Moshe are, too."

"Oh. That makes sense. Here, I have this canvas jacket and I doubt I'll need it. It'll give you some protection against bites. Be safe, Bea." She handed over the jacket. "Come on guys, the chickens are probably roosting in the trees unless someone has already loaded them."

Bea flew down the hill where Brian and Moshe waited near the rafts. Several of the little boats already bobbed along the waves, the setting sun casting a glare that made it hard to see. Carrying the raft above their heads they ran toward the surf. Decomposed corpses lay along the beach, some still moving feebly, others motionless. Moshe and Brian took care to step on every rotting skull along the way, pounding it when they got a "juicy" one.

"There is something seriously wrong with the Y chromosome," she muttered under her breath. Out loud she said, "Guys, stop it. Let's go."

They paddled furiously until they got past the breakers where the evening wind seemed to make them soar across the waves. Debris, planks and bodies sloshed in the water around them. The huge, hulking ships towered in the distance, menacingly dark with the setting sun behind them. A few boats had already reached their target and figures climbed the twisting grappling rope ladders, swaying with the movement of the ship and struggling to hang on.

So far, both ships remained silent. Half-expecting to be shelled at any moment they covered the last few yards and drew up beside the other rafts. Their ladder hooked on the third try but only one of the hooks latched. They tried to pull it down for another try but the hook held fast.

Looking back they saw more boats heading away from shore. They needed to finish this as soon as possible. The plan was to clear the boat in stages obviously starting with the deck. Once that was safe, the children would board. After that they would move on below deck. They expected that stage to be…complicated.

"I'm going first. Once I'm up I'll fix the other hook."

She was halfway up when the ship pitched, slamming her into the metal hull, knocking the breath out of her. She gripped the ropes, wrapping them around her forearms until she got her breath back. Above her the hook scraped along the railing, sliding several feet to the right. She looked down and was surprised to feel terrified at how far the little boat was below her. She had never feared heights before.

Focusing on the railing looming above was better. She took a deep breath and climbed slowly, fearing another pitch of the ship, forcing her legs to stop shaking. After an eternity she gained the top. There were several figures clustered along the rails in the distance but she couldn't tell what they were doing. She yanked the ladder up and fastened both hooks securely. Brian began to climb with Moshe close behind. The wind caught them and they swayed far out over the water. What she thought were screams of terror turned out to be those of delight instead and she rolled her eyes as they clambered over the railing, still laughing.

"Come on. Weapons ready," she said, pulling out her knife. The boys followed and they made their way across the deck, learning to adjust their steps to the motion of the ship.

The figures near the rail were their own people, David and Ian among them. They finished flinging a body over the side then came back for three more that lay prone on the deck, all wearing filthy blue uniforms. Broken skulls leaked black fluid onto the deck. They stepped around the noisome puddles and pitched the bodies into the waves.

"There were just a few of them up here. Piece of cake," David said. "The interesting part will be next."

"Yeah, can't wait," Ian said. "Come on; let's get the kids up out of the water."

But the boats weren't there. Looking back toward the shore they saw only two boats heading their way. There should be five. They searched the dark water for the others but-

Bea exclaimed, "I see them! In the water, they must have gone down. They're still alive, Look, you can see them waving!"

The ladders still hung from the railing but their rafts had broken free of their moorings and were gone. Ian muttered a short prayer, kicked off his shoes, and dived over the side. David, Cam, and more men followed. Bea stopped the boys.

"Don't. Someone has to be here to haul the children up. They're too small to climb."

They could do nothing but watch as the men fought through the waves, trying to push those floating in the water into the remaining rafts which were now dangerously overloaded. One began to go down. They soon saw why.

Dead, water-swollen hands pulled on the sides of the boat, trying to reach their prey inside. Water rushed into the little craft and they flipped, spilling the occupants into the cold water. The wind caught the children's terrified screams and carried them out to Bea and the boys.

Something moved in the corner of Bea's vision and she looked to the right. A small flotilla of lifeboats with Chinese markings rounded the side of the ship, headed toward the hapless passengers. Paddling as if their lives depended on it, the blue-uniformed soldiers shouted as they raced across the waves, trying to catch the passengers' attention.

Reaching the scene they used the paddles to pull the passengers in, reaching out and snatching others away from the grasp of the hideous, ravening dead. Once they had a full boat, they fought through the floating debris of planks and dead, making for the ship where they tied the children to the ladders so Bea and the boys could haul them up. Their mothers struggled up next and collapsed onto the deck then gathered their children into their arms.

Screams broke out as one woman realized her daughter was not among the children. She ran to the side, desperately scanning the waves before diving in. The dead were waiting and she didn't re-surface.

Bea waited with Anna and Daniel, both lying on the deck, exhausted and shivering. She took off Virginia's canvas jacket and wrapped it around them. She hadn't seen Virginia in the water and feared the worst. Moshe and Brian, still waiting at the rail, suddenly *whooped* and ran to the ropes. Bea ran too.

David, swaying on the tossing ladder, climbed up and over the railing, falling onto the deck, exhausted. His skin looked blue and he shook uncontrollably. He looked at her intently for a moment then reached for her. She gasped when he encircled her waist and pulled her toward him but his lips were surprisingly warm and he kissed her hard. He tasted like salt and honey.

Ian climbed up next and he leaned over the side, shouting something encouragingly. He and the boys pulled the ropes and Virginia reached the rail and climbed onto the deck, still holding her son in her arms. Bea exclaimed and started forward then stopped. Greg's eyes were closed; his head lolled across Virginia's shoulder.

Virginia sank to her knees. "He slipped out of my arms when the boat flipped. Please, God, please."

Greg's hair, soft as down, was sodden and dripped water onto the deck. He didn't move. Virginia turned him over, rubbed his back hard then turned him and kissed his pale, cold face. His arms flopped back as she held him closer in desperation, still rubbing his back, trying to warm him.

Ian, a look of dawning horror on his face, took his boy and began to compress his chest, pinching his nostrils and breathing into his mouth with short, quick puffs. Greg lay limp and cold. Ian, hands shaking now, tried again but the baby didn't respond. Virginia took him in her arms and began to scream, rocking her baby back and forth. It was a long time before she stopped.

~

Bea, wearing rubber gloves and a surgical mask provided by their Chinese hosts, pulled another moldering husk of a body out into a cramped corridor and scanned the walls as she dragged it along. She didn't want to get lost again. Private Tsou, noticing her confusion in the lower regions of the ship had taught her the Chinese character for "Exit" last night and she was eternally grateful. The ship was a giant and confusing labyrinth to her.

Within minutes of rescuing everyone from the water last night, the Chinese opened up the passageway to below-decks and started rooting out and destroying their infected crewmen. This ship was identical to their own and they were familiar with the layout, even in the near-dark. The crew was busy until late in the night. Once they were done, the Americans volunteered to extract the infected remains. The Chinese allowed this but David noticed they were very cautious about letting them near certain sections of the ship.

There was no time to worry overmuch about it. The deck was freezing after dark and they desperately needed to get the children below. They had sustained heavy losses and now numbered fewer than twenty souls. Most of their lost had been women and children and they had also lost Cam. No one had seen him go under but one of the children said the giant red-headed man had pushed her into a boat but she didn't see him anymore after that. No one had seen Barry, Pam, or Colonel Hamilton again either.

Mei made a point of working with Tsou last night and gleaned as much information as he was willing to give her. Apparently after he returned to the ship and gave the letter to his captain, he added his own personal plea for mutual assistance. The captain angrily ordered him confined to quarters. In spite of this, over the next two days he was able to talk to enough of the crew to spread the proposal around. There had already been a near-mutiny a few days ago in which the captain had been unable to confine (or execute) all of the rebels as the crew was already so reduced that no one was expendable.

The morning of the evacuation Private Tsou and his co-conspirators made their move. The captain was relieved of command (at gunpoint) and tied up. After they disabled the ship and its weapons they released him and left him there. Tsou and a few others were already leaving for shore when they saw the refugee boats going down in the water.

Mei relayed this information to David and others but she was uncharacteristically downcast since they had boarded the ship. It was understandable. They had all been through a lot and she was probably as exhausted as anyone. Nevertheless she spent hours with him and Private Tsou, interpreting while the three of them discussed their next moves. David still wanted to go north in hopes of finding a non-infested refuge with a water supply and tillable land.

At the same time she was caring for Virginia and she was the only one able to calm her enough to get her into a cabin. She didn't say so but Bea suspected Mei had sedated her. Every time she tried to visit, Virginia was asleep.

Sighing she finished dragging the body up to the deck and Brian helped her toss it over the side. They skipped the sections near cargo hold number four last night, leaving them locked and off limits but this morning they had gone in and taken down the few infected still there. This body was the last one.

The day had turned gray and the waves tossed restlessly. The ship had moved a short distance out to sea but the shore was still visible. The beach was dark with the roving dead and the water still thick with them. Multitudes of sharks hunted today, sleek dorsal fins slicing through the waves.

Only one of the chickens had made it out to the boat. It pecked about the deck, clucking disconsolately.

Ian was out on deck, holding his daughter in his arms. Her arms were around his neck and she was crying. Ian held her tightly and stared out at the waves. He looked ten years older than he had yesterday.

"Ian, is there anything I can do? Have you eaten today?"

Ian looked surprised. "I honestly have no idea." He asked Anna gently, "Have you eaten anything today, baby girl?"

She shook her head. "No, I want to see Mom first. I want Mom to wake up."

Ian held her even tighter. "I don't think it's safe for Mom to wake up right now. We have to wait a little longer."

Bea begged, "Please come below and eat something. Fitz got a lot of our supplies out and on board. At least come drink something warm."

"Maybe, in a little while."

Giving up, Bea went below, eventually finding her way to the galley where she encountered Fitz, who was in his element, distributing rations, assigning bunks, and happily predicting an eminent outbreak of Legionnaire's disease, E. Coli., or both at once. He and the ship's cook achieved a wary truce over meals only after the cook produced a delicious won-ton soup for all of them and no one had gotten sick, despite Fitz's dire warnings. Bea wandered back to her assigned sleeping quarters.

The ship, despite the lingering smell of dead bodies, was something of an improvement over the camp. Everyone had a bunk, a few had cabins. They had electricity and showers along with computer access. The Chinese were extremely reluctant to allow them on the computers and when Brian broke through their security to log on and changed the operating language to English they were very angry and threatened to lock him up until Mei intervened.

He managed to change the majority of the system back to Chinese, leaving just two computers set up in English. That was the easy part. Gaining access to the failing internet took several hours and even then the connection was sporadic and slow. Systems were breaking down around the world.

All at once the floor beneath her feet shuddered. She steadied herself and held onto the bunk until she regained her equilibrium. The entire ship now hummed with a slight vibration. They must have re-started the engines. She ran back to the deck, emerging just as the anchor was raised and they began to move.

David had had his way and they sailed north. Except for the big cities, which they planned to avoid, population numbers dropped farther up the coast and rainfall was generally reliable. Earlier today she printed off maps then they had carefully marked target locations. The future of cyber access was uncertain in this new world and it was best to have hard copies of anything important.

The coast slid slowly by. Everywhere she looked were crushed and burnt buildings, splintered wharves and docks, and the dead. Hundreds of thousands of teeming, shambling dead. Borrowing Mei's binoculars she focused on the dark masses of bodies swarming the shore. Here too, the slow, decaying shufflers were being supplanted by the newer, faster version. There seemed to be no end to them as they continued to pour over the low hills above the beach, surging out into the breaking surf. The once beautiful coastline, the subject of songs, paintings, movies, and television for so many years, affording so many the "California life", now belonged to the dead.

Chapter Fifteen

The days slipped by, one after the other as the massive ship made its way slowly up the Pacific coast. The skies were the pale blue of early spring with sunshine only occasionally obscured by fat, drifting clouds. Smoke from countless fires on the mainland was often visible in the distance but the sea breezes usually blew it away long before it reached the ship.

The dead still thronged the coast and each day they found them in the water around the ship, repulsive and fell, clawing in vain at the metal hull. Hoping to escape them at least long enough to fish, they moved farther out to sea and cast nets improvised from nylon webbing found down in a cargo hold. Each cast brought in a variety of fish but also pulled in hideously bloated bodies, often limbless, eye sockets blank but mouths still searching, biting the rope and struggling for release. The crew threw back the entire catch. Eventually they stopped trying and rationed the food ever more severely. They each got one bottle of water a day. There seemed to be no escape from the infected.

Often they came upon other boats, though none as large as this one. They usually hailed them by bullhorn but seldom got more than a wary wave in response if they got a response at all. Once a gun cracked and a bullet went over their bow, a message easily understood. They drifted on.

Virginia, accompanied by Ian, Anna, and Daniel, spent a little more time outside each day. The little family was broken and grieving as were so many others. Some of the men had lost their entire families.

Nevertheless, life on board developed a routine. Brian and Moshe scratched out the lines for a shuffleboard court on the deck and used metal plates from the galley as pucks. It was a welcome distraction for the children. Their Chinese hosts were not pleased when they noticed the damage to their ship but allowed the games, occasionally joining in. Despite this they kept a distance between themselves and the refugees and David sensed there were divisions in their ranks. He got the definite impression that some of the crew did not want them on board. A particularly hostile group, a faction led by a Private Chang, tried to confiscate their weapons the first night but with Mei's help, David made it clear they were on board only temporarily and wanted to be able to leave quickly when needed. They kept the guns for now.

The demographics of the group were troubling. David knew that populations with too many men and very few women were inherently unstable. Men will compete for women, sometimes violently. The Chinese had already shown Mei constant flattering attention when she treated their burns and occasional small injuries. They branched out to the few other women who had survived most of whom seemed oblivious (like Virginia) or amused. This, coupled with the food shortage, made him as well as Ian very eager to find habitable land and get off this boat.

This morning, according to the map, they were somewhere above Tillamook. There were dead here staggering amongst the washed-up debris on the bank but far fewer in numbers. Seagulls circled and landed, tearing into and devouring the dead that were no longer able to walk. A pack of dogs descended from the low cliffs and, scattering the shrieking gulls, began to feast.

Coming down from a morning visit to the deck, Bea ran into Mei emerging from the infirmary, papers and charts tucked under her arm. She was frowning at something she held in her left hand then stuck into her jacket pocket when she saw Bea.

"How is Virginia?" Bea asked.

"The same. She's sleeping too much. Sleep is good but this isn't normal."

"You're not giving her anything to make her sleep?"

"No." Mei started to say something else then stopped. She seemed distracted and looked as if she had been crying.

Shouts rang out somewhere farther down the passageway. They heard laughter and Brian and Moshe rounded the corner, bowling them over.

"Sorry! Gotta go!" They were still laughing as they ran.

One of the Chinese crewmen ran into view and stopped, talking angrily to Mei, demanding something. She shook her head and said something that caused him to stalk furiously away.

"What was that about?"

"He said the boys stole food, noodles, cookies, not much. He wants them caned."

"I'll talk to them but that sounds a little extreme." Bea gave an incredulous laugh. "Caned? Was he serious?'

"Extremely. You should talk to them very seriously and right away." Mei finished picking up her scattered paperwork. "Who's up on deck?"

"David and Ian."

"Oh. That's good then." She hesitated just a moment, squared her shoulders, and went above.

Bea turned to go and find the boys when her foot hit something small and plastic. Mei must have left something in her haste. She picked it up. It was a pregnancy test stick. And it was positive.

~

David watched as the tiny port town of Hypatia drifted into view. From this distance it could have been a picture postcard. White picket fences bordered gardens surrounding cedar-shake sided buildings. Whiskered seals sunned themselves on the rocky beach where waves splashed into white foam like steam from a fumarole.

Ian, Virginia and Anna also gazed out at the shore. The view was almost achingly normal, America as it used to be. America the beautiful.

Virginia was pale and thinner. It often took her a few minutes to reply to questions and sometimes she didn't reply at all, just nodded and looked into the distance. No one could break through her gentle distractedness. Ian's eyes often filled with tears which he ignored or wiped away without comment. Their daughter was Virginia's shadow. She had developed a stutter and spoke very little anymore, except in whispers. Daniel trailed after her like a lost soul.

They all had to get off the ship. Over the last few days, their hosts had become ever more restrictive with food, locking the galley unless it was meal time and even threatening to confine Moshe and Brian to the brig if they snatched any more snacks throughout the day. The single surviving chicken had disappeared and no one could account for its absence. David thought it had probably fallen overboard.

They were also pressing Mei for information on the cure for the Z-virus. David begged her to stall as much as possible since no one on board was actually ill and the cure was truly their last ace. She said they were hinting very strongly that they were willing to care for the women and children but the men would soon need to make other arrangements.

Footsteps rang out on the metal steps and Moshe burst excitedly onto the deck. David feared another contretemps with the Chinese and prepared to try to smooth over another situation and extend their increasingly shaky welcome on the ship.

"Listen to this! They made it! The people in the Tower of London!" Moshe exclaimed.

"What?"

"The BBC people are back online. Hurry!"

Ian and Virginia stayed on deck but David allowed Moshe to drag him below where Brian listened to a radio stream on the computer.

"This is BBC London broadcasting from our new location atop Britain's White Tower. We apologize for the brief lapse in communication but we are back and find our new digs quite cozy.

The Ministry of Health has advised the public against using water from any municipal source as all groundwater is contaminated and unsafe for consumption. We expect this situation shall continue into the indefinite future. Bottled water is the beverage of choice unless any of you have a few bottles of double-malt whisky. In that case please email me immediately and I shall try to reach you. We've been without alcoholic refreshment for days. In all seriousness, mates, don't drink the water.

London as we once knew it is no more. Thousands of bodies fill the streets and the Thames is choked with the corpses of our countrymen…"

Bea wandered in and David moved aside to make room for her around the console. She shook her head and stayed near the door, listening intently to the broadcast. Something was up but he didn't know what. She wasn't hostile but seemed genuinely disappointed with him for some reason and that rankled.

He was seeing a new side of her on board the ship. She spent an afternoon playing Chinese poker with their hosts, smoking one of their cigars on a dare (and quietly getting sick over the gunwale later), in an attempt to lessen the growing tension and animosity.

The day after the boys pulled an all-nighter that resulted in breaking one of the deck cranes, she improvised pirate costumes for the children as well as herself and led them on expeditions to root the boys out from any place they tried to hide and sleep. Both boys were exhausted and begging her to stop by the end of the day but she made sure they stayed up late that night, too. The pranks had stopped for now.

She attracted a good bit of attention as well. The scarcity of women in their little group would have ensured *that* even if she didn't look- well, the way she looked. The white bikini had never made a re-appearance and she dressed discreetly, deftly avoiding being cornered by any of the growingly aggressive Chinese soldiers. David missed the white bikini though.

They all knew it was time to leave. Fitz once again was making sure they had bug out supplies in their packs. He found spare gun oil in one of the cargo holds and all their weapons were cleaned and loaded.

The broadcast concluded with the classic BBC pips. Good to know others were still alive, that fragments of western civilization still existed, at least for now. They were so remote that they might as well be on the moon (also once within the reach of mankind) but the proof of their existence was comforting.

Bea caught the boys before they left and appeared to be admonishing them to behave. They protested their complete innocence and good intentions but didn't seem too alarmed until she took them by the arms and pulled them aside. David was close enough to hear her say,

"Don't you dare blow me off again, either of you. These men will kill you if they think you're a hindrance to their survival and in their eyes you're both starting to look like one. Straighten up."

They left the room, walking dejectedly, shoulders drooping but once out of sight the sound of laughter and running footsteps echoed back. Bea made a strangled sound in her throat and headed topside, her angry footsteps loud on the metal ladder.

David followed.

The ship was anchored. David didn't know why since the regular meetings he and Mei used to have with Private Tsou and the others had ceased. He wondered if they were going to attempt to net some more fish. He didn't see any dead in the water but of course that didn't mean they weren't there. Ian and Virginia must have gone below. Bea stood with Anna by the rail, holding the little girl's hand and looking at the ridiculously beautiful little town. There was even a picturesque lighthouse painted with black and white stripes perched on a cliff. The seals' barking was a welcome change from the menacing moaning of the dead.

"Population is just under 2,000, primarily Caucasian, Hispanic, and Black, education level averages 14 years of school completed and the median income is $50,000 per household. Or that's how it used to be." Bea spoke, still staring at the shore.

"Wikipedia?"

"No, Census Bureau website. I'd never thought about living on the coast before but this might be a good place. I wonder if the dead are here, somewhere out of sight. I would hate to be literally between the devil and the deep blue sea like we were in SoCal."

"Going by previous experience, I'd bet there are some here. Still any time the population numbers are smaller there's a better chance of clearing them out and making a go of it."

Several of the Chinese emerged on deck, pulling one of the fishing nets with them. They all smiled at Bea but only nodded to David. Securing the ropes to the deck crane, they cast the net, all of them watching it sink out of sight.

Bea spoke in an urgent tone. "We've got to get off of here. The boys are living on borrowed time. Mei said the crew has had enough of them and I can't get them under control. I'm worried about Mei too." She finally looked up at him. "I think they think that she will stay with them after we go. She has medical skills any group needs and it's obvious they want her. You have to watch out for her, David." The last sentence was spoken very emphatically.

David nodded, "I agree. You need to watch out, too. Groups of men without women are prone to volatility and aggressiveness. China already had a huge gender imbalance, almost as bad as India's. They were aborting their girls because with the one child policy, they felt they had to have a boy since traditionally it's the son who makes sure the aging parents are taken care of. Now we have a similar problem. Of course for all we know there is a large group of female survivalists just up the coast. Probably not though."

The crane started again, making them jump. Slowly the bulging net rose into view, lifted up and over the rail. The ropes broke, spilling their catch. Hundreds of silvery fish skidded across the metal surface.

A body struggled in the midst of the flopping, twitching fish. Eyeless and bloated, gnashing broken teeth in its rotted mouth, it slid along the deck, coming to rest at Anna's and Bea's feet. The abdomen gaped wide and dozens of gray, slimy eels were attached to the exposed organs, burrowing their way deeper and deeper into its flesh.

Bea screamed and kicked it, her foot sinking into its shoulder before it spun a short distance away, the eels slithering along with it. The soldiers were quick and punctured the creature's brain with a steel spike with a hooked blade just beneath it. Bea had seen them several times before. They looked something like a halberd but Brian said they were modified grappling hooks.

Anna still screamed and before Bea could interfere, Private Chang stalked over and slapped the little girl. David punched him, knocking him to the deck and leaped forward to hit him again. The rest of the crew surrounded them, threatening them with their hooks. Bea picked up Anna and shouted at them to leave her alone.

225

Bea held the little girl and glared at the crewmen. Anna cried and spat out watery blood as Bea shushed her and stroked her hair. She finally quieted but didn't get down. The Chinese ignored them now and cleared the deck before going below. No one would be eating fish tonight.

A sound rumbled across the water, an engine sound. They looked behind them and saw a boat, a pleasure craft, bouncing across the waves. A man, very tall with broad shoulders and a head of very red hair, stood at the wheel, driving with one hand and waving frantically with the other.

Bea shaded her eyes against the rising sun. "Is that Cam?"

David looked. "Either that or we're under attack by a rogue Viking."

The boat drew closer and cut the engine. David threw one of the rope ladders down and soon Cam stood on board, sunburned and smiling.

"You left me, you heartless gits!" he said, crushing Bea to his chest and planting a smacking kiss on her cheek.

"How did- Cam, where the hell did you go? We were there until dawn searching the waters while the boat was cleared. We didn't know what happened. I mean, you're too big for a shark to get his mouth around, much less a zombie," David said.

Cam, blue eyes sparkling, grinned. "I got caught in a current. I was putting the kids in the boats and I got pulled under by one of those poor dead bastards. A strong one. I punched the daylights out of him but it was like a love tap as far as he was concerned. He kept coming over and over and finally I figured all I could do was outswim him. Bloody cross tide pulled me north and washed me up under some pilings on an old pier. I must have crawled up the beach some but I don't remember much other than waking up in the sand the next morning. The dead were there a little farther up the beach but they hadn't sensed me yet. I managed to slip into one of our boats washed against the

226

pilings and row out to sea but it was losing air and I had to keep bailing. Finally this beauty of a boat drifted my way. It had an owner but he wasn't much for conversation so I pitched him out and here I am."

"Wait here. I'm going below to let everyone know." Bea left, still carrying Anna. She found Virginia and relinquished her to her mother with a quick explanation of what had occurred on deck. Virginia frowned and inspected her daughter's face. There was a red mark and the beginnings of a bruise. She took her back to their cabin.

Bea ran into Mei and the boys coming from the infirmary.

"Mei, Cam is alive. He just showed up in a boat that-"

Mei's eyes widened and she ran. Bea and the boys followed.

Outside, Cam's face was lit with a tenderness Bea had never seen before. Mei ran to him and, crying, kissed him, light, scattered kisses all over his face. He picked her up and enfolded her in his arms, crushing her against his chest as he kissed her and carried her across the deck. They stayed there for some time.

~

The vast ship, a vessel that once carried the wares manufactured and sold in an intricate economic system that encompassed the world, harbored many hidden nooks and crannies. Deep below deck, sheltered in a small cargo hold that still held packing crates and packing blankets, David and Bea sat in the near dark. His arms were wrapped around her and she leaned back against his chest, feeling warm and safe for the first time in a very long time. His face rested against the side of her head so every time he spoke it tickled her ear.

227

"So it wasn't you then, it was Cam all along," Bea murmured.

"It must have been. I didn't have a clue though, about Cam. Mei kept that pretty quiet."

"She hasn't been herself for several days but I thought it was because she's pregnant. I've been really worried about her, when I wasn't thinking about how mad I was at you."

David sat up straighter, "Mei is pregnant? Did she tell you that?"

"No. I saw the pregnancy test she dropped. I assumed that you- well you know what I assumed. What do you mean, 'too'?"

"Bea, that may be a mistake. I don't think that- well it's not impossible but- Virginia is pregnant. Mei has been taking care of her ever since Greg died and I think she actually suspected it before Virginia did."

"Oh no. Do they know when? Was it before she was infected? It must have been."

"Ian and Virginia were almost divorced right when the virus broke out. They had been separated, off and on, for a few months. Ian never told me why they split but he was the most miserable s.o.b. to work with the whole time. He was in D.C. when the truth about the virus became widely-known and he pulled in every favor he could to get transport home to her and the kids. I'm not sure if she got bit before or after he got there but once he knew, he called me and I helped arrange a pick-up, you know that part."

"So she was probably pregnant when she was bitten."

"Almost a certainty but she had no idea."

"She also was pregnant throughout the malaria treatment. Dr. Osawy missed that."

"Maybe. Or maybe the doctor didn't care. The thing is, aside from the possible effects of the Z-virus on the baby, there are also the possible effects of the malarial fever."

"We have to find a place soon. Virginia won't be able to travel forever and then newborns are a lot of work. Noisy too. Maybe we should try going ashore here. Our hosts are sick of us anyway. Especially of the boys. Now they're branching out to Anna."

"I think we should try. We have to be prepared for anything though. Once we're off the ship the Chinese won't wait for us to decide whether we like the town or not."

"Fine. We leave tomorrow if everyone will agree. I'll go tell Brian and Moshe to get ready. I've left them alone too long already."

David pulled her close again and pressed his lips against the nape of her neck. "Right now? Five more minutes."

She caught her breath at his touch and smiled as she brushed his lips with hers. "Five more."

~

One deck above them, in the ship's galley, their Chinese hosts concluded a meeting. Breaking out several bottles of jealously guarded rice wine they prepared to relax and enjoy an evening of the Chinese equivalent of shooting the breeze. Glasses clinked and masculine laughter rang out but Private Tsou begged off, saying he planned to go to bed early. Walking quietly and constantly looking over his shoulder he headed toward the bulkhead area where the infirmary was located.

Mei was there, double-checking their supplies and making sure they were packaged properly for transport. She had been berating herself for days for not stocking pre-natal vitamins. It would have been so easy to pick some up during one of their foraging missions back at the camp. Hearing footsteps she looked up.

Private Tsou slipped into the room and closed the door. Mei's heart began to race. She had never felt frightened by the attention the crew paid to the women, just mildly annoyed. She was frightened now but determined not to show it.

"Do you need medical attention, Private Tsou?" She spoke in the classic Mandarin her parents had taught her.

"No, but I thank you for the skillful care you have shown me in the past, honored lady. I also wish to tell you that you and your fellows are no longer safe on this vessel. Tomorrow evening, you and the other female members of your group will be confined to the hold and the men will be placed ashore. It was only with great difficulty that I was able to persuade the crew not to kill them."

"Thank you for this information. I will inform my friends but I will not reveal it was you who told me." She hesitated. "I have something for you, Private Tsou. It's the cure for the virus."

His eyes widened and she continued, "It must be given as early as possible to the infected individual and the fever that results must be allowed to burn in order for the virus to be destroyed. It has been used successfully only twice that I am aware of and the cure is not a certainty. It must be kept in cool storage and I am uncertain of its shelf-life. Do you understand?"

He bowed and accepted the small Styrofoam package and turned to leave but she stopped him.

"Private Tsou, would you like to leave the ship and join us?"

"I thank you for your kind offer but it is my hope to return to China and to my family. The last time I heard from my wife she told me our daughter was safe and she was taking her to stay with family outside the city. My best chance for seeing them again lies in remaining on my ship." He bowed again and left.

Mei filled two backpacks with supplies and slipped out into the corridor. Bea wasn't in their shared room so she shoved the packs under a bunk and went to look for Cam. They had spent the entire day together, the joy that they had found each other making it difficult to break away but Fitz had finally assigned him a bunk and Cam fell into an exhausted sleep, not even waking for supper.

The door at the end of the passageway opened and Bea and David emerged, releasing their entwined hands just a little too late to prevent her from seeing it. Bea actually blushed.

Mei refrained from smiling. She had had suspicions about the two of them for a while.

She spoke in a low tone, "We need to talk."

David went to find the rest of the group while the women woke Cam. After a few brief disagreements they settled on a plan. They would leave tonight.

Chapter Sixteen

Virginia wandered in a dark landscape of grief, searching for a way out, but there was no escape. Every morning she awoke and sometimes it was a few seconds before she remembered that her son was dead but then the knowledge came and with it the crushing sadness that kept her separated from everyone around her. She and Ian were often mute when alone, unable to speak of this death that had taken the light from their world. With everyone else she said the things she thought she should say but later had no memory of the conversation.

The news that they were leaving left her indifferent. She listened as they outlined the plan but made few comments. Nodding to the whispered instructions she then left for her cabin to gather all the children's belongings, calmly folding clothes and making sure nothing was left behind.

The mildness was deceptive. Inside, she felt enough grief and rage to set the world on fire and happily burn with it. Her baby was gone and she wanted the desolation she felt to encompass everything, for heaven to weep unending tears for the little life that was no more, for the little boy who would never grow up. She held his blanket in her arms and rocked back and forth, searching for memory of his voice, his scent, the velvet warmth of his neck. Tears, which never seemed to completely stop, dropped unheeded onto the bedraggled, beloved cloth. Folding it then pressing it to her cheek, she tucked it tenderly into her pack.

Bea and a few others were taking the children on deck, ostensibly to play shuffleboard before bedtime, while Virginia and Mei gathered packs and supplies. The ship had landing craft but they were using the inflatables stowed in the hold. They were quieter.

Something clattered to the floor and she picked up her knife, her grandfather's KA-BAR knife that was meant to be passed on to Greg. She held it tightly for a moment then began to methodically stab the thin pallet that served as a mattress. Stabbing, tearing, ripping the bed apart, she finally stopped, looking around with a small sense of satisfaction at the mess she had made. It was a start to the havoc she wanted to unleash everywhere. She slipped the knife into her boot, picked up the backpacks and left to join the children on deck.

As soon as she emerged into the corridor, someone grabbed her arms roughly, spun her around and slammed her against the wall. A hand clamped her mouth as her captors fumbled to tie her hands. She bit down hard, capturing the thumb between her teeth, not stopping until she felt bone and her attacker cried out. When the hand was pulled away she didn't scream but managed to twist around and go in for a bite of the man who still held her arms. He pushed her away and she rolled to her feet, coming up with the knife in one hand. Blood ran down her face.

Bringing the knife up in one fluid motion, she buried it in his neck then tugged it free. He went down and his companion tripped over the body as he came after her again. Virginia recognized Private Chang. The knife went deep into his belly and, thinking of the red, slap mark and bruise on her daughter's face, she forced it up, stopping only when she hit the sternum. His life poured out onto the floor, a hot rush of blood and viscera.

A few feet down the corridor she came upon Mei, tied up, gagged, and struggling furiously to get free. Her eyes widened in fear at the sight of Virginia but she stopped struggling while Virginia cut the plastic cuffs and untied the gag.

"Virginia, what happened to you?" She couldn't imagine anyone covered with that much blood could be unwounded.

"Nothing. I'm fine. What about you?" She extended a bloody hand to help Mei up. Mei took it reluctantly.

"Just bruised. They jumped me as I left the infirmary. I think these guys had a plan of their own. Let's go."

A few feet further they came upon the blood-soaked, lifeless body of Private Tsou. His throat gaped wide and blood pooled in the corridor. Mei's breath caught in a sob but Virginia's eyes hardened. She took Mei's hand and, stepping over the blood, pulled her along.

On deck they found the children huddled together near the bow, unhurt. The women lay trussed and gagged, Bea among them. They cut them free.

Bea gasped, "Brian and Moshe, they're in the water. The crew threw them in. Oh please, God, let them be okay!"

They ran to the side and scanned the darkening water but saw nothing. They had no flashlight, no searchlight. They listened and thought they heard a faint thumping somewhere.

"Did you see any of the men below?" Bea asked.

"No, but they should be here soon. Give it two more minutes. If they don't make it up with boats we'll-"

"There's no time," Bea interrupted.

She ran to the side of the boat and took off her shoes, prepared to dive in when she felt a hand on her arm. Virginia shook her head and put a finger to her lips.

The faint thumping grew louder and was accompanied by muffled sentences and exclamations. The rope ladder that Cam climbed up earlier was still on the rail and it shifted and twisted with weight. They looked down and saw two figures inching their way up.

"...fine. We'll find the rifles again and..." The voices were lost in the wind but the two figures climbing were clearly Brian and Moshe.

234

Bea laughed in relief. The boys gained the deck and sat shivering in the cool, evening breeze.

"They just threw us over. We didn't even have a chance to defend ourselves! And they took our weapons. Ian and David are going to be mad."

"I think they'll forgive you. Now be quiet, everyone." Virginia went back to the hatch, listening for sounds of movement below. After a few minutes she moved aside.

"They're here."

The boats were soon over the side and tethered while the group climbed slowly down. The sea was calm tonight and a bright moon lighted their short journey to shore.

"How did you get out of there with no one seeing you?" Mei asked Cam, holding on the side of the boat while Moshe and Brian paddled. "They're usually all pretty busy at this time of evening."

"Ah. That would be the grog," Cam said.

"The what?" asked Moshe.

"Grog. Alcohol, wine, whiskey, whatever you want to call it. The fine gentlemen of the crew were having a bit of a tipple in the galley. I was scouting out our way to the top and took the opportunity to lock them inside. They're angry but they'll eventually think to shoot a hole in the door or wall and they'll be fine. Which is more than I can say for the three chaps I found in the corridor. You wouldn't happen to know anything about that, Mei?"

"I guess they suspected Private Tsou wasn't on their side and they killed him. I was attacked and tied up. From what I heard them say, not all of the crew wanted to wait until tomorrow and were going to secure the women tonight. They also were going to kill you guys. I can't help but wonder if they knew he had warned me. I feel responsible."

"You're not responsible for that. God rest his poor soul. And the other two blokes?"

"I'm pretty sure that was Virginia. She was attacked, too."

"I thought as much, considering the state of her."

"That wasn't her blood. She's struggling, Cam. She lost her son. She's been almost catatonic until now."

"I suppose angry is better than catatonic. We're not the same people we were before all of this, are we?"

They ran the boats aground then dragged them through the surf, placing them among the rocks above the high-tide mark. Virginia took a moment to splash her arms and face clean and they moved on.

The seals that had thronged the rocks earlier were elsewhere and they had little difficulty climbing the narrow line of cliffs overhanging the beach. They emerged in a park, empty swings moving eerily in the breeze, the merry-go-round spinning slowly. There was a faint, salty aroma of dead things, not unusual near a beach. No dead were in evidence yet.

They moved on. The street contained several boutique stores, among them an upscale beachwear store, a yogurt shop, and a bakery. Just past a post office was a YMCA, beyond that, the lighthouse. The YMCA looked very new and a large American flag snapped in the ocean breeze. Glass front doors were broken and they stepped through the frames. Little piles of sand and dry leaves covered the tile foyer.

Cam and Bea wanted to press on, get farther away from the ship. Almost everyone else wanted to find shelter for the night, especially those with children. A vote was taken; the majority won.

They knew something had gone wrong here before they reached the front desk. Dark stains streaked the floor. Chairs and tables were overturned. Shell casings lay here and there. Stuck to the wall among the plaques honoring various board members and benefactors was a clump of brain and scalp with a few blond hairs still attached and dangling. The body they belonged to lay below, little more than bones and dried flesh, nothing above the neck.

A community bulletin board sported babysitting offers, bicycles for sale, and a reminder of an upcoming bake sale. There was also a reminder that hand washing was very important in helping prevent the spread of colds and viruses. They smelled mold and chlorine and came upon the indoor pool. A few bodies struggled feebly in the murky water. They moved on.

A janitor still performed a staggering perambulation around the wooden floor in the gym. Cam split his skull with the cleaver and they dragged the body into the pool area and closed the door.

Yoga mats stored in a supply closet were perfect for sleeping but they found nothing with which to cover up. Still, the place was fairly clean and had room for all of them. There was no drinking water. They found buckets and decided to fill them with water from the pool to flush the toilets.

A few precious bottles were in packs and children were given sips as they lay down on the yoga mats. Prayers were said, a comforting routine to most of them, and they were soon asleep.

Virginia lay awake next to Daniel and Anna in the near-total darkness, listening, thinking she heard dragging footsteps and occasional moans. Was she imagining things? Were there dead hunting them? The gym was secure with its only windows near the ceiling but she had no way to look outside. Ian and Fitz had first watch at the entrance doors and she knew she had to get up in four hours but she couldn't fall asleep. She placed her hands gently across her belly, searching for the expected swelling curve but couldn't feel it. It was still too soon. Nevertheless she wrapped her arms protectively around her middle and fell asleep.

The faint, rosy light of dawn woke her. No one had roused her for her watch and she felt completely disoriented. The children still slept beside her. She instinctively searched for the small figure that would never be with her again. The pain of realization was as sharp as ever.

She pulled on her boots and slipped past the sleeping bodies into the hallway. Fitz and Ian were near the entrance, still keeping watch. Looking for a bathroom she found instead a door at the very end of the hallway, marked "Lighthouse." It wasn't locked and hoping curiosity didn't always kill the cat, she opened it, crossed a short breezeway then ascended a twisting, metal staircase. Reaching the top she stepped out onto the encircling viewing platform.

Foamy waves broke in ceaseless *booms* on the rocky shores. Dark figures cavorted playfully in the water, the seals coming ashore and climbing onto the wet boulders, their ponderous bodies surprisingly quick. Gulls screamed, swooping down and plucking fish from the water with deadly accuracy. The Chinese ship was gone. They hadn't been interested enough in them to follow them onto land. To the east she glimpsed the top of a mammoth, white windmill, turning lazily in front of the rising sun.

A binocular viewing stand swiveled 360 degrees. To her surprise no coins were required and she peered through the view finder, slowly turning to look inland at the sun rising over the low mountains to the east. She stopped abruptly then focused the viewer lower.

Dark figures swarmed over the hills. At this distance they looked like colonizing ants or a coven of black locusts but of course they weren't. She shivered in dread and ran for the steps.

"Do we make a stand or do we run?" was the question on everyone's lips. No matter what Virginia or Ian said, they couldn't make these exhausted survivors understand they couldn't win against the numbers that approached. The charming little seaside town lulled them into a false sense of security and most of them wanted to stay. They seemed to think they were weaklings if they didn't try to hold this town and some of the men were in the process of whipping themselves into a frenzy about it.

David stood frowning over a map. Taking a route farther north would also take them close to the Cascade mountain range and his parents. They weren't really all that far away now. He'd never reached them again by phone but he refused to consider them not being okay. They were tough and smart and resourceful.

Ian was still trying to persuade the men to leave. "You have no potable water source, an uncertain food supply, no escape route other than the sea and the only boats you have are the rafts. This is not the place to make a stand. We haven't even scouted out the area yet. We have to go. Even now it may be too late."

He closed his eyes briefly and released an exasperated breath. He had kept watch all night, wanting Virginia to rest, desperately wanting to protect the child she carried, deliberately not waking her. He was too tired to argue with the increasingly hostile group and he wanted to leave and keep what was left of his family alive.

Fitz lumbered into the room, returning from the lighthouse. He caught Ian's eye and shook his head. He had been scanning the sea, looking for possibly derelict ships they might be able to row out and board.

Minutes ago Virginia had given up on the group and, gathering the children, she waited for the signal to go. She knew Bea and the boys and probably David and Fitz as well, would go with them. She wasn't counting on anyone though and was surprised and pleased when Mei, holding two packs, joined them.

"Cam, too?" Virginia raised an inquiring eyebrow.

"Yes, he's staying with Ian and David in case they get any real grief from the rest of the group. He wants me to slip out unobtrusively. He's afraid they'll try to stop the only nurse from leaving."

Virginia nodded. They were going to take the High Street north, following that until they came to the coastal highway. They should be able to find transportation after that. It still nagged her that they had seen so few of the townspeople. Where had they gone?

They were also seriously in need of drinking water. She was thirsty and so were the children and she hoped they would come upon a market that hadn't been raided. They could make it for a while without food but not water.

Loud shouts then whistling and hand clapping rang out from the gym. A door opened and shut then David, Ian, and Fitz joined them. With nothing more to be said, they walked out through the door frames into the street where the boys and Bea waited.

They passed a travel agency and an ice cream shop. Two cars, both with flat tires sat in front of a corner market that was just a burned out husk. Just over a hill the gargantuan, white windmill sliced the air, impelled by the ocean breezes. They crested the hill.

Below them, where the main street connected with the coastal highway, the people of the town had made their last stand. Not understanding the nature of the enemy, they blocked the main entrance to the town with their vehicles and prepared to defend their territory in a logical and organized fashion.

The dead knew nothing of logic or organization. They no doubt flowed around the little roadblock like water around a rock and attacked the defenders with no plan other than the urgent need to consume and kill. All of them, attackers and townspeople, dead and reeking, now staggered in a rotting mass at the bottom of the hill. The windmill with its constant *whoosh* kept them there, clawing at the smooth base.

The group instinctively ducked as soon as they caught sight of the dead. They stayed down and spoke in whispers.

"…as quietly as we can, we head to the right of the blockade. There are three cars in the front that aren't blocked in. We just have to hope one will start. Ready?"

They moved in smoothly without attracting attention and Bea slid behind the wheel of a minivan. The engine chugged briefly then emitted nothing but clicks. They moved on to the green jeep but no keys.

Virginia kept watch on the dead during the process, keeping Anna and Daniel close. A golf club, a nine iron, lay abandoned on the ground and she picked it up, testing the swing. A dead man, very tall, stopped shuffling on his skinless feet and cocked his head, ear turned toward the cars. In a sluggish, awkward turn he began to make his way over, reaching pavement and dragging along a shovel still gripped reflexively in rotten fingers. The metal scraped along the pavement, attracting the attention of two more dead, one carrying a string of drying entrails in her hand. Both executed a graceless pirouette and fell in behind the tall corpse, teeth gnashing.

Fitz moved to stand beside her. He picked Daniel up and put him on his back while Anna jumped into Virginia's arms. As the corpses advanced, they put the children in the bed of an ancient pick-up and waited.

Virginia swung the club hard, black liquid spraying out from the tall corpse's shattered skull. He went down and Fitz jerked the shovel from his hand just in time to puncture the brittle skulls of the two following.

To their right, Cam, Mei, and Ian were similarly engaged against a larger group. Taking the children Fitz and Virginia wove through the parked vehicles and joined them, clubbing and slicing the attacking dead. Cam decapitated three with his cleaver. Now coming forward in waves the dead climbed onto the car hoods, reaching for their prey. A dead teen with a nose-ring gripped Virginia's ankle and pulled her down, her head crashing into the front windshield. Stunned, she grabbed the wipers as the creature dragged her toward its ravenous mouth. She kicked, collapsing the gray face but it didn't go down. A mouth bit down on her boot in a bruising chomp and her body slid sideways. More eager hands grasped and pulled. She lost her grip on the wipers just as an iron grip on her collar pulled her back on the car. She looked up at Cam gratefully, turned and pulled her knife from her boot and pierced the teen's skull. He went down.

She climbed on the roof of a Subaru and scanned the area, leaning down and bashing in the skull of an elderly woman who got too close. Near the back of the car blockade she saw the boys opening the doors of an SUV with tinted windows, climbing in and closing the doors. An engine roared and the vehicle bumped into one behind it, knocking a space big enough for them to drive out and around onto the grassy median. Bouncing over the uneven terrain they skirted the blockade and stopped next to the car Bea and David were trying to start.

Bea looked up, rolled her eyes and tugged on David's arm. They climbed into the SUV but about ten cars and a hundred zombies were between them and the rest of the group. Moshe honked the horn.

Cam grinned and tucked his cleaver into his belt. Taking a child under each arm he jumped from car to car, finally reaching the SUV and handing them over. The rest of the group followed. The dead had trouble navigating through the tightly packed vehicles and were easily left behind.

They stopped at the crest of the next hill. A few dead staggered up the hill after them but they were no threat anymore. Mei trained her binoculars on the more distant hills. The dark stain spreading across the landscape was getting closer.

The SUV's powerful engine ate the miles easily. Mei drove, ousting a disgruntled Moshe who felt he should be allowed to drive since he had found the vehicle. Ian, Cam, and David slept.

Stores along the highway were few and all had been looted at some point. They needed water desperately now. Anna and Daniel had cracked lips and their faces looked pinched. Water had been rationed while they were on the ship even more severely than food and dehydration was a real specter.

Virginia leaned her head against the cool window glass. The road continued to rise and her ears popped in the increasing altitude. She tried to swallow but her throat felt like sand. The countryside flew by and the day began to darken and she found that she was afraid, deathly afraid of what the night might bring. Civilization had more or less banished the terrors of a darkness that could only be alleviated by the sunrise. Electric light had driven away the fear of the unknown with the flip of a switch. But no more. Once again darkness was a terrible foe that must be survived behind the shelter of strong walls and doors. Terrible things that lurked in the dark were all too real.

As the sun sank behind cliffs to the west, Mei pulled off the road at a gas station. She had an idea that any place this remote might have a generator back-up and they could fill up. Anything was worth a try.

Wind whipped the fine grit in the parking lot and stung her eyes. The station was looted like every other place they had tried. There was no evidence of violence; the shelves had just been emptied. The cash drawer was open and full of bills. She tried the small sink behind the counter. No water. She licked chapped lips and searched under the sink for water, soda, anything that might have been overlooked.

Outside, Cam walked the property. No generator out here. The lot ended at a sloping cliff, protected by guard rails. Below that a dry valley stretched out into flatter land east. He stood watch, searching for movement. Ian and David joined him.

Two deer grazed on the sparse clumps of clover growing below. Both were females and after a few minutes two fawns emerged from the bushes and joined them to nurse. The men were very still and the animals didn't notice them.

Fitz joined the group. "We should kill them for the meat."

"Soon enough we'll probably need to. Right now I don't want the children to see me kill Bambi and Bambi's mom," Ian whispered.

David remarked, "Bambi would be pretty tasty right about now."

They continued watching the deer. One of the does suddenly looked up and cocked an ear. All of the animals became very still, just barely twitching those sensitive ears. After a moment they leapt and fled in a bounding run until they were completely out of sight.

In the distance what looked like smoke or dust formed and gradually drew closer. A sound almost like the crunch of dead leaves rose from the valley. A dry, rustling sound. They soon saw bodies in the dirty, clouded air.

A herd of dead, thousands strong, swarmed across the valley. Sinewy, desiccated bodies fanned out, churning up clouds of dust in their wake. Lurching and staggering they were an abomination befouling the once peaceful landscape.

Ian heard a gasp and looked behind him. Daniel stood there, his hand over his mouth. He crouched instinctively and crept over toward the men. Ian put a finger to his lips and pulled him close.

Eventually the infected were gone, heading for whatever drew them in the first place. A few stragglers remained, either they were slower and couldn't keep up or they were distracted by something in the valley. Their odor reached them and the men turned away.

They knew they weren't safe here but they evaluated its potential. They had the high ground as well as a building they could make fairly secure. As they stood debating, Mei walked around the corner with two six-packs of beer held high.

"A beautiful woman and beer, it must be a sign from God. We have to stay here now," Cam said.

"Don't be sacrilegious," said Mei.

"I wasn't," Cam said solemnly.

Night fell quickly. Everyone drank the warm beer with thankfulness and relief but Virginia fretted over the children drinking alcohol. She touched her belly with a small pang of guilt. What was happening to her child? This baby had already been exposed to so much. Mei had been very upbeat about the baby's development. She knew the placenta provided a layer of protection that many toxins were unable to breach but she was still afraid. A feeling of love and protectiveness overwhelmed her.

"I wouldn't worry too much about the beer Virginia," said Bea, trying to reassure her. "Children have drunk beer throughout history. They often had no choice, water supplies in cities were so contaminated. The Puritans' children drank 'small beer' every morning along with their milk. The alcohol content in this stuff is pretty low."

It wasn't enough to really satisfy any of them but they made the best of it and settled in for the night. Virginia returned from outside to find Anna and Daniel already bedded down, covered with contributed jackets from the rest of the group. Fitz was telling them a bedtime story.

"...and what do you think the G.I.s did then? They'd just finished fighting that bastard Hitler and they weren't going to put up with this crap in their own home town. When the sheriff's deputies took those ballot boxes in for a private count the soldiers went and got their weapons and came back for a re-count."

The story went on for some time, something about corrupt politicians of the 1940's in a small town called

Athens and brave soldiers who fought for truth, justice, and the American way. He finished with-

"...and that's why we have the 2nd Amendment, the right to keep and bear arms. Now go to sleep and remember the immortal words of General Chesty Puller."

"What?" asked Daniel.

"Well, to paraphrase, *'They're in front of us, behind us, and we're outflanked by an enemy that outnumbers us millions to one. There's no way in hell they can get away from us now.'*"

He left and Virginia kissed the children goodnight. Anna whispered, "Mom, do you think Greg can see us now? If I tell him I love him will he hear it?"

Virginia nodded. She couldn't speak.

"We're a broken family now, aren't we?"

She nodded again, finally managing to say, "We are, darling, but not completely. Not as long as we still have each other."

Anna sobbed and Virginia held her for a long time before she cried herself to sleep. She placed her down gently next to Daniel and covered her with a jacket. She lay down beside them, gun at hand, keeping watch until very late when she too, finally fell asleep.

Chapter Seventeen

The Columbia River is at any time an awesome spectacle of nature. Over 1,200 miles long it has multiple hydro-electric dams once skillfully managed by the Army Corps of Engineers to provide electrical power. Snaking through Canada, Washington, and Oregon, it was one of the rivers that Lewis and Clark described in their journals as teeming with salmon and beaver.

Something far darker filled it now. The group trudged forward, hungry and thirsty, tormented by the surging water that sparkled so enticingly. They had already seen bodies, both dead and undead, bobbing by in the torrent.

Heavy rains and snowfalls in the area had already swelled the local dams well past their capacity. The McNary and Dalles dams burst several days before the group reached the banks of the roaring water, dismayed to find the bridge they expected to cross had been swept away.

According to the map their next best opportunity to find a bridge was in Alconquin, a considerable trek to the east. Low on gas and knowing they wouldn't make it all the way, they set out along the river road, driving the SUV dry then abandoning it by the side of the road.

David convinced them to try for the Seattle area. His parents had a large property just outside the city and he knew they would have room for all. He was also eager to make sure they were okay. Somehow he couldn't believe they wouldn't be there, his mom out in the garden, tying up pole beans, dead-heading the roses, his dad "resting his eyes" as he napped under the grape arbor.

Daniel, riding on Fitz's shoulders, first noticed the smoke. Gray feathers of ash drifted through the air. Not long after, they heard the crackle of burning wood and saw the first few tongues of flames licking along the ground, burning up last year's dead leaves. They were forced to turn back, the heat and smoke burning and stinging their eyes.

They didn't get far before they were cut-off. The fire had crept in behind them.

Retreating to the shore they waded out into the shallows, using sticks to push away the dead that floated too close. Bea screamed when a passing corpse grabbed her leg and pulled her under. David pulled her up and Cam sliced off the dead arm. The corpse, caught again in the current, floated away.

The top branches of trees on the bank had already caught fire and flames moved along the forest floor.

David looked intently at the woods. The flames moved in odd, staggering patterns. Realization dawned.

"They're coming our way! The dead! Hurry!"

They stood back to back, weapons held ready but looking into the woods and seeing the number of burning bodies shambling their way, they knew the outcome. Still, they intended to go down fighting.

A deep, hooting whistle floated across the water. David thought he was hallucinating when he heard a bell ring as well. He looked up and saw a boat, a ferry, headed their way.

A woman shouted through a bullhorn, "I can't come any closer without running aground! Can you swim out?"

"We have small children! Can you launch a raft?" David shouted back.

"Someone will have to be out here to help me, I only have a skiff that I can't launch by myself," was the shouted response.

Cam plunged into the water and made for the boat with strong, sure strokes. A heavy plank whirled by in the current and struck his head. He went down.

"Cam!" Mei screamed, jumping in after him.

The woman on the ferry tossed a lifebuoy out. Mei's head surfaced and she looked around, frantically searching. She dove under again.

The dead, some still in flames, reached the bank. Virginia held the children close and fired. She hit the two closest dead on. They went down in the water, drifting in the shallows. Ian shot two more.

A random spark drifted down and landed on Anna's head. Virginia splashed water to put it out. She felt the heat now, burning their faces, sucking the oxygen from the air.

"David, you and Bea go. Take the boys, too. We'll wait for you to launch the skiff. Hurry, please!" Virginia urged.

They swam out and climbed the netting draped over the side. Just as they boarded, Mei's head popped up again but this time she screamed, fighting two dead pulling her down. Fitz dove in and swam out but though he searched he couldn't find her again. Finally, exhausted, he climbed the boat's netting.

David and Bea were already launching the skiff, securing it to a line so it didn't drift away. Ian swam out far enough to grab the prow and pull it in. Virginia and the children climbed in and together they paddled for the ferry boat.

They never made it. A wall of water from upstream smashed into them, breaking the rope and sending the little skiff downstream in a churning maelstrom, then smashing the ferry against the far shore. Grounded but still upright, the boat was the only protection they had and they huddled on the deck, searching the water until darkness settled in. Bea screamed their names until she was hoarse but no one answered. They were gone.

~

The fire burned for most of the night before cooling rain doused the flames, finally soaking the smoldering cinders until they were sodden and harmless.

As dawn broke, the group searched the scorched wasteland for signs of survivors. Haley, the boat's captain, came with them. She was a surprisingly small woman with steel-gray hair. Extremely familiar with the area, she had navigated the river for years.

The dead were present in huge numbers but most were still on the other side of the river. The ones who stumbled into the still-roaring waters were quickly swept away.

Mid-morning they came upon a body half buried in the silt and mud of the bank. Approaching warily they froze when one eye opened but the iris was bright blue and looked at them with recognition. Cam rolled over then sat up, groaning and wiping mud away. His other eye was bruised and swollen shut.

"Mei?" he croaked with difficulty.

"Not yet," Bea said. "We're still looking. We lost Ian and Virginia, too. "

Brian and Moshe, farther down the bank, shouted and waved to get their attention. They were pointing at something on the opposite bank.

David trudged closer through the mud and soon he saw what they were yelling about. The skiff was on the bank, pulled up above the water line and empty. Dead stumbled along near it. Though he tried he couldn't see any resemblance to Mei, Ian, or Virginia, nor were any of them child-sized. Whoever they were, they were burned beyond recognition.

They returned to Cam. Trying to stand, he staggered and fell in the mud then, trying again, he made it up the bank. Finding Fitz, they sat, debating their options.

"You can't get back to the other side and even if you could, there's no way you could evade the dead. I think your friends are gone," Haley said. She was in despair over her boat. She had been trying to get to one of the small tributary rivers to dock when she came upon them yesterday.

"A lot of us are trying to ride this thing out on the river. The only problem is the dams are starting to burst and the water is too dangerous. I thought a tributary would be safer. I guess I'll never know now."

"We're trying to get to my folks' place just outside of Seattle. You're welcome to come with us," David offered.

"Thank you but no. I have family close by but farther south. They'll be looking for me if I don't get back soon and I don't want them in any danger. Are you folks going to be alright? You know you're very close to the city now? Don't go too far in, Seattle was hit hard."

She left.

They followed the bank as it wound north. Around noon they spotted a group of dead crouched around something on the ground. They approached cautiously but satisfied grunts and moans drifted in the still air and the dead paid them no attention. They were clearly eating.

Preparing to go around they all heard a sound, almost a sigh, as if a last breath of air had been softly exhaled. With a feeling of dread they drew closer, weapons ready.

Mei lay in the mud. Her eyes were open and her body jerked as the cadavers pulled away strips of flesh and meat. One of them pulled an arm free from its socket and broke the bone with a sharp *crack*. Another reached into her abdomen and dug around, pulling a dripping piece of dark meat free.

Cam *roared*, there was no other word to describe it, and grabbed two of the ghouls with both hands, smashing their heads together until they cracked. The third he picked up and slammed repeatedly into a tree, not stopping until the head was little more than splintered bone. He dropped the remains and crouched in the mud. Birds fled as he screamed until his voice faded to hoarse rasps.

They had no way to bury what remained of her poor body so they consigned Mei to the mighty flow of the river, carrying her away to a muddy burial somewhere. Moshe said a prayer before they moved on.

They wandered through a charred, bleak countryside. The rain stopped but the still gray sky was a backdrop for the blackened trees. Twice they had to stop and let Cam rest. He was very pale and his lips almost blue. Bea feared he had internal injuries but had no idea what to do about it. There was nothing to do but keep going, hoping he would make it long enough to get treatment somewhere, somehow.

David was not familiar with the forest here and was simply heading north in the hope they would eventually find a road with directional signs.

By mid-afternoon he knew they were lost. They stopped for a break and Cam stretched out on the ground, immediately falling into a doze. Bea sat next to David on the damp ground. "Ian and Virginia. Do you think they got away?"

"They were, *are* two of the most stubborn people I know. Someone pulled that boat up on the bank. If there was any way to get out of there they would have found it. They know we're heading north. We might get to my folks and find them already there."

They woke Cam but it took him a while to gain his feet and when he did Fitz had to support him. They trudged on, passing into a green section of forest untouched by the fire. Thirst was a constant torment and they licked the precious drops of moisture left from the night's rain on the spruce and hemlock branches.

A rustic cabin, probably someone's hunting lodge, lay just ahead in a green copse. Wooden, moss covered shingles and round glass windows gave it a hobbit-like air. They approached with caution but there was no sign of habitation, dead or otherwise.

Cam groaned and leaned against the door, "I'm knackered, mates. Leave me if you want, I'm going inside. If there's no bed, the floor will be fine."

Musty air greeted them but there was no smell of the dead. The single room contained two sets of bunks, a plank table with two chairs, and several oil lamps. Bea wiped away some of the grime from the windows, brightening the room a little. A cedar chest held blankets and she covered Cam who had already rolled into a bunk.

Fitz rummaged around the back of the cabin and returned with two plastic buckets. "I'm going out to scout for a spring, creek, anything that might have clean water. Brian, Moshe, come on. Bring your weapons," he ordered.

The cabin was decent shelter but the size and the dimness made it feel claustrophobic. David and Bea sat outside, letting Cam sleep. Birds called and the evergreens gave off a fresh, clean scent. Out here nature was untouched by the tragedy visited upon humanity.

Fitz and the boys returned, Fitz with a face like a storm cloud, the boys' faces white and strained. They had hiked down into a hollow and were soon rewarded with the sound of water splashing over rocks. A narrow stream of water, crystalline and cold, fell from a high rock ledge. They washed out the buckets and were just about to fill them when something splashed heavily into the shallow pool.

The legless torso of a girl splashed haplessly in the water, clawing at the surrounding mud until she climbed out among the mossy rocks. Sensing them she clambered forward, dragging intestines behind her. Brian instinctively stomped her skull in revulsion, popping her eyes and scattering her mostly intact brain in the water. Looking up they saw legs dangling from the ledge. The stream was contaminated. They tried but couldn't scale the cliff to see if the water was clear upstream.

"At some point we're going to have to take a chance and drink the water," Brian said disgruntledly.

"Yeah, but not that water," Fitz said. "How's Cam? We need to go."

253

Bea sighed and got to her feet. The old door screeched as she pushed it open. The room was darker now and Cam still slept, an unmoving lump beneath the blanket. Licking painfully dry lips she called, "Cam? It's time to go."

He jerked awake and holding the bed post, felt his way to a standing position. His legs trembled and he leaned against the wall. Bea's heart sank. He was too weak to go on and they couldn't carry him.

She would stay with him. The rest could go on ahead then… what? There weren't any vehicles that could make it in this terrain. Would anyone be able to find them again in time to help? She and Cam would both probably die here if he didn't recover enough to walk out soon. They were nearly mad with thirst already.

Cam fell and scrabbled for the bedpost, trying to get back into the bunk. She knelt down, slinging his arm around her shoulder, trying to raise him enough to tumble him back into the bunk when she realized what he was doing.

Before she could stop herself, she exclaimed, "Cam!"

His arm clenched her neck in an iron grip as he turned slowly and faced her. Gnawing on the wooden bedpost, he had splintered the flimsy pine and now chewed hungrily on the slivers before spitting them out. One tooth fell to the floor. Baring a gap-toothed snarl beneath dead eyes with black goo oozing from his mouth, he snapped at her, missing her cheek but catching her hair and yanking hard with his teeth.

In agony, she screamed and fell prone on the wooden floor. Cam fell with her, still squeezing her neck in the crook of his arm. The position he held her in made it impossible for him to reach her with his mouth but in his current state he couldn't understand that. He kept biting at the air all while tightening his grip on her throat. The light dimmed and she saw silver streaks shooting in front of her eyes. Sounds began to recede.

Something hot and wet splattered against the back of her neck just as a gun popped somewhere near the door. The arm holding her neck twitched and stopped squeezing but didn't let go. Cam collapsed on top of her, knocking the breath from her body. Someone called her name and rolled the huge man off of her. She could breathe again. Strong hands lifted her up and David looked at her anxiously, wiping the blood and brain matter from her neck and shoulders. Fitz and the boys stood in the doorway, identical expressions of shock on their faces.

"Are you hurt? Did he-"

She couldn't speak, just shook her head and began to cry, deep, shuddering sobs she couldn't control. The horror of the day, of the last several days had caught up with her. David held her, rocking her in his arms until she finally stopped. He took her face in his hands and kissed her lightly on the mouth.

"Can you walk?"

She nodded.

"Then let's go."

Night was falling again as they approached a low, stone house set in the curve of a valley and surrounded by a forest full of spruce and fir trees. David's heart was in his throat as they walked the graveled driveway, weapons held high over their heads. No lights shone in the windows but smoke billowed from the chimney.

A shot rang out and a bullet sliced the air over their heads as a figure standing on the front steps racked a shotgun and shouted, "There's nothing here for you. I'm armed and so is everyone else here. Keep moving."

David kept his rifle high above his head, "Dad?"

The shotgun went down and was laid to one side as the tall man ran toward the drive. He clasped David so tightly he couldn't breathe. Finally breaking free, laughing, David took Bea's hand, introducing her and the rest of the group. A woman, gray hair caught back in a sleek pony tail, emerged from the house, eyes wide as if she couldn't quite believe what she saw. Tears streamed down her face and she smiled.

"Welcome."

~

World Health Organization
Geneva Bureau
Update- Z-Virus (revised)

The new Director General would like to thank all of the individuals who contributed to the recent laboratory sessions. Research into the nature of the virus has told us little so far, but it is hoped that serological testing will reveal courses of treatment that will allow us to issue protocols. Polymerase chain reaction testing has yielded no results. For now diagnosis remains clinical and treatment is still confined to isolation and restraint of infected individuals.

There is little new information to impart at this time. We are working on consolidating laboratory resources and reinforcing our present location against the continued assaults of the dead. Basic necessities such as water, food, and access to health care continue to dwindle. Electrical grids have broken down leaving the few communities that still exist here cold and in the dark.

Industrialized nations where superior infrastructure and transportation allowed the virus easy and rapid dissemination have been particularly hard hit. It is very difficult to predict when or if they will recover from the virus-triggered devastation.

The usefulness of refugee centers has been very limited as even the most rigorous admission and screening procedures have failed to keep the virus out. The few camps that did not fall to the virus have fallen instead to cholera, dysentery, and meningitis. Mortality rates rival those of the Z-virus infested areas.

Please continue to check the website for updates.

Epilogue

One year later...

A truck, sides splashed with dried mud, labored up a winding mountain road. Cresting the hill, it rolled into the main square of a small town. Skeletal, decayed remains lay layers deep in the streets. Long abandoned vehicles surrounded them, dead drivers still inside. The truck wove through, rolling over the bodies and breaking the brittle bones, crushing them into even smaller mounds of blackened flesh and bone shards.

The truck paused briefly next to a defunct fountain in a central square. The surrounding mountains were breathtakingly lovely, some of them snow-capped. Faces pressed against the truck windows, looking out. Cottony, white clouds scudded along the horizon, blown by the sharp spring gusts.

The truck rolled on. Turning left it soon reached a residential section, passing under oaks, leafless now but ancient and towering. The street was blocked by a phalanx of vehicles. Dead leaves lay in piles around them, as if they had been abandoned there for some time.

Making a sharp left the truck backtracked, eventually reaching a golf course. Bouncing across the once manicured greens it made for a break in a split rail fence taking them through a suburban yard and into an older neighborhood. Houses, burned to empty shells, dotted the street here and there. Dead bodies, emaciated and leathery, lay on the ground. The dirty truck pulled into the driveway of a red-brick house and stopped.

A man, dark-haired and bearded climbed out, a shotgun over one shoulder, a knife in a sheath at his belt. He closed the truck door and walked the perimeter of the house, looking around him as he went. Three bodies, unrecognizable in decomposition, sprawled across the front walkway. He rolled the husks off the pavement with one foot, exposing feeding beetles that scurried away into the grass.

The front door was not locked and he went inside. After a few minutes he re-emerged and went back to the truck. The passenger side door opened and two children climbed out, also looking around warily. Two houses on the other side of the street had burned to the ground and the rusting, derelict hulk of a Lexus lay sideways in one of the yards.

Hands reached out from the truck and handed the man a blanketed bundle which he held close as a woman slid to the ground. The March winds whipped up and blew dark hair around her face and she smiled and tucked it behind her ears before taking the bundle back into her arms. Along the walkway narcissus bulbs poked pink tips above the ground.

The children raced ahead, disappearing inside. Ian and Virginia heard footsteps stomping up the staircase and they followed, carrying their son. They were home.

~

World Health Organization
Geneva Bureau
Update- Z-virus (revised)
General Worldwide

The Z-virus is one of the most transformative events ever to impact our world. Every form of government, every institution of the planet has fallen to the pandemic. It is expected that in most parts of the earth, all sciences, all literature, all that humanity has created will soon be lost forever. Many cultures, perhaps even entire races of people have already or shall soon disappear.

Sporadic assaults and limited battles are occurring daily in most regions as survivors fight for valuable resources such as water, access to food distribution centers, medical supplies, as well as military weapons depots. The failure of the industrialized nations to secure their military stockpiles will unleash additional, lethal instability worldwide.

Radioactive clouds continue to sweep across the Chinese continent and it is strongly suspected that the sterilizing effects of the radiation are prolonging the "life" of the dead there and in other countries that chose the "nuclear option."

Recently, incomplete reports filtering out of China indicate the virus may have jumped the species barrier. Smaller vermin, especially rats, have been observed swarming in unusually large numbers and attacking herds of pigs and cattle. Extermination efforts here in Geneva have met with limited success and we believe this will be the case worldwide. At this posting we see no evidence of infection in the local vermin.

Attempts to detect antigenic or genetic responses to the virus have yielded no positive results. If the human body is making an attempt to create an antibody we have found nothing to indicate success. The few labs still functional are rapidly losing supplies and use of equipment as electrical power becomes more and more intermittent.

History tells us that any virus this lethal will soon mutate to a more benign strain. We have yet to see any evidence of this with regard to the Z-virus and it may be that humanity is experiencing an extinction event.

Our fortifications at this location have failed and we fear we will soon succumb to the months long assault on our facilities here. Already the dead have breached the courtyard gates and reached the lower floor of the building, cutting off any escape route.

May God have mercy and be with us in our hour of need.

From the author

I hope you enjoyed *Dead Coast* and the entire *Living Dead* series. If you did, posting a review on Amazon is a great way to help other readers find it for themselves.

You can find more of my work at Amazon's L.I. Albemont page

Want to reach me?

You can find me at my blog http://lialbemont.blogspot.com/

If you want to contact me directly, email me at lialbemont@gmail.com.

Made in the USA
Lexington, KY
28 November 2013